SWEET JUSTICE

VICKI THARP

SWEET JUSTICE

Sweet Justice is a work of fiction. Names, characters, places and incidents either are the product of the author's imagination or are used fictitiously, and any resemblance to actual persons, living or dead, business establishments, events, or locals, is entirely coincidental.

Original Cover Design by Designs EE

ISBN 978-1-948798-55-6

Copyright © 2022 by Vicki Tharp

All rights reserved.

No part of this book may be reproduced in any form or by any electronic or mechanical means, including information storage and retrieval systems, without written permission from the author, except for the use of brief quotations in a book review.

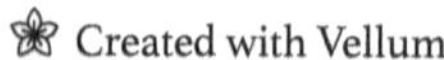 Created with Vellum

1

---

*J**ustice.***

Did any word sound sweeter?

Too bad Finn had nearly lost all hope of finding it after all these years.

To add to the frustration, he was an FBI agent with resources civilians didn't have access to.

Still, he hunted.

And as of—he glanced at his Bvlgari watch—an hour and a half ago—he possibly caught his first break in a very long time.

The loud rap came at his back door, and he knew who stood on his porch before the doorknob turned. Oscar Finn stood from the kitchen chair, the leather sticking to the dried sweat on his legs and bare back, feeling like he'd stripped away the top layers of his skin.

Ronan Tran opened the door, disappointment on his face, not surprise.

Ronan had come dressed for an upscale drinks night out in Alpine—designer slacks, Brioni button-up with the sleeves rolled up to mid-forearm.

Alpine, Wyoming was a bit of a drive over windy mountain

roads from their location in Murdock, but it had been too long since they'd taken a night off. Especially since controversial shock jockey, Nathan Quest had been gunned down on Murdock's mostly quiet streets a few months before.

"You haven't even showered," Ronan said.

Finn reached for his tank and slipped the sweat-dampened shirt over his head. Ronan's eyes dropped to the pile of papers on the kitchen table. Finn couldn't remember making the conscious decision to shove the table against the half-wall to keep the piles from falling off the other side. But since Finn tended to down his meals standing at the kitchen counter, it wasn't like he needed the tablespace for eating.

"I just—" Finn cut himself off. Anything he added to that sentence would only make Ronan ask more questions, and Finn didn't have it in him to argue on a Friday night after a long week. He hitched his thumb over his shoulder in the direction of his bedroom. "Give me fifteen minutes, and I'll be ready."

"You completely forgot we had plans, didn't you?"

Finn didn't bother denying the truth. Ronan, no doubt, saw it on his face. They'd been friends since grade school. Not even Finn's ex-wife knew him inside and out the way Ronan did.

Ronan tossed him an aggrieved smile. "You confirmed two hours ago. You were heading out for your run, and then we'd—"

"I know." Finn went to brush by Ronan to take his shower, even though the last thing he wanted to do was go out. But Finn had agreed to go, so he wouldn't go back on his word.

Ronan caught his shoulder. "Sit."

His friend had that quiet, no-nonsense tone that tended to get peoples' attention. Even Finn's.

"You telling me as my boss or as my friend?"

"Jesus Christ, Finn, does it matter?" Dropping his hand, Ronan took a step back. The exasperation hit Finn almost as hard as Ronan's earlier disappointment had.

Instinctively, Finn knew there'd be a breaking point when Ronan decided being his friend was no longer worth the effort even after Ronan had stuck by Finn's side all through the years. Even during the darkest times after his sister's death.

Finn's ex-wife, Sondra, had found her breaking point a lot sooner. Ronan would find his as well.

Ronan was a stubborn, persistent fuck, but it was only a matter of time.

Finn dropped into the chair he'd vacated at the end of the table next to the wall, and Ronan pulled out the one beside him.

With his thumb, Ronan's riffled the stack of papers of the police file in front of him that included some of his sister's crime scene photos. A photo of his sister's body before the coroner had her removed her from the scene flicked by. "Oscar, I—"

"You did *not* just first-name me," Finn said.

Ronan almost smiled. "Thought it would get your attention."

Finn scrubbed his hands over his face and caught a whiff of himself. "Can you hold that thought? I really need a shower."

Ronan followed him down the hall of the three-bedroom bungalow Finn had bought, gutted, and restored after his divorce. Not that he was home enough to enjoy it. He could have afforded newer and much better but having wealth didn't mean he had to have more. He had all he needed right here.

You don't have Soto.

But that wasn't something that would ever change, so he shoved that unwelcome thought out of his mind. Money couldn't buy everything. Least of all, a woman like Soto.

She has a first name. Maria. Maybe if you used it instead of treating her like one of your men, you might make some headway.

No. She worked directly under him. *Did. Does.* Hell, he didn't even know anymore. He couldn't allow himself to think about the possibility of her not returning to his joint task force once her medical leave ended.

You certainly don't have a problem thinking about her when you can't sleep at night, when you reach your hand down and—

"It's been twenty-five years." Ronan followed Finn into the bedroom and straddled the corner of Finn's bed when he sat. "You really think you're going to find who killed your sister after all this time? The police never found anything."

In his bathroom, Finn stilled. Ronan's words landed like a nauseating kick to the balls. They made his stomach queasy, and sweat form at his hairline. Good thing Finn hadn't had dinner yet. He tossed his running shirt into the hamper and almost told Ronan about the text Massey Yates, the computer guru over at Steele-Wolfe Securities, had sent him.

But considering Ronan's words, he thought better of it. "The police never found anything because they didn't even try."

Finn wasn't telling Ronan anything he didn't already know. He hooked his thumbs into the waistband of his running shorts and stopped. He looked at Ronan pointedly over his shoulder. "Do you mind?"

"I've seen your junk before. I've had bigger. And you never had any modesty anyway. Don't change the subject. I'm trying to talk some sense into you. Maybe I should have tried harder when you got the hair-brained idea for us to join the FBI years ago."

"Maybe you should address your boundary issues." Finn dropped his shorts and underwear because Ronan clearly wasn't going anywhere. He started the shower and stepped in before the water warmed.

Ronan didn't say anything for a bit, then Finn caught movement out of the corner of his eye.

"I don't have a problem with boundaries," Ronan said.

Finn turned and looked through his shower's frosted glass. He couldn't see Ronan clearly, but he could make out his friend's general shape. "You standing in my bathroom doorway while I shower would say otherwise."

"I'm not here to talk about me."

"I thought that's why you wanted to go out? To get some advice about that woman you—"

"That was before I walked into your house and found your sister's files all over the kitchen. Again."

He didn't have the balls to tell Ronan that he'd taken the files out several months before and had been working on them almost nightly. If they both hadn't been so busy, Ronan would have been over to his house earlier and found out for himself.

Finn finished rinsing and turned off the water. Ronan tossed him a thick, fluffy towel off the warming rack. He rubbed his face dry when all he wanted to do was scream into the towel. No matter what people said, he wouldn't—*couldn't*—give up until he brought his sister's killer to justice in whatever form that took.

She deserved no less.

He wrapped the towel around his waist and stepped out of the shower. He glowered at his oldest friend. "You're starting to sound like everyone else. I thought you were on my side. On Ali's side."

"Fuck you." The hurt flashed in Ronan's dark eyes as he tossed Finn a fresh pair of gym shorts and a T-shirt. Finn couldn't say he was disappointed that Ronan had given up on the idea of going out. "I've been by your side from day one. I joined the FBI because of you. And I've fucking looked the other way for you, for Ali, when you and I both know it could have cost us our careers."

Finn leaned in, a tight leash on his words when he said, "I never asked you to do any of that."

"No. You didn't. But you're my friend. You didn't have to ask."

Whatever head of steam Finn had been building dissipated. "Turn around so I can get dressed."

Ronan rolled his eyes and turned his back to Finn. "Just because I'm bi doesn't mean I'm into you."

Finn only caught the hint of frustration in Ronan's voice because he knew his friend so well. "You know damn good and well it has nothing to do with that."

"Then what's it have to do with?"

"Expecting a little privacy in my own damn house." Under normal circumstances, Ronan wasn't argumentative or defensive. It was one of the things that made him so effective at his job. Something was up, but Finn would circle back around to that later.

Finn pulled on his underwear and shorts and reached for his T-shirt. "I'm decent."

Ronan turned around. "I'm not finished with you. Where's your Scotch?"

"Same place it always is." Finn followed Ronan down the hall.

Ronan veered into the den as Finn continued into the kitchen. Ronan trailed after him a couple of minutes later, carrying two crystal whiskey glasses and one of Finn's finer bottles of single malts. Maybe it was a good thing they weren't heading into Alpine. Now, if they climbed too far into that bottle, they wouldn't have to worry about finding a ride home.

MARIA SOTO PULLED up to the Steele-Wolfe Securities' building Friday evening, surprised to find cars in the parking lot, the roll-up doors on the lower level open, and the obstacle lights as bright as the Vegas Strip.

Wyatt Wolfe, her soon-to-be boss and co-owner of Steele-Wolfe with his wife Geneva and partner Gil Brant, had requested she meet him inside to sign the final hiring documents.

She should have been excited to start this new chapter of her career, but if she were honest, she'd spent enough years with the DEA, assigned to the local joint task force that even as she welcomed the change, a part of her heart would remain with the task force.

You mean with Finn.

Dios mio. Yeah, him, too. She wasn't afraid to admit that, but a person couldn't subject themselves to unrequited love forever.

No, it was time for her to move on. There were plenty of men out there that could love her despite what she did for a living.

What about finding someone who loves you because *of what you do for a living? Don't sell yourself short, chica.*

Yeah, well, she'd held out for that with no luck, so she would settle for the other if, or when, the time came.

She climbed out of her red Rogue dressed for a workout at the facility after signing her employment documents, not expecting nearly everyone else from Steele-Wolfe to be there as well. But it wasn't like she wouldn't have to share the facility with them every day, so she might as well get used to it now. It would be harder to hide the limp she develops after a hard workout, but she'd dealt with that for a few months now.

A month before, medical had cleared her after her under-cover task force operation had turned into a shootout that left her with a bullet wound to the leg and two suspects dead. One from the hands of one of the suspects, one from hers.

But being medically cleared didn't mean that she didn't hurt physically.

Or mentally.

Steele-Wolfe had offices on the facility's second level, leaving the lower level for workout equipment, sparring mats, and various equipment. In the entryway, she considered taking the elevator to spare her leg the strain of the stairs, but since she thought about doing that, she made herself hike the stairs.

She made it to the top with barely a twinge. The last time she'd climbed those steps a couple of months before, she'd stepped onto the floor with a limp she couldn't hide. At least this time, she hadn't opened the door to find Finn on the other side.

The time before, she'd come to talk to Wyatt, unsure if she wanted to leave the DEA and her home with the task force. But after running into Finn—now her former boss—she'd recognized it was past time to move on.

Emotionally, that is. He'd made that abundantly clear.

Along with window offices, the upper floor also had a few dorm-style rooms, a kitchenette, and a large communal diamond-shaped conference table with banks of monitors overhead, so everyone had a good view of shared information.

Massey, the company's computer tech, and another man she hadn't met yet had a stack of electronic equipment laid out on the conference table and were packing it all into protective travel cases.

Massey was sitting in his wheelchair, organizing all the cords. He had the kind of smile that pulled you in and made you want to be his best friend, especially when he focused that smile on you. "Here for good, now?"

"All done but the signing."

The other man stepped over with minimal assistance from a cane and offered his hand. "Isaac Lang. I'm only filling in while Gil is on paternity leave."

She'd heard about Lang. He'd been Gil's handler when Gil had been deep undercover with the ATF. Lang had barely escaped with his life when a bullet ripped through him, nicking his spine and nearly leaving him paralyzed from the waist down. Looked like she wasn't the only one looking for work in the private sector.

Then again, everyone at Steele-Wolfe, except Massey, had former ties to law enforcement in one way or another.

"Glad to meet you." Maria shook his hand. "I hope to see you around. Where are you two headed?"

"Savannah. A surveillance case," Massey said. "Heading out in the morning, but we shouldn't be gone more than a week or two."

Wyatt hung up his phone and walked out of his corner office to greet her. His welcoming grin settled some of the nervous gremlins kicking around in Maria's stomach and making it ache.

"I've got the papers in the office. Shouldn't take long. Then we can meet everyone on the obstacle course. Winner gets a six-pack."

Maria had no chance of winning, but she didn't want to skip out on a team-building experience on her first day of employment. She had nothing to prove to Wyatt. He knew her limitations... *mostly*.

By the time they finished signing all the paperwork, Isaac and Massey had cleared out with the equipment, leaving it on a dolly downstairs beside a white van.

"You don't have to do this," Wyatt said as they walked to the obstacle course. "It's all in good fun, and no one will think less of you if you don't want to participate."

"Oh, hell no," Maria said, not sure if that comment was more for Wyatt or herself. She hated having the injury, but she refused to back out of a friendly wager. And who knew, maybe she'd surprise herself. She'd worked with weights. She'd worked up her stamina for running. But she hadn't yet pushed herself the way an obstacle course would.

She had a lot to prove.

More to herself than anyone out there watching.

At the obstacle course, Massey had switched from his wheelchair to his crutches. Isaac stood nearby, taking the money for friendly side wagers, egging everyone on. Gil and Jericho would face off first on the course. Apparently, not even being on paternity leave could keep him from a little friendly competition.

"Get him, Dad!" A six or seven-year-old kid sat in the grass, not too far away from the start, next to a baby's car seat on the ground with a light blanket snuggled around a sleeping baby. How the baby could sleep with all the laughter and good-natured ribbing, Maria would never know.

"Stay with your sister," Gil said. "This will only take a couple of minutes."

The kid rolled his eyes. "*Duh.*"

Still, Gil caught Geneva's eye, and she nodded, indicating she'd keep an eye out as well.

Gil walked over, ruffled the dark mop of hair on top of the kid's head, and approached the starting line. Wyatt raised an arm as he took a stopwatch out of his pocket. "On your mark..."

Jericho and Gil dropped down like they were in the starting blocks, grins on their faces. Jericho wasn't a small man, but Gil was the type of big that made other big men look small. Jericho playfully shoved Gil in the shoulder a fraction of a second before Wyatt dropped his hand. Gil didn't falter.

They tore off in a sprint, over the rows of belly busters, across the easy balancer, under the belly crawl, over the inclining wall, through the monkey bars, swinging over the water hazard, and finally to scale the vertical wall with the climbing rope.

Everyone else hurried down the side of the course, cheering the men on, not caring who won. Gil gained headway when he could sprint, surprisingly fast for a man of his size, but Jericho outperformed him on the areas requiring more upper body strength. That was where his relatively smaller frame allowed him to excel.

On the last obstacle, Gil hit the vertical wall first, but Jericho scrambled over it like a monkey, dropping down to the raised platform on the other side and jumping the few feet to the ground, sprinting across the finish line a step ahead of Gil.

They both bent at the waist, catching their breaths, sweat rolling off their bodies even as the night caught a chill. The little boy came running down with the biggest smile on his face, not caring that Gil hadn't won. "Daddy!"

"You were supposed to stay with your sister." Gil's head popped up, catching the boy in his arms, his eyes immediately traveling down the length of the obstacle where he'd left the baby. He found Geneva walking up the course with the sleeping baby on her shoulder.

"I hope it was okay," she said. "I told Jack I'd watch the baby."

"It's fine." His son jumped down, and Gil took his daughter, his hands engulfing the little girl. The gentleness Maria witnessed by this hulk of a man had the back of her eyes stinging.

Ohmygod. She needed to get back to work and bury herself in a case if the sight of a man holding his baby made her want to cry.

All that time off work was making her soft.

You know there's nothing wrong with having emotions, right?

Maybe not, but being in a male-dominated profession, she'd learned to bury hers deep under a thick layer of cynicism and sarcasm.

Cassie and Geneva raced next, having trouble getting through the course not because they didn't have the strength but because they couldn't stop laughing and badmouthing each other.

"Go, Cassie!" Massey hollered, waving a crutch in the air. "You go, girl," he added when she sprinted through the finish line as Geneva came over the top of the climbing wall.

Maria glanced back at Massey, then a few feet behind him where Isaac stood, his attention on Massey.

Isaac caught her watching, his face flushing red under the vapor lights. Man, if only Finn looked at her the way Isaac looked at Massey, all lust, need, and hunger.

Maria glanced away, feeling like she was intruding.

"Can I talk to you a minute?" Gil's good humor had vanished.

At first, Maria thought Gil was talking to her but realized he was looking straight past her. She turned. Isaac stood with his hands on his hips, and a *what's your problem?* expression on his face. He stepped into the grass as Gil bore down on him with the baby nestled against his neck. His voice a harsh whisper as he took Isaac aside.

Cassie and Geneva walked by, giving each other a high five. Wyatt clapped Maria on the shoulder, jogging backward toward the starting line. "You and me next."

It wasn't like she wouldn't take her boss up on the challenge. But she wouldn't go easy on him either. If he wanted to win, he'd have to work for it. She grinned. "Wouldn't miss it."

He pointed down at her feet. "Your shoe is untied."

She squatted to tie it. With everyone walking back to the start, she couldn't help but overhear Gil and Isaac's hushed but heated conversation.

She caught Isaac's words in the middle of a sentence. "... I don't know what's going on in that thick skull of yours or what you think of my prowess when it comes to men, but I can assure you even *I* can't turn someone gay."

"Damn it, you know that's not what I meant," Gil ground out, the baby starting to fuss on his shoulder.

"Then what do you mean?"

"Maybe it would be better if I took this case with Massey. I—"

"You're on paternity leave. And that's beside the fucking

point. You don't think I can keep my work and private life separate. You don't think I can maintain boundaries," Isaac's voice rose above a harsh whisper catching the attention of everyone at the start of the obstacle course, though they were probably too far away to hear the words.

Maria hurried up and double knotted her shoelace to give them their privacy, though they didn't seem overly concerned about who heard.

Then Isaac's voice dropped again as he leaned in and added, "You don't think I know that Massey isn't into guys. I know that. I'm fine with that."

"You say that now. But you're going to be holed up with him for—"

Maria started walking away, and Isaac's voice rose higher.

"Fuck you. And fuck the fuck right off."

Isaac went to brush by Gil, knocking into his other shoulder as he passed, startling the fussy baby awake. The baby started crying.

Gil patted his daughter's back. "I don't want to see you get hurt, Isaac."

Isaac turned around, giving him a double-barrel shot of the bird. "I could do without your concern."

Isaac strode ahead, and with Gil's long strides, he quickly caught up to Maria as he patted his baby, talking softly to his daughter as he tried to get her to settle. "I'm sorry you had to hear that."

"It was kind of hard not to. Want a bit of advice?" She didn't expect he did, but she'd give it a shot.

"Yeah." His response didn't even sound sarcastic.

"Do you trust your friend?"

Without a fraction of a second's hesitation, he said, "With my life."

"Then trust him to navigate whatever he's got going on. Who knows. Maybe Massey is into him, too."

"Massey is straight."

"Massey told you that?" One thing Maria had learned was that sexuality was a wide spectrum. You couldn't make assumptions about a person.

"I've only seen him date women."

"Doesn't mean he's straight."

That shut Gil up. "You're right. Maybe I should butt out of something that isn't any of my business."

Maria grinned at him. "Always a good policy."

Gil shook his head but chuckled to himself, his baby girl squirming in his arms. Finally, Gil peeled off course and headed for the diaper bag.

As Maria stretched her legs, she heard Gil call out to Isaac, "Hey man, I owe you an apology."

She glanced up to see Isaac straighten, a crooked smile on his face. "This ought to be good."

She headed for the starting line—too far away now to make out Gil's words—preparing to get her ass kicked but determined to make it as close a race as possible.

2

At the start of the obstacle course, Massey replaced Wyatt as the official starter, leaning his weight on one crutch and holding the other one up with the tip high in the air.

"Wyatt is embarrassingly slow on the balance obstacle," Jericho called out to Maria, his breathing still slightly elevated after his exertion. "You can make up time there."

"Hey," Wyatt chided. "I can hear you."

Cassie laughed. "The truth hurts."

Wyatt shook his head, but his smile never faltered.

This was what Maria had been looking for. A team. A *family*. One where you fight and squabble and give each other a rash of shit, knowing full well that you have each other's backs. It may not be the joint task force she'd worked on under Finn's command, but she'd found her new home.

Maria believed she could make up time on the straightaways between obstacles as well. She'd been a sprinter on the track team in high school. She had after-burners when she needed them. That speed had also served her well on the streets when chasing down a perp.

As soon as Massey dropped his crutch, she sprinted for the belly busters, a bit of a challenge for someone of her short stature, but she could jump as well as sprint, so they didn't slow her down too much.

Maria picked up speed before the easy balancer, scampering across the narrow log without slowing. On her right, Wyatt cussed already a few strides behind her. He lost his balance and fell off the apparatus but scrambled back on, allowing her to dive into the belly crawl before he could jump off the far end of the balancer.

She made it through the incline wall and the monkey bars ahead of him, but barely. His superior upper body strength and wingspan through the monkey bars helped him gain on her even with her speed.

She willed her lungs to expand faster, her legs to pump harder, ignoring the twinges in her injured quad, reminding her she wasn't yet a hundred percent healed.

Little Jack ran along beside them, cheering both of them on. Followed close behind by Jericho, Geneva, and Isaac with Gil and the baby. Massey pulled up the rear.

Maria and Wyatt made it to the climbing wall at the same time. Their final obstacle. She grabbed the rope and started pulling herself up, her legs on the wall, walking up step by step. Her injured leg shook with the strain, and a shock of pain shot up her thigh and skittered up her spine.

Her grip slipped, and she lost her footing. She caught her full weight with her hands on the rope. She slid and crumpled to the ground, burning her hands on the rope.

She hissed in a breath. Wyatt had one leg over the wall, balancing on top. "You okay?"

If she didn't die of embarrassment, she would be fine.

She put her hands high on the rope, prepared to make another attempt. She'd already lost, but that didn't mean the race had ended. Swallowing down the gasp of pain from the rope burns, she started up the wall.

"You don't have to do this." Wyatt stood on the platform on the other side of the wall and looked down at her.

She couldn't answer, not when she concentrated so hard, fighting against the burns on her hands and the salvos of pain shooting up her injured leg. Everyone crowded around, encouraging her climb. She hated being the center of attention. She should have quit when she'd fallen, but there wasn't much she could do about that now.

The muscles in her arms burned, and her breath came out in harsh, guttural gasps. As she neared the top, Wyatt reached a hand down to her. She didn't need a hand. She would either do it under her own power or not at all.

"Stubborn. I like that about you." Wyatt took his hand back. His warm chuckle of appreciation washed over her as he stepped out of the way to allow her to grab the top of the wall.

The edges bit into her fingers. She squeezed tighter, swinging her leg up to catch her heel on the top of the wall. Her heel slipped, her body swung down. She now hung from the wall by her fingertips. She didn't have enough upper body strength left to pull herself up.

"You've got this." Wyatt's quiet assurance gave her much-needed encouragement.

Maria dropped to the heavily padded ground to regroup. Finally, she stood, her hands on her knees as she caught her breath and waited for the burn in her muscles to subside.

"One more try," Jericho said. "One more is all you need."

Gil's baby gurgled in happy agreement, and everyone laughed, easing the tension. Maria straightened, wiping the sweat from her hands onto her shorts.

"You don't have to kill yourself," Isaac piped in. "It's a friendly competition."

Massey shot him a look.

"What?"

"She's fine."

"I never said she wasn't."

That exchange only made Maria smile more. She'd just signed on with the firm, and already her colleagues were protective of her, each in their own way. Yeah, she'd known she'd made the right decision before scribbling her name on the dotted line, but this proved her instinct had been correct.

She was where she needed to be.

She was home.

Determined to try one last time, with her strength dwindling, she backed up the thirty feet to the end of the water hazard and got a running start. If she didn't have momentum on her side, she didn't think she'd make it.

Wyatt clapped from above. "Let's go."

"Make that wall your bitch," Massey hollered out.

She laughed as she took off running. Momentum took her halfway up the wall before requiring more of her strength. Hand over hand, step by step, she climbed the wall, her shoulders screaming, her arms shaking, her knees wanting to lock. She caught the top edge and got a solid hook with her heel.

"Come on, come on." Wyatt gripped the wall as if to keep himself from reaching for her and yanking her over the wall. With one last effort, she heaved herself up, resting her upper body across the narrow top part of the wall.

She'd made it.

Maria rolled and let herself drop onto the platform on the other side in a controlled manner to the whoops and hollers of everybody on the ground. She laid flat on her back and caught her breath.

Jack climbed the platform stairs. "That was awesome! Wait until I tell my friend Billy. He won't believe it!"

"Yeah," Wyatt said as he reached a hand down to help her up. "That was awesome."

Maria took his proffered hand, linking her grip with his. "Yeah, awesome." She couldn't hide the self-deprecating sarcasm, even though she'd been learning how to take a compliment. Sometimes she had a hard time giving herself the credit she deserved.

He pulled her to her feet. After regaining her balance, he didn't let go until she met his eyes. "I didn't hire you because I thought you could beat me in a race. I hired you because you don't give up."

FINN AND RONAN kept their thoughts to themselves through the first glass of the single malt as the full moon rose higher in the sky, bathing them in pale light. In the distance, a pack of coyotes yipped, and an owl hooted. Thirty yards from the end of Finn's back yard, the ground fell away, and the shadowed ponderosa pine trees parted. In the daytime, he had one hell of a view of the Rockies. The view had been what had sold him on the property when he first saw it.

Drinking, sip by sip, Finn couldn't get Ronan's words out of his head. Did Ronan think he should pack up Ali's files and walk away?

"Look me in the eye and tell me you don't think Ali was murdered."

Finn's words almost came out as a dare, but if Finn were being honest, he didn't want to take it that far. Probably because he didn't want to hear the truth.

Ronan twisted in his Adirondack chair and poured two more fingers of scotch into each of their glasses. "Ali was a librarian.

Despite what the movies want to make you believe, their lives aren't all that dangerous."

"That's exactly my point." Finn rested his elbows on his knees. "She didn't have any enemies. No jealous or disgruntled boyfriend. There was no reason for someone to want her dead. So for someone to want her dead and then go to the trouble of staging it to look like an accidental drowning or suicide—"

"*Finn*. They found the empty bottle of benzodiazepines on her bathroom counter. Her tox screen showed she had enough benzos and alcohol in her system to kill her even if the drowning hadn't. With little else to go on, I can see how the detectives and the M.E. concluded it was an accidental drowning with an overdose."

"You think—"

"I *think* that despite the shoddy work the detectives did on the investigation, they might have gotten it right."

"Are you fucking kidding me?" Talk about a gut check. "They didn't even go as far as to find out that the prescribing doctor on the pill vial didn't exist."

"Wouldn't be the first time that someone got a fake prescription filled."

Finn swirled the drink in his glass and downed it in one swallow before reaching for a refill. He didn't make a habit of drowning his feelings in eighty proof, but sometimes he needed it. "You playing devil's advocate, or are you just being an asshole?"

"I'm trying to be real. I'm trying to be your friend. Not sure which of those two options that makes me. Regardless, she could have taken those pills. The overdose could have been on purpose or accidental. I don't know. But it's a hell of a stretch to say she was murdered."

Finn slammed his glass down on the stone-topped table between them. Ronan startled. The scotch splashed over Finn's hand. Finn shook the liquid off and stood, unable to continue the conversation sitting down. "What about the secret tunnel at the library where she worked? What about that?"

Ronan scoffed and set his glass down with a slow, precise deliberateness—the glass he hadn't touched since after the first refill—taking the time to formulate what he had to say and how he'd say it. Finn had seen that measured manner of Ronan's many times over the years, in his personal life and professional. It usually kept Ronan from saying something he couldn't take back.

Linking his hands in his lap, Ronan leaned back, not looking nearly as relaxed as he wanted Finn to believe him to be. "The tunnel has been debunked."

"Has it?" It wasn't a question, as much as it was a challenge.

"No one has ever found a secret passage from the bowels of Franklin Public Library to CIA headquarters."

"Why do you think it's called a *secret*?"

Finn let his head fall between his shoulders and blew out a breath. He knew how he sounded. He'd dealt with enough conspiracy theorists in his day to know he sounded exactly like one. If he didn't reel himself in, Ronan might worry about his fitness to continue his job.

Would losing your job be such a bad thing? You could work on Ali's case full time, not in snatched moments here and there. It's not like you need the money.

While he didn't need the money, he needed the stability and the routine of his job, if only to keep Ali's case from completely taking over his life. He'd lived that firsthand and had an ex-wife to show for it.

"You know what you need?"

Besides justice for Ali? Finn didn't know, but he had a feeling Ronan was about to tell him. Finn stalked back to the small table and refilled his glass. "What's that?"

"A woman." When Finn opened his mouth to protest, Ronan raised a hand and said, "Hear me out. You were a different person with Shondra."

"Apparently, not different enough. She still left."

"She'd probably take you back if—"

"No. We're much better off as friends. And she's seeing a great guy that makes her happy, which makes me happy."

"That sour face says otherwise."

Finn flipped him off. His friend didn't deserve any more of a reply than that. Ronan raised a brow at him, assessing him as if Finn were one of their suspects that they'd dragged into an interview room.

"You think I'm unstable," Finn said. It wasn't a question, and it didn't come out as one.

The silence dragged on. A critter scurried through the underbrush, rustling leaves. Finn couldn't picture another man who could withstand Ronan's blistering scrutiny without wanting to confess, even if he hadn't done anything wrong.

He waited Ronan out because he didn't want to say anything that might confirm Ronan's suspicions.

"What's going on? What's the real reason you completely forgot we'd made plans? That's unusual, even for you."

Finn tried to change the subject. "I thought we were getting together to talk about *your* problems."

Ronan stood, and Finn had to wonder if Ronan planned on leaving for now or for good. "Don't play that game. Talk to me."

If you can't talk to Ronan, who can you talk to?

Nobody. At least nobody that wouldn't think putting him on a seventy-two-hour psyche hold wouldn't be a bad idea.

To keep from having to maintain eye contact, Finn picked up the glasses, the half-consumed bottle of scotch, and carried them inside. "I got a text from Massey Yates while I was on my run."

Ronan tapped a finger to his temple as if trying to place the name. Then he snapped his fingers. "Wait, isn't he that conspiracy theory kid that keeps sending emails up my chain of command?"

"He's not a conspiracy theorist." At least Finn didn't think he was. "No one is taking him seriously. He's trying to find someone who will."

"You believe him?"

"I don't *not* believe him. A far-fetched theory doesn't mean there's no validity to it. But his text wasn't about DeadMoney. Not exactly."

Ronan propped a shoulder against the wall and crossed his arms. "Then what was it about?"

"It was about that congressman that died yesterday. Greg Fitzhugh."

"I heard about it. The Feds are on it. From what I heard, they took his personal and work laptops looking for a suicide note."

"Massey seems to think he could be another victim of the DeadMoney betting pool on the dark web. The same way that shock jockey, Nathan Quest, and that director—and accused pedophile—Christian Novak, was."

Ronan had that *oh, come on* expression on his face that negated his need to say the words. "Quest was gunned down in a hail of bullets like a modern-day version of a mob hit. Fitzhugh was found—"

"Facedown in his pool. With his swim trunks on backward the same way Ali's bikini bottoms were."

That got Ronan's attention. As much as Ronan had encouraged Finn to move on, he'd also been nearly as invested in helping Finn find Ali's killer. Ronan straightened, some of his skepticism taking a back seat to his professional and personal curiosity. "Where did you hear that? I don't think that information has been released to the public yet."

"It hasn't. But Massey found out. Unofficially. He has a lot of friends out there, and he has a way of getting the information he wants."

"Legally?"

Finn shrugged. It would probably be best for everyone involved if they didn't continue that part of the conversation. He waited a beat for Ronan to put all the pieces together. Finn didn't have to wait long. "You're thinking this could be the guy. You think someone killed the congressman, and that same person also killed your sister."

"I have to check it out, at least."

"A congressman is dead in D.C. You don't think every swinging dick in the FBI won't be all over that case? If you go there, you'd only be in the way."

"I have to go." By the pinched, *here we go again* expression on Ronan's face, he'd already guessed that, even if he clearly didn't like it. Still, Ronan wouldn't be Ronan if he didn't try to talk some sense into Finn.

Finn tried to beat him to the punch. "I haven't taken time off since—"

"Since your last cluster-fuck of a goose chase that nearly cost both of us our careers." He didn't allow Finn to apologize for that debacle *again* before continuing. "Your task force is already overworked and down by one."

"I already told you, I'm not ready to add someone—"

"If you're waiting for Soto to return to your team, you can stop. She cleared medical a month ago, and she still hasn't returned."

Soto had cleared medical? Finn polished off the last of the scotch in his glass and chased it down with the remainder in Ronan's. "Why didn't you tell me?" More importantly, why hadn't Soto told him herself?

"I thought you knew."

"She'll be back. She'll come to her senses and—"

Even as Finn said it, he knew it wasn't true.

Knew she had other opportunities that didn't involve the task force... *him*.

"*Fuck*."

Ronan blew out a hot breath and turned, heading for the front door.

Finn followed. "Where you going?"

"I'm leaving. I can tell you've already made up your mind to take your days off. Nothing I can do or say will change that."

"You'll cover for me?"

Ronan shook his head even as he said, "A week."

"Make it two."

Ronan huffed out a laugh even though it looked like he'd rather land a right hook to Finn's jaw. He opened the door. "Fine. Two. But take someone with you." From Ronan's authoritative tone, Finn was talking to his boss, not his lifelong friend.

Finn didn't refuse, but he said, "I don't need a babysitter."

"Then consider it back up." Ronan walked out the door without waiting for Finn's response.

Finn almost had the door closed when Ronan added, "Oh, and Finn?" Finn opened the door wider. "Don't make me regret this."

3

———

In the lower level of the Steele-Wolfe facility, Maria took full advantage of having a top-notch place to work out. She didn't have to show up for work until Monday but continuing to regain her strength since the shooting remained her top priority, which explained why she was at the facility with both front and rear bay doors open to the rising sun.

Not that she was the only one there. Massey and Isaac had arrived early to finish packing Massey's wheelchair-accessible van with all the gear they needed for their assignment in Savannah.

Jericho and Wyatt were upstairs prepping for Jericho's departure later in the day.

She couldn't wait to get her first assignment and sink her teeth into an investigation. The last year working undercover on the streets as a sex worker in a sting set up by her joint task force with the FBI, the DEA, the ATF, and the local sheriff's departments had taken their toll. In the end, they'd gotten a lot of bad people off the streets.

The shooting had brought the investigation to an abrupt conclusion. She couldn't say she was happy to have been shot, but she was glad the assignment had ended. It was supposed to have only been for a month. Instead, like all things governmental, it had dragged on for more than a year.

With boxing gloves tied at her wrists, she worked the heavy bag since the rope burn on her hands prevented her from lifting weights. And if she were honest with herself, her shoulders, arms, and especially her injured leg needed a chance to recover from the obstacle course the night before.

A vehicle pulled up. Maria paid it no mind and concentrated on the set of her feet and her form as she worked on her jabs and uppercuts.

The familiar, expensive cologne registered a split second before Oscar Finn said, "What are you doing here?"

Her next punch landed wide, her gloved hand sliding off the side of the bag. She reached out to steady it, but she didn't stop. In fact, she imagined one *oh so sure of himself* FBI agent stood in front of her in place of the bag.

Not that she wanted to hit Finn. She wanted to do other things to him. But he'd made it clear that that would never happen. What better way to manage her frustration than taking it out on his imaginary pretty face?

"What does it look like I'm doing here?" She didn't miss another punch. Jab. Jab. Uppercut. Kidney punch. Sweeping kick at knee level for good measure.

"You know what I mean."

She did. No need to make it easy on him, though. She landed a few more solid punches that reverberated all the way up her arm.

"Would you stop a minute?"

He wasn't her boss anymore. Wasn't *anything* to her anymore.

She didn't stop.

Taking a strategic step back to land another brutal combination, Finn did the most ill-advised thing she'd ever seen him do. He stepped between her and the bag. She tried to stop the punch, but she noticed him too late. She managed to pull her punch a bit, and Finn blocked the brunt of it with his forearm.

"What the fuck, Finn?" Maria's lungs heaved from her exertion, and sweat poured down her body, snaking through every crease and crevasse. She had her hair in a bun, but tendrils had escaped, sweat plastering them to her forehead and the side of her face.

He simply raised a brow at her, not a thread out of place in his bespoke Italian suit. He rarely looked creased. Fabric that expensive didn't dare.

Instead of answering, he looked her up and down. That wasn't lust in his eyes. It wasn't disgust either, which kept her from dotting one of his eyes.

"What?" she asked, at a loss for what he wanted from her.

"Can you put something on?"

She held her arms out and glanced down her body. She wore a teal sports bra that complimented her darker complexion. Her black compression shorts ended mid-thigh. All the important bits were covered. "What's wrong with what I'm wearing?"

She heard footsteps behind her and turned to see Geneva walking into the bay with what looked like a box of pastries from town, wearing her paramedic uniform as if she'd come home straight from her shift.

"Oh, hey, Finn," Geneva said, holding out the box. "Want a pastry?"

"I'm good, thanks."

Maria held up her gloved hands, and Geneva pulled one of them out with a napkin and set it on the nearby weight bench.

"Thanks," Maria said.

"What are you two doing?" Geneva asked.

"We were discussing what I'm wearing."

Maria thought she heard Finn groan.

"What's wrong with what she's wearing?" Geneva eyed Finn. "I think she looks fierce. You've got the curves, woman. No need to hide them."

Maria grinned, and they bumped fist to padded fist. Then Geneva swung her attention back to Finn, and by the man-eating look on her face, he wasn't going to enjoy what she had to say. "And Finn, I mean this in the nicest way possible because I consider you a friend." Finn stiffened as if bracing for the blow to land. "But you need to get that stick out of your ass."

Finn huffed out a breath, the fractional smile toying with one corner of his mouth.

Geneva spun on her heel and headed for the stairs.

Maria held out one of her gloved hands. "Help a girl out?" She'd worked up an appetite, and the danish called her name.

Wisely, Finn didn't say anything else about her outfit. He untied the strings at her wrist and pulled the glove off her hand. He caught her wrist before she could pull her hand away. Uncurling her fingers, he stared down at the rope burn on her palm.

"What the hell happened?"

"Obstacle course mishap."

He rushed to take the other glove off and tossed it aside. The rope burn on that hand looked worse than it felt. At least that's what Maria tried to convince herself. "It's not so bad."

Finn ghosted his fingers over the scabbed-over wound on her right hand. His touch should have hurt, yet it only sent a shiver of pleasure down her spine. She'd been totally gone for this man for so long that even the most innocent of touches made her body respond.

Not for long, though. Soon, she'd get him out of her head and move on with her life. It was more than past time for her to do that.

Wyatt came bounding out the door to the stairwell. It slammed with a loud clang behind him. "Geneva said you were here," he said to Finn. "What's up?"

"I've got a case."

"We're a little short-staffed at the moment, but I'll see what we can do to help."

Jericho came out of the stairwell carrying a computer bag over one shoulder and a stuffed duffel in his hand. Wyatt turned to him. "You have a sec?"

He raised the duffel. "Let me put these in the car, and I'll be right over."

Maria went to gather up her gloves when Wyatt said, "You too, Soto."

"*Wyatt.*" Finn nearly whispered as if trying not to let her overhear, but she was only a few feet away, making it impossible to pull off.

Maria loved the way Wyatt's brow rose. A challenge? A dare? "You have a problem with that?"

Finn straightened. "Not at all."

A lie, but Maria and Wyatt both let it go.

Without asking for them to follow, Wyatt headed for the stairs, catching the door as the elevator pinged and Geneva, Isaac, and Massey stepped out. Geneva kissed Wyatt before heading back up to their houseboat.

The houseboat they lived in was on a pond in the middle of Wyoming. And don't forget the cow, That-a-way, with its horns pointing in the same direction, that roamed the place like a dog, sleeping on the end of the dock on a stack of old blankets and greeting guests as they arrived. The old cow was more interested in the alfalfa cubes people offered.

"Let me know when you get there," Wyatt called out to Massey and Isaac.

"Will do," Isaac said as he followed Massey to the van.

Jericho returned from loading his vehicle, and he followed Wyatt, Finn, and Maria up the stairs. She hadn't completely caught her breath, and sweat still lay damp on her bare skin. After stepping into the office space, Finn removed his suit coat and held it out to her. She almost turned and walked away, but she was more afraid to sit at the conference table stinking from her workout than proving a point to Finn.

Besides, she hadn't thought of bringing a T-shirt with her. She'd had no plans other than to work out and head back to her place immediately after.

"Thanks," she reluctantly grumbled and took one of the seats at the conference table. Finn sat across from her, Jericho to her side, and Wyatt at the head.

"What can we do for you?" Wyatt asked.

"I have a case I promised my SAC I'd get assistance on."

"I'm not sure what we can do for you. Most of my team is heading out into the field. What's your time frame? Can we put it on the back burner for a couple of weeks?"

Finn twisted his head from side to side as if trying to relieve the tension in his neck. "It's personal. I'm taking two weeks' leave. That's all the time I have."

Maria sat up straighter. She'd known Finn for a number of years through the task force. Knew and respected the type of man he was from her time with the unit. But to say she knew him well would be a lie. At least not in a personal sense. Hell, she didn't even know where he lived.

Not that she hadn't been tempted to follow him home on occasion to find out. Luckily, she had enough self-respect not to dive down that rabbit hole. And who was she kidding? He would have spotted the tail, and she would have hated for him to confront her about it because what would she say?

"I've got Maria." Wyatt shifted his gaze to her, the words barely out of his mouth before she and Finn both said, "No."

Jericho leaned back in his chair and crossed his arms over his chest, an *I'm going to need to get popcorn* grin on his face. "This should be good."

"How about Jericho helps me, and Soto goes in his place? She's very good at what she does."

"I can stay," Jericho offered.

"No. You're going." To Finn, Wyatt said, "And you don't have to sell her to me. I'm the one who hired her. But Jericho has been gearing up for this assignment for weeks, and he's had training in negotiations that we need if we're going to pull this case off successfully."

Maria bristled. "You don't think it takes top-notch negotiating skills to convince a john twice your size not to beat you up or kill you?"

The room went silent. The men squirmed in their seats. Finn looked apoplectic. Wyatt looked resolved. Jericho looked impressed.

"And that was just a normal Tuesday night," Maria added.

"Despite that, there isn't the time to bring her up to speed," Wyatt said.

"What about Brant?" Finn asked, not giving up easily.

As much as Maria didn't want to work with Finn, it also offended her that he tried so hard not to work with her.

"Paternity leave," Wyatt said, "And before you ask, no, I'm not pulling him off it. He's more than earned it."

Finn's head dropped between his shoulder blades, but not for long. It was one of the few signs of vulnerability she'd ever seen him allow himself to express.

"Look, I know you're in a tough spot, but if you want help, Maria's all I have. It's her, or no one."

Finn took that in for a moment, then stood, extending his hand to Wyatt. "Thanks. I appreciate you trying to help."

Nodding to Maria and Jericho, Finn turned and left.

Was it *that* bad working with her that he'd rather have no help at all than have her?

The door to the stairwell closed behind Finn. Jericho turned to her. "What the hell was that all about?"

As soon as Finn stepped out into the cool morning air, he realized his mistake. Soto still had his suit coat. He should go back inside and get it while he had the chance, but he didn't trust himself not to change his mind and take what Wyatt had offered.

The help he needed.

And it wasn't like Maria hadn't been an amazing agent to work with. Her instincts were dead on. He loved to watch her work through a problem and develop a solution the whole team could get behind.

Loved to watch her period.

That's the problem, isn't it? You want to do more than watch. You want to touch, you want to kiss, you want to bring her into your whole world.

Wanting and knowing that it was a shitty idea at the same time didn't make it any easier. And knowing that she wanted him as well...

She hadn't come out and said it in so many words, but she'd made herself clear. If the attraction had only been one-sided on his part, he could have navigated that without issue. He wasn't a Neanderthal. He could control himself.

But he'd learned over the years that he had no control over her. Not that he'd want it. It was just that if they both wanted a relationship—or both *thought* they wanted a relationship—that could wind up disastrous.

He'd already put his ex-wife through the wringer, and he

thanked the stars above that they'd come out on the other side as friends. He refused to put someone else through that hell as well.

Soto has seen a lot. She's not like Shondra. She understands what you deal with because she's dealt with similar circumstances in her career.

Except there was a huge difference between dealing with death on the job and dealing with death on the job and coming home to Finn's never-ending investigation, to his *obsession.*

No. He was doing Soto a favor by walking away. And if that meant having to buy another suit, then so be it. It wasn't like he couldn't afford it.

He drove home. The neglect of his lawn became much more noticeable in the light of day. He ignored it and the knowledge that the lawn signified a bigger problem. He wasn't only pushing his chores to the next week and the next.

He was pushing his life further and further down the road.

He wasn't living.

He was existing.

And it wasn't sustainable.

Ali would be pissed at him for that. She'd loved life. If the shoes were reversed, she would have found a way to live for both of them.

He unlocked his door and stepped inside. Maybe he would do that. Make sure he lived—*really lived.*

After he'd found who'd killed her.

He wasted no time changing into a pair of athletic shorts and a T-shirt and going on a run while he had the chance. He had a flight to D.C. in the morning and planned on hitting the ground running—his investigation, that is.

Besides, he needed time to clear his head and get the vision of Soto's perfect ass in her compression shorts out of his head. He'd seen her in plenty of skimpy outfits when she'd come back to the office straight off the street or before heading out to it, but that had always been in the work environment, and he'd never let his eyes linger, even for a second.

But damn. Walking into the facility and seeing her there had stopped him short. With no one else around, he'd taken that second—and then another—to appreciate her.

He slipped through his backyard's rear gate and started running down the steep trail abutting his property. It wasn't a very well-traversed trail. Some of the more dedicated trail runners knew about it, but mostly he had that portion of the trail to himself.

Which also meant the less populated trails were overgrown. Leaves and small branches snapped and whipped him as he ran by. He kept the image of Maria in his head while he ran. Thought of all the delicious, naughty things he wanted to do with her.

All the places he wanted to touch and kiss and lick.

All the dirty things he wanted to whisper in her ear.

All the nerve-tingling things he wanted her to do to him.

For the longest time, he'd never allowed himself to jack off to those fantasies until one day, he said to hell with it. Not sure if that had made not having her better or worse, but he'd had a hell of a good time in the process.

Even as he huffed his way up the ridge that overlooked his house, the sweat rolling down his back, and his quads screaming and his lungs billowing for every last molecule of oxygen, by entertaining those thoughts of her, he'd managed to give himself a hard-on.

Christ.

The thin fabric of his running shorts didn't hide anything, and running while aroused wasn't pleasant. He stopped at the top of the ridge, catching his breath and taking in the scenery, trying to get his mind off a beautiful ex-DEA agent.

To forget that perfect ass, he shifted his thoughts to what he hoped to accomplish in the next couple of weeks. Those thoughts did the job the scenery couldn't—it killed his boner. He took off up the trail, pushing himself harder and faster, anything to clear his mind.

Would he ever have peace?

Would his sister?

He was less than a mile from his home when he ran down a more populated trail along the backside of some houses. Now that he was closer to civilization, his phone chimed with an incoming text.

Soto: I still have your suit coat.

Finn stopped and leaned against someone's privacy fence. The dappled light from the leaves overhead made his screen difficult to see.

Finn: Keep it. I don't need it.

He shoved the phone back into the case strapped to his arm and continued his run. His phone chimed again, and he ignored it until it chimed a second time. He stopped in the middle of the trail as a woman ran from the other direction. Stepping aside, he gave her a nod. He'd seen her on the trails before but had never exchanged more than a wave or a nod.

His phone chimed in his hand.

Soto: Like I have a use for it?

Soto: I know you have more money than Midas, but even he wouldn't want to toss a perfectly good suit.

Soto: ??

Finn: You can leave it at the office. I can pick it up when I get back.

Her reply came almost immediately.

Soto: The office is out of my way. I'm in the area. I might as well drop it off on my way home. What's the matter, you afraid to let me know where you live? I may have had a thing for you, but I'm not that desperate. Trust me. I have options.

Her thumbs must have flown over the keyboard. She better not be driving while texting. And about her knowing where he lived... he was a private man. He liked keeping it that way. But, he knew a challenge when he read one.

Finn: You better not be texting and driving.

Soto: Duh.

Finn chuckled, but he didn't exactly know why. Maybe it was because of the way she loved to push his buttons. His ex-wife had been good about calling him out on his bullshit, but she'd never pushed him out of his comfort zone the way Soto did.

He swiped the sweat out of his eyes and fired over his address. He could almost see the self-satisfied smile on her face. Fine. She may have won that round. At least he'd have his suit coat back.

Back at his house, he closed and locked his gate and walked up the steps to his back deck. He'd left a towel on one of the Adirondacks because he usually came back with his clothes soaked through and layer upon layer of trail dust stuck to his body. He'd taken the valley trail, crossing a stream and slipping and sliding through muddy parts left wet from snow runoff even that late in the summer.

He toed out of his muddy running shoes, glanced over his shoulder to make sure no one was standing on the ridge that overlooked his property, and stripped naked. He knocked the bigger chunks of dirt off with the towel before securing it around his waist. If he hurried, he'd get a good shower in before Soto arrived.

Sliding open the rear door, he padded into the den. The doorbell rang, and Finn froze. No way she could have gotten to his house that fast.

She said that she was in the neighborhood.

She knocked with the meat of her fist. The kind of knock

that law enforcement used to let the people inside know they weren't fooling around.

He tried to hustle past the front entry and down the hall to his bedroom without being seen. One glance at the sidelights on either side of his front door, and he knew he couldn't get away with that.

Soto stood in front of one of the sidelights still dressed in her workout clothes, her nose pressed to the glass and her hands cupped around her eyes to block out the sun's glare.

He rolled the top edge of the towel down one more time to make sure it stayed put and headed for the door.

She knocked again, even though she saw him coming. He unlocked the door and opened it partway.

"Hello," he said.

"*Hello?* You sound like you don't know why I'm here."

He held out his hand, and she draped the collar of his suit coat over his fingers. "You might want to send that to the cleaners. I was kind of sweaty when you gave it to me."

"Thank y—"

She pushed her way inside, not waiting for an invitation. He hadn't expected her to do that. It caught him off guard. Short of closing the door on her, he didn't have a choice but to let her in.

The entry led straight into his den. She brushed past him and made a slow turn next to his rustic wood and iron coffee table he'd bought from a local artisan.

"Wow." She stopped spinning and leveled her eyes at him. Her assessing gaze dipped down and back up again.

He used every ounce of willpower he had to keep from squirming under her perusal. If she'd been wearing sunglasses, she would no doubt have slipped them down the length of her nose and ogled him over the top of them.

"I guess you don't always wear your suit."

As bad as his running shorts were at hiding an erection, the thin towel wasn't significantly better. Unsure of how to respond, he let the comment go.

"Wow, what?" He was almost afraid to hear her answer.

"What?" she said absently, then tore her eyes away from the trail of dark hair beneath his belly button and snapped them back to his face when she realized what she'd been doing. "Um… I didn't expect your place to look so… so…"

He stepped closer. "So, what?"

"Normal?"

He laughed, and the tension eased. "What did you expect?"

"I don't know. Quadruple the square footage for one. A high stone fence and a strong security gate."

"A tuxedoed butler to greet you at the door with caviar and champagne?" he added.

"I'll admit, I'm a little disappointed about that. Not gonna lie. I'm getting hungry." Her stomach rumbled on cue, and she covered it with her hand. "Sorry about that."

"I live alone. I don't need that much space, and living with help is not all it's cracked up to be."

She turned and headed for the kitchen. He tossed his suit coat onto the back of the couch, and as much as he didn't want her going in there, short of blocking her way or grabbing her arm, he couldn't stop her *and* play off what she was about to see as if it were no big deal.

"I like what you've done with the place." She walked through the space. "Looks like you opened up the ceilings, put a half-wall into the kitchen…"

Yeah, the half-wall hiding the case files and the product of years of investigation on the table. In seconds, she'd know the truth of it. He was in deep.

Soto stepped into the kitchen. Her steps faltered when her eyes dropped to his kitchen table. "Um…"

He walked in behind her, not sure if he was more embarrassed to be standing in front of her filthy, sweaty, and nearly naked or for her to see the disaster that was his life.

Even if he refused to apologize for either.

"This is what you wanted help with? There must be years of investigative work here."

"Nineteen years, to be exact."

She rifled her thumb through the same stack of case files that Ronan had, the file naturally falling open to the most viewed page—the crime scene photos of his sister.

"Who is she."

He didn't want to get into it. Especially with the way he was dressed. And, if she couldn't help him, there was no need to tell her. "It doesn't matter."

"It doesn't matter," she repeated. "Yeah, clearly."

She met his eyes, the question remained, but she didn't press.

He stepped back, offering for her to leave without directly telling her to get out of his house. "Thanks for dropping my suit coat by."

She blinked at him. Once. Twice. He half expected her to put him in a headlock until he cried uncle and told her the truth. No one who knew her would put it past her.

Instead, she nodded and headed for the door with one long last look at the table. If she thought he'd lost his mind, she didn't say so.

He walked her to the door and opened it for her. As he was closing the door behind her, the knot between his shoulder blades eased. Then she braced her hand on the door and stuck her head back in.

"You're really going to let me leave without telling me who she was?"

He closed his eyes, not sure he was up for seeing the

sympathy in her eyes when he divulged that kind of information. "That was the plan. The hope."

"She mattered."

More than anyone knew. Except him.

The silence dragged like a bag of jagged rock. Heavy. Immovable. "She's why you're an agent."

It wasn't a question. She must have seen the truth of it in his now undoubtedly red eyes.

"Who was she?" Maria pressed.

The sting immediately came to the backs of his eyes, and he blinked to keep the tears at bay. It had been a long time since he'd shed a tear over his sister, but the way Soto had asked as if she understood, he... *fuck.* Was he going to tell her?

She dropped her voice. "*Oscar.*"

His first name dropping from her lips caught him off guard. No one called him Oscar.

Ali had.

He swallowed down the maddening lump in his throat. "She was my sister."

Soto didn't spew the empty platitudes well-meaning people often said to him when they find out, not that he went around telling many people, mainly for that reason. Completely unexpectedly, she said, "You're a good man, Finn. She would have been proud of you."

She stepped away. Finn closed the door and slumped against it. The tears he'd valiantly held back earlier now fell like rain.

4

─────

As Maria drove back to her place, two things kept going through her mind. Jericho asking, 'What was that all about?' as Finn had walked out of Steele-Wolfe Securities without the help he needed because he didn't want to work with her, and those haunting four words Finn spoke... 'she was my sister.'

She didn't know what she'd expected Finn to say. Maybe the case files were from an old, unsolved case of his from early in his career that he couldn't get out of his head. You stay in law enforcement long enough, and you'll have a case that haunts you. That one case that keeps you up at night, making you wonder what you could have done differently, or better, or, or, or. There was always another *or*.

But his *sister*.

Maria's heart hurt. Nineteen years of investigation. He'd only been an agent for about fourteen years. He had to have been looking since before he started college, long before the FBI. How had Maria not known that? How had no one on the task force known that?

Since when had Finn ever talked about anything personal?

She couldn't even remember anything that had come up in conversation, except maybe that he had family money. Even then, it wasn't because he'd volunteered the information. It had come after someone had jokingly accused him of being on the take because the FBI didn't pay well enough for their agents to afford fancy suits and cars.

Instead of defending himself, he'd simply said, 'there are other ways for someone to have wealth.' And then he'd changed the subject.

Family money had been the consensus since he didn't seem to care what the stock market did.

And he was too *by the book* to be on the take.

Finn may not want her help with the case, but one thing she'd learned about these complicated, drawn-out investigations was that sometimes you needed a fresh pair of eyes if you wanted to knock a stale case wide open.

She stripped out of her workout clothes, now stiff with dried sweat, and turned on her shower. The water touched her sore palms, and she hissed in a breath. A reminder of what Wyatt had said to her. *I didn't hire you because I thought you could beat me in a race. I hired you because you don't give up.*

Yeah, well, maybe it was time to put some of that don't-give-up-ed-ness to good use. Did she want to work on an investigation that forced her to work with a man who had refused her help?

No.

But after seeing all the work he'd done to find his sister's killer, after he'd gone to Wyatt admitting he needed help, after looking at the pain in his eyes he wasn't quick enough to hide, she had to put her reservations aside and do the right thing. She'd never forgive herself if she didn't at least try.

Quickly, she dressed in a pair of her black tactical pants and one of her old DEA T-shirts and checked the refrigerator for food that could spoil. Since she always avoided going to the grocery store for as long as she could, the contents of her refrigerator consisted of condiments, beer, and a dried-up slice of pizza.

Ay Dios mio, had she devolved into a twenty-year-old frat boy?

She suppressed a shiver, dumped the pizza into the trash, locked up, and dumped the trash in the can outside. For years, she'd always carried a *Go* bag. A bag that she kept in her car in case she ever needed to leave at a moment's notice. She'd recently repacked and updated the bag's contents shortly before signing on with Steele-Wolfe, so she didn't waste any time executing her plan.

And going from decision to her car in less than fifteen minutes didn't provide any opportunity to consider what the hell she was getting herself into. Which, considering her unresolved feelings for Finn, was probably for the best.

As soon as she hopped into her car, she gave Wyatt a heads up. He backed her plan, only requesting daily updates. Before heading over to Finn's, she made a critical stop at Sakana's, a local sushi restaurant in Murdock.

Yeah, sushi in the middle of Wyoming seemed like a dodgy prospect, but Sakana's pulled it off. Stomach complaining, she drove the twenty minutes out to Finn's place, pulling into his long driveway and parking in front of his garage. She didn't know how long they'd be gone, and she didn't want to leave her vehicle on the street.

She exited her car, grabbing the overstuffed bag of takeout. Finn had a wrought iron fence between the side of his house and the garage, but it was more decorative than a security measure at four feet high. She tried the gate. Locked. She hooked the bag's straps over one of the stiles sticking up. She braced a hand between them and hopped the fence with practiced ease.

She knocked on his back door, hoping—for her libido's sake —that he wouldn't come to the door nearly naked.

LIKE HE HAD TOO many times before, Finn poured over the pages of his investigation. He scanned the file he'd put together on suspicious 'accidental' drownings in D.C. in the few years before and after his sister's death. He had hoped to find evidence that didn't make him look nuts.

Not that he cared what anyone thought besides maybe Ronan. He'd given up on updating his parents years ago. All it did was make his mother cry, and his father shake his head and tell him to let Ali rest in peace.

But how the fuck was he supposed to do that when her killer was still out there?

His stomach grumbled. He hadn't eaten since... since the night before. And that hadn't been much more than an uninspired roast beef sandwich eaten, as usual, at the kitchen counter.

That morning he'd skipped breakfast in a rush to meet with Wyatt. After leaving disappointed, he'd gone on his run, and the rest was history. At least he'd taken the time to clean himself up before diving back into the investigation.

When his stomach growled again, he knocked back another slug of his now cold coffee to shut it up.

He heard the car come up his driveway, surprised that Ronan would show up at his place twice in as many days, but his friend was probably stopping by to check on him to make sure he'd kept to his word.

At least Finn could honestly tell Ronan he'd tried even if it were probably better that he go it alone. Ronan might disagree with him, but like always, he'd eventually give in. Ronan always did when it came to Ali and Finn's never-ending quest for the truth.

The knock on the door came as a bit of a surprise since Ronan usually let himself in, but Finn was too engrossed in the file to pay it much mind. He hollered out, "It's open, asshole."

The back door into the kitchen opened. Finn didn't look up. He heard the rustle of plastic bags a second before Soto said, "I bring sushi, and I'm the asshole?"

"I—" Finn sputtered and stood. He was so hungry. He half wondered if she were a mirage and his mind was playing tricks on him. "What are you doing here?"

She held up the bag from Sakana's. "Sushi, remember?"

"But—" His brain refused to kick into gear, his thoughts slipping like over-worn sprockets. "The gate was locked."

Soto rolled her eyes. She had a way of rolling them that said, *you're a fucking idiot* without her having to say the words. "I've hiked up my mini skirt and sprinted after perps in four-inch platforms. Your four-foot fence won't slow me down."

He took the food from her hand, set it on the counter, and removed all the containers. She'd gotten salmon and tuna sashimi, rainbow rolls, California rolls, and spider rolls. She dug through his refrigerator and pulled out two bottles of water.

"I know you didn't just drop by to bring me food, so why are you here?"

"Can we eat first?" Her eyes dropped to the overcrowded table. "The den?"

He did the mental calculation in his head. If he ate at the table, he could get that much farther instead of sitting in the den where he couldn't read while he ate.

"You're kidding me, right? You want to keep working," Soto said as if she'd read his mind. "Fine."

She set the water on the table and moved files over, careful not to stack things on top of each other. While it looked like complete chaos to anyone else, he knew what each pile contained and knew where to find what he was looking for. He appreciated that she'd naturally considered that.

He brought over the containers of food. With the bare minimum of table space, they stacked the containers on top of each other. They'd have to work their way down the stack, but that wouldn't be a problem.

They each took a seat, and he passed out the chopsticks. The groan of bliss when Soto slid the first piece of sashimi into her mouth went straight to his groin.

And that's why working with her is a terrible, horrible, stupid idea. She can't even eat without you making something more out of it.

She waggled her chopsticks in his direction. "If I'm going with you, you should bring me up to speed."

Going in for another bite, Soto plopped that piece into her mouth as well, luckily for him, sans sound effects. He'd hate to go over the details of his sister's murder with a boner.

She didn't ask if she *could* go with him. She was *telling* him. The distinction wasn't lost on him, but he'd also worked with her enough over the years that even though she couldn't be more than five-foot-four, he'd learned early on not to let her size fool him. She had Big Dick Energy, and she knew how to use it.

Finn didn't fight it, but he did have to stifle a smile. He gave her the Cliffs Notes version as he dug into the food. She listened with practiced intent. He could see her filing each tidbit of information away bit by bit. There was more. Oh, so much more. But you couldn't get the nuance of the case until you'd scoured all of the documents.

And if he were honest with himself, he'd taken the investigation down so many rabbit holes that he didn't know what was relevant and what was wishful thinking.

By the time he'd finished, only the spider rolls remained, the empties in the takeout bag on the floor between their feet.

She took out the original case file from the D.C. Metropolitan Police Department and opened it to the first page. "How did you get this file? You know someone in the department?"

"No. No strings pulled. My father had even been with the State Department back then, and he either couldn't, or I suspect *wouldn't* get copies of the case during or after the investigation had been completed. I had to file a FOIA request when I turned eighteen, and that's the file they sent. A year later."

"What the fuck? A year?" She ran her thumb along the edge of the file. The original, anemic file when it came to content. "And what investigation? Comic book amateur sleuths could have done better. This isn't an investigation. This is half-assed filling out forms and calling it good."

He heard the frustration in her voice. If she were perturbed now, wait until she read through the file.

"Did you speak with the detectives?"

"They'd retired by the time I got the file, but I managed to track them down finally." He dug into the middle of one stack of papers to his left, pulled out a blue file folder, and handed it to her.

Not much of anything useful in it, but he'd crossed that *T* in his investigation. Then he rummaged around until he found the interview he had with the medical examiner, the morgue techs, and even the embalmer at the funeral home. He gave her all those files as well. It wasn't even a drop in the investigative bucket, but she had to start somewhere.

She stacked all the files he gave her under the police report and ate the last piece of the spider roll before he could. "When do we leave?"

"Our flight is at nine in the morning. It was the earliest one I could schedule."

"Do I need to buy a ticket?"

She talked about using her own money to buy a ticket to help him out in his investigation. Like he'd ever let her do that. "No. I'll take care of it."

"All right then." She opened the file to the first page. "Better brew a big pot of coffee. Looks like we're going to need it."

5

Finn shook Maria awake. The kitchen was nearly dark except for a small lamp Finn had brought to the table. The sun was peeking above the horizon. Maria shook her head to clear the fog.

Behind her, the coffee pot gurgled with a fresh batch. Her stomach lurched. If she never saw another coffee bean again in her life, it would be too soon. As it were, her kidneys were threatening to go on strike. Plus, the coffee hadn't been doing its job if she'd fallen asleep face-down in the files.

She had to clear her voice before she could speak. "How long have I been asleep."

He shrugged, the harsh light from the lamp only making the dark circles under his eyes look worse than they were. "An hour. Maybe two?"

"What time is it?" She fumbled for her phone, but her hand had fallen asleep, and she could do little more than slap at the dead screen. Great. She'd forgotten to plug in her phone.

"Nearly six."

"*Six!*" She bolted to her feet and started scrambling to gather her things. "Why didn't you wake me? It's a three-hour drive to Cheyenne. If we don't get a speeding ticket, we might—"

"Hey, hey, hey." Finn stood and gripped her wrists, carefully avoiding the abrasions on her palms. "Relax. We have time. We're flying out of the Alpine airport."

"Alpine?" What was he talking about? "All they have is a little municipal airport."

"I have a plane there."

Maria busted out laughing. She didn't even know if it was all that funny, but she laughed until she snorted. "Oh, my God. Of course, you do."

He dropped her wrists and went to the cabinet to get travel mugs for their coffee. "It's not exactly mine. It's a jet pool. You pay in every month, and you get a certain number of hours of flight time. It's not that big of a deal. People do it all the time."

Said the man with money to burn.

"When was the last time you flew commercial?"

Finn's beautiful mouth opened and closed, his brows drawing together the way they did when she asked him questions he'd rather not answer. "Does that matter?"

"I guess not." She hitched her thumb over her shoulder. "I'm going to get a change of clothes out of my car and take a quick shower before we go."

"There's a guest bathroom in the hall. Everything you might need should be there."

By the time she'd returned with her clothes, Finn had disappeared into his bedroom with the door solidly closed. She heard water hitting the drain pan. She tried not to think about Finn naked, especially now that it was so easy for her to do that after yesterday's towel incident.

But if nothing else, the whole private plane thing underscored how far apart their worlds were. He's over there in designer clothes and fast cars, and she's happy knowing that her new job will cover her mortgage and the last of her modest car payments.

He'd never know what it was like to struggle to pay all of his bills.

Maria had never forgotten how her mother had worried about all their expenses, even if she never remembered going without.

At least now Maria was financially stable, if not rolling in dough. She had savings to fall back on. She'd taken a risk going with Steele-Wolfe Security instead of returning to the joint task force or asking to be reassigned. Even though Wyatt paid well, she'd taken a step down in salary.

The upside? If the company did well, she would have greater financial opportunities.

And she didn't have to come to work every day and sit across the table from Finn.

This case notwithstanding.

Without wasting time, she showered and changed, opting for a comfortable pair of jeans and a blouse that made her tits look great even if she'd resigned herself that there would never be a her and Finn. All those years, it had been nothing more than wishful thinking.

Though the one definitive thing she'd learned during her time on the task force was that it was a hell of a lot of fun pushing Finn's buttons.

MARIA YAWNED in the driver's seat beside Finn. She'd insisted on taking her car and driving to the airport, which suited Finn just fine. He hadn't had a good night's sleep in days, and pulling all-nighters at his age wore on him. Not that he was as old as he felt, but he certainly couldn't push himself for days on end the way he'd been able to do in his twenties without having it take its toll.

"I get why you want to solve your sister's case. And obviously, you've been working on it for years. But why the big push now? What's in D.C.?"

"Massey sent me information on a case there. Congressman Fitzhugh." Finn pulled eye drops out of the pocket of his suit and tried to wash away the grittiness in his eyes. He pinched his eyes with his thumb and forefinger. When he opened them again, he had to blink Soto into focus.

"He's that congressman that died the other day?"

"Drowned in his pool."

The uncomfortable silence stretched out. Soto had something on her mind. Maybe she didn't know how to say it to him.

"Spit it out," Finn said. "You've never had trouble telling me what you think before."

"The case has never been this personal before."

He turned in his seat to more clearly see her as she drove. She had her hair up in a messy bun on top of her head, and he loved that she didn't feel the need to wear makeup. Not that she needed any. She was beautiful the way she was. But they weren't driving to Alpine for him to sit there and admire her face.

"If this is going to work—you helping me with this case—you can't go easy on me. Or try to spare my feelings. I don't need or want a *yes* man or woman. I want another set of eyes. I want input whether you think I'm going to like what you have to say or not."

She glanced at him before returning her eyes to the windy road as if wanting him to see the sincerity on his face. "Okay, here goes." Again, that quick glance. "Are you sure you're not chasing ghosts? How many people drown in their pools each year? Do you track down every one of them? What makes the congressman so special? And why do you think his death could be connected to your sister's?"

"They were both found in the pool with their bathing suits on backward. At least my sister's bottoms were."

Soto braked, then caught herself and sped back up. Luckily, early on a Sunday morning, the road between Murdock and Alpine wasn't heavily traveled. "The autopsy I read showed no indications of sexual assault on your sister, and I assume the same will be found on the congressman. If the congressman had a lethal amount of drugs in his system, that could account for the backward clothing. It's not like people are super detail-oriented when they're high as Benjamin Franklin's kite."

"My sister didn't use."

"Says the majority of family members about their loved ones. Your sister didn't live at home. How would you know for sure? You were what? Ten when she died?"

"Twelve."

"It's not like she would have been telling her kid brother about all the drugs that she did. She would have hidden that shit."

Soto wasn't telling him anything he didn't already know, but he *knew* his sister.

At least the thought he had.

"Did she have any drug screens through her employer? Something to compare to get a general idea what the norm was for her?"

"She was a librarian. It wasn't like she was operating heavy machinery. No one was going to die if she misapplied the Dewey Decimal System. I doubt her work had random drug tests."

The sun had risen, casting a warm, pinkish glow on the Rockies. They would be early to the airport, but Finn hoped they could change the flight plan and leave early if the pilots were ready. It felt like every second counted, while at the same time, it already felt like he was three laps behind in a four-lap race. If the congressman had been killed, there was no reason to believe the killer would have hung around town waiting to be caught.

And *if* it was the same person who'd murdered his sister, that meant not only was the person a professional, but if they were still doing contract hits after all these years, they knew how *not* to get caught.

"I thought she worked for the Franklin Public Library."

"She did."

"That's a federally funded library. They could have had a program in place for all their employees, irrespective of their jobs."

"Good point." Finn took out his phone, started a new note, and titled it *Things I've Overlooked*. He didn't know if there would still be records of something like that after all these years, but it would be worth checking into.

As they approached the outskirts of Alpine, Finn pointed up ahead. "The turnoff for the airport is right after that gas station."

Soto slowed, and despite what Finn had said to her about speaking her mind, she had more to say. He could feel it in the tension in the car. He waited her out. Maybe she needed a minute to figure out how to phrase her words.

After a mile or two, she slowed and pulled through the main gates of the airport. There wasn't so much a central terminal as a row of hangers. He directed her to a hanger in the middle of the row with a Bing Brothers Corporate Charters sign.

She parked, and they retrieved their bags from the back of her Rogue. They each had their bags, but he'd also brought his garment bag for his suits. He couldn't think of any place he went without it. And, of course, his laptop. He'd provided one for Soto as well, having loaded the case files on it from his laptop.

Long ago, he'd scanned and digitized all of the casework he

had to work on while he traveled. But he was old school enough to like to have the real things in front of him while he worked at home. Something about being able to see the pages in his head, the notes scrawled in the margins, the bent corners, the food stains. He could see them all in his head. And being able to put his hands on pieces of paper made him feel closer to the information somehow.

It might make him weird, but that was how it worked for him.

She took her bag out of his hand when he went to carry it for her, and he let her without comment. She was more than capable of taking care of herself.

It was a short walk into the hanger. One of the things he loved about chartered flights was skipping all the lines at the airport. A grounds crew guy recognized him as soon as they walked through the door.

"Mr. Finn. Good to see you again."

"How are you, Sam?"

"Doing well, sir, thank you. I'll stow your luggage. There was a mechanical issue with the plane you'd reserved, so you get the long-hauler. Good news is you'll have a little extra room today. The crew's doing their preflight right now."

The man pointed to two doors beside the office for Soto's benefit. "Restrooms are in there. There's coffee in the office, or if you prefer, there's a pot started on the plane. The onboard fridge is stocked if you're hungry. I'll put the computer bags in the overhead compartment. You can board anytime."

"Thank you."

Soto glanced around, taking in the hanger. One of the Bing Brother jets was outside the hanger with portable stairs pushed against the passenger door. Before, Finn had only flown in that plane when he'd taken trips out of the country. It had a couch and comfortable seats, a galley, a lavatory... and a bed in the back.

He almost groaned when he thought about that bed. Not because he pictured himself joining the mile-high club. As tired as he was, a three-hour or so nap on the flight over sounded decadent.

"I'll be back." Soto headed to the restrooms.

Finn waited for her and escorted her to the plane. The swirling breeze blew the scent of coffee down the steps. The first thing he did when he boarded was head for the coffee. He'd mistakenly left their travel mugs in the car.

He pulled the pot out of the built-in coffee maker and held it up. "Want some?"

"Do Canadian geese want to murder people?"

Finn chuckled. "I'll take that as a yes then."

He poured both of their coffees into cups, put on a lid, and handed her one. She took her coffee black, the same way he did.

"Food sounds tempting. The bed and breakfast I stayed in last night had no bed and no breakfast. My Yelp review is going to be brutal."

"Sorry. I have a guest room. I should have—"

"I'm teasing. I'm a big girl. If I'd wanted your bed—*a* bed—I would have asked for one. Besides, I didn't go to your place to sleep. I went there to work."

"Why did you? Why did you want to help?"

6

————

Maria leaned against the bulkhead dividing the galley from the seating area, contemplating how to answer Finn as to why she'd decided to help him. "Honestly... I don't know." She thought about it more. "Because you let me?"

The pilot and co-pilot came through the cockpit door to greet them. The woman's co-pilot didn't look old enough to make a model airplane, much less fly one. They introduced themselves, and the pilot said, "We'll be going wheels up in fifteen."

"Thank you," Finn said.

The pilots secured the passenger door and returned to the cockpit. When they were alone again, Soto returned to their previous conversation. "You've got two weeks. I'm all yours."

Oh, man, that came out wrong.

What the hell was wrong with her? She quickly added, "I didn't mean it that way. I meant, according to Wyatt, he can let me help for as long as you need me during that time."

"Look... Soto..."

The way those words came out, it sounded a lot like the

beginning of one of those *It's not you, it's me* kind of conversations. Could she have made a bigger ass of herself? "I want to help. I know you're not interested—"

"I never told you I wasn't interested."

Wait. What?

Soto laughed. The joke was on her. If he wanted her to be honest with him, then he'd better watch out. "You can't even stand to look at me half the time."

He tilted his head, the confusion on his face almost comical. He took the coffee cup out of her hand before she could take a sip and set his and hers on the galley counter behind him. He placed his arm on the end of the bulkhead above her head, standing closer than he'd been seconds before.

She swallowed hard. The way he looked down at her now, she couldn't say she didn't recognize the heat in his eyes. With a glance at the cockpit door as if he feared the pilots were standing in the doorway watching... *judging*... he dropped his voice and said, "It's not that I can't stand the sight of you."

"Then what is it?"

"It's that erections in the workplace are unprofessional, and while I love the tailor that makes my suits, that thin wool would have done little to hide it."

"Prove it."

What are you doing? Take it back. Right the fuck now. If you take it back fast, you can play it off as a joke. A bad one, but still a joke.

Instead of backing away, he eased closer. "And how do you suggest I do that?"

"Kiss me."

Now you've gone and done it.

Maria wanted to close her eyes and hide behind her eyelids, hide from his intense scrutiny. But even though she'd obliterated whatever line she shouldn't have crossed, she didn't want to take her words back. She wanted to see what *By the Book* Finn would do when pushed.

Or shoved.

She didn't close her eyes. Instead, she watched a variety of emotions flash behind Finn's heavy-lidded eyes before he finally took that step back.

Yeah, that's what she'd thought.

Great. Now she was stuck in a steel tube with the man she'd made a fool of herself over.

"Do you ever break the rules, Oscar?"

She liked how using his first name got his attention. Liked that he hyper-focused on her as he puzzled out the question beneath the question.

If he figured it out, maybe he'd pity her and fill her in as well because, at the moment, she had no idea why her mouth wanted to get her into trouble.

"I do my best not to. I'm not perfect. No rule is black and white. But no. Not usually."

She smelled his cologne, a subtle, subversive scent that you could only smell if you got close enough...

Like now.

It made her flash back to the day before when he wore nothing but a towel, with the scent of dirt and sweat and clean mountain air all over his body.

So many naughty things she wanted to do with the man who was all about composure and rule-following.

She wanted to see what it would be like if he let himself lose control, let himself get out of his head long enough to really *feel.*

Maybe that's why she pushed his buttons.

Or maybe it was much simpler than that. Maybe she just wanted him to kiss her.

"It wouldn't be right to kiss you," he said.

"There's no rule that says you can't."

"Not officially. But technically, because I hired Steele-Wolfe, you still work for me."

Maria appreciated a man with a dedication to his integrity. However, she was having difficulty figuring out what she liked about it right then.

A part of her wanted to take him by the ears and plant a kiss on his lips that made him forget his name.

And all of his damn rules.

"I won't say anything to HR if you don't."

Not that Steele-Wolfe had an HR, but she was sure Finn got the gist.

The slight smile softened his expression, and he lost one of the worry lines creasing his forehead.

He skimmed his knuckles down the side of her face, a reverence to his whisper-soft touch. It sent a rush of delicious goosebumps dancing across her skin.

"It won't change anything." Even as he said it, he leaned nearer.

"Then why are you scared to do it?"

A chuckle escaped him with an audible breath. "You don't give up, do you?"

"That's what they tell me. I'm not looking to be the asshole here, so seriously, if you don't want—"

His voice dipped, the bass dropping out of his voice, and whatever he said got lost beneath the whine of the jet's engines as they spooled up.

Maria raised on her tiptoes, closing the distance between them.

He brushed his lips against hers. A sound escaped the back of her throat, part sigh, part groan, all indulgence.

She wanted to sink into him, but she didn't want to take more than he offered.

To be this close, to breathe him in as he did the same to her after all those years, was heady stuff.

She wanted more. More now. More later. And as much as she'd pushed for this one taste, she wouldn't—*couldn't*—be the sole driving force behind what else might or might not develop between them.

As an *oops* baby, growing up, having to fight for her place in the family had taken a toll.

By the time she'd been born, her mother had already separated from her father.

It seemed like her mother had already been done with anything that reminded her of Maria's father. And from what relatives told Maria, her looks and personality made her her father's mini-me.

Her siblings had taken after their mother, so that must have made them more palatable to be around.

Seemed like from her earliest memory, Maria had to fight for anyone's attention.

Some fights start out as a losing battle.

For once, she needed to be someone's priority. Needed to be considered first, not someone to be tolerated until the relationship grew untenable.

But she didn't want to think about her mother right then.

She wanted to remember every second, every delicious detail of this kiss.

Finn angled his head, taking the kiss deeper. Their tongues touched. She tasted the coffee they'd chugged that morning in their hurry to get on the road.

But beneath all that, she tasted his hunger. Felt rather than heard the low growl in his chest under the hand she'd placed over his hammering heart.

This isn't happening.

But it *was*.

A la verga.

The intercom squawked, and the pilot came over the PA. "Please take your seats and prepare to taxi."

Maria expected Finn to jump back, not linger and press his forehead to hers.

After a shared breath, the plane started to push away from the hangar, and Finn took a step back.

He cut his eyes away, and a knot formed in her gut. Fuck. Did he regret it?

He better not fucking regret it.

They took their seat at a four-seat grouping. Two on each side of a table facing each other. Finn took the rear-facing seat, and Maria took a forward-facing one and buckled in with a snap.

Finn stared out the window, the front of his dress shirt a little crumpled from her hand. She must have balled it into a fist.

The plane lined up with the runway. The engines revved. Maria glanced at him. He must have felt her eyes on him because he refocused on her. The look in his eyes made her heart kick once in defiance. She raised her chin. "Don't you dare tell me it was a mistake."

FINN BIT back the very words Maria dreaded hearing before they could fall unceremoniously and thoughtlessly from his mouth.

They would be a lie, anyway.

An excuse to ignore what he really wanted and not have to face the reality that if he started anything with her, it could end very badly.

And wasn't having her as a friend much better than finding out she couldn't stand the real, imperfect Oscar Finn?

The way she held his gaze, the rebellion flaming in her warm, brown eyes, he watched as her internal shields crept up, ready to protect herself from whatever she expected him to say.

Even if he thought it would be better to lie to her and let her suffer the rejection now, he couldn't look her in the eye and say it, couldn't watch those shields go up and lock closed, couldn't watch, even if he thought it would be for the best.

He was too tired to pretend he didn't want her.

Did that make him a selfish asshole?

Thankful that the table between them hid what that kiss had done to him, he considered how to answer her.

"No." He let the simple word hang there, mixing with the whine of the jet's engines as they climbed higher and higher into the sky. The clouds streamed past the windows, obscuring the ground below. "It wasn't a mistake."

Her chin came down a notch, but she didn't smile. His forced declaration obviously didn't make her feel any better. He needed to say more if he didn't want to screw things up completely. Jesus, he was bad at this.

No wonder Shondra left him.

"If I hadn't wanted to kiss you, I wouldn't have."

He couldn't read the subtle shift in her expression. If he had to guess, he'd say he was only digging a deeper hole. "What I mean..."

One of her perfect black brows rose as if to say, *This ought to be good.*

Before he lost his nerve—or regained his senses—he said, "What I mean is I'd wanted to do that for a long time. And me wanting more doesn't negate the fact that I'm not an easy person to be with. I have more than my fair share of flaws. If you don't believe me, you can ask my ex-wife."

Soto's sputter almost made him laugh.

"Wait, you were married?"

"And divorced. Is that so surprising?"

"How long were you married?"

As much as he hated to go into his failed marriage, at least it got rid of his boner. "Six years. Divorced for three."

She sat back, the wheels churning. "You were married during part of the time I was on the task force. Why didn't I know this? Why didn't anyone know this."

"My marital status had nothing to do with my work."

The incredulous look on her face made him wonder if it were such an outlandish thought that someone had wanted to spend their life with him. Or at least thought they had wanted to until the reality of him—and his relentless drive to find his sister's killer—had set in.

"No. But your marriage never even came up. Like, *I have to leave early to pick my wife up at the airport*, or anything like that. You didn't even wear a ring."

"Neither one of us had one. We didn't feel like a piece of jewelry made our commitment any more or less than."

The plane reached altitude and leveled off. The pilot turned off the seatbelt sign. Finn unbuckled and stood, unsure why the conversation made him so uncomfortable. "Want that coffee now?"

"Sure. They have any food in there? I'm starving."

"I'll see what they have."

Instead of waiting in her seat for him to return, she followed him into the galley. He should have known she wouldn't have been distracted that easily.

He dumped the now cold coffee he'd poured before takeoff and fixed them each a fresh cup. From the refrigerated storage, he pulled out two sausage breakfast sandwiches and heated them in the microwave.

Soto—or was it Maria now that he'd kissed her? No. Better to stick with Soto. No need to further blur the lines the way the kiss had—blew on her coffee then took a sip. "Who's idea was it not to wear rings?"

"Shondra's." If that raised brow were any indication, he'd surprised her.

Soto's eyes narrowed. "Wait. Is that why you were such an asshole during the Turner investigation three years ago? You were going through your divorce?"

"I wasn't an asshole."

"Your team would beg to differ."

The microwave dinged, saving him from having to respond immediately. He handed her her food. He picked up some napkins and returned to his seat. They ate their breakfast in silence, not because the food was that good, but because Finn didn't quite know what to say, and Soto was gracing him with the opportunity to respond.

He swallowed a bite and wiped his mouth. "Was I that bad?"

"There was talk behind your back. Mostly the team wanting to help if they could, but of course, you refused to let anyone in."

Finn let the part about not letting anyone in go without comment and latched onto the other part. "*Mostly?*"

"There were the few who threatened to cuff you, hold you down, and see if they could pull the extra-long stick out of your ass."

"*Extra?*" Finn laughed. Even though he and Shondra were in a good place now, having his marriage fail still stung, and being able to laugh about it helped a bit. "I'm sorry I was more of an asshole than usual."

"I'm sorry you didn't feel like you could tell us. We were a team. We would have been there for you. We would have picked up as much of the slack as we could."

"It wasn't your slack to pick up. That was on me."

"And you're not an asshole. Mostly. I enjoyed working with

you on the task force. Leaving was the hardest decision I'd ever made."

"Yet you did."

She hesitated as if deciding how much she wanted to reveal. Something shuttered behind her eyes, and he knew whatever came out of her mouth next would be the sanitized version—a partial truth. "It was time for a change of scenery."

Finn let her end it there. They finished their breakfast, his having gone cold, the bread stale, and the sausage rubbery. His stomach churned, but he choked it down because he had no idea when they'd next get a chance to eat.

After cleaning up their breakfast, Soto got out her laptop to keep familiarizing herself with as many aspects of the case as she could while she had the chance. Finn made mental notes of what he wanted to do when they landed. Securing a rental car and driving out to the scene being the first of many things.

If he got lucky, he might know one of the federal investigators and be able to get some information. It would be easier that way, but he'd do whatever he had to do to ensure all leads were followed.

It might all be a goose chase, but Ali was worth the effort of finding out.

Soto jerked awake in her seat, her eyes opening, then drifting closed again. She hadn't had much more sleep than he had, and she was obviously on fumes. She would be no good to him if she didn't at least shut down for a short period of time.

He stood in the aisle and tapped her on the shoulder. She woke, and he held out his hand to her.

Though sleepy and a bit confused, she trusted him enough to put her hand in his. "Where we going?"

Her sleep roughened voice shot to his groin, and he had to remind himself, yet again, that it would be best to keep things between them professional.

Is that why you had her take your hand? To keep it professional?

He ignored his inner voice and led her to the back of the plane as she rubbed her face and tried to wake up. He opened the rear cabin door and let Soto precede him inside.

"Oh, wow," she said, brushing her hand over the luxury bedding in the jet's single room.

It had a bed larger than a twin but probably not even full-sized. It had windows on either side with the shades already drawn. It had a couple of nooks in the headboard to hold a cell phone or a book, but not much else.

She turned and sat, her eyes trying to close again though she fought it.

"Get some sleep. We're going to have to hit the ground running."

She toed out of her shoes and snuggled into the pillow, not even trying to talk him out of it. Her eyes opened, and she said, "You need some sleep, too. The bed's big enough for the two of us. We can draw a line down the middle like siblings in a car if that would make you feel better."

By that stubborn set of her jaw, she was only half kidding about the line down the middle.

As tempted as he was, he turned her down. "I've got... work," he decided on. Even though as tired as he was, he could probably sleep standing up.

Finn settled in his seat, his laptop open to his case files. He started reading a file he'd read a hundred times before.

But still, he read, hoping that he might catch something he hadn't noticed before, something that would break his sister's case right open.

Wishful thinking, but maybe one of these days, it would come true.

A bump of turbulence jarred him awake. Glancing at his watch, he realized he'd only returned to his seat fifteen minutes before. He closed his laptop and scrubbed his hands down his face, already feeling the crick in his neck.

He glanced at the rear of the plane. The sliding door to the cabin stood open, the empty side of the bed inviting him in.

What would it hurt to lay down and get a couple of hours of sleep?

She'd offered. Could he allow himself that much?

Did he dare?

It wasn't that he didn't trust himself. It was that he didn't trust himself not to want more.

Finally, his exhaustion won out over his good sense. Maybe he would find it again once he got a little sleep. One could only hope.

At the cabin door, he slipped out of his shoes, hung his suit coat up in the tiny closet, and stretched out on the bed beside her, the mattress dipping under his weight. In the few minutes since she'd laid down, she'd curled up on her left side, facing away from him.

He laid flat on his back, careful to maintain the little space between them. As soon as his head hit the pillow, his eyes drifted closed, his mind going directly to the place he didn't want it to... images of him and Soto in the bed, but this time, neither one of them had clothes on, and that carefully maintained space between them had been obliterated, their bodies now slick with delicious sweat as they both chased their climaxes.

7

———

Maria awoke to a ping on the PA as the plane's engine speed slowed a fraction at the beginning of its descent. The pilot announced they would be landing in thirty minutes.

Behind her, Finn groaned and stirred. Sometime during the flight, he'd come to bed, thrown his arm around her waist, and tugged her into him... and his erection.

Not that she was complaining, but if he knew that he'd snuggled up against her while he'd slept, he'd probably have a bit of a freak-out. Which in Finn speak meant that he'd grumpily pretend like nothing happened when something had.

Not that Maria expected anything to come of the close contact besides more awkward silence, but at least she had physical proof to back up Finn's words when he said he was interested.

To be fair, this wasn't the time to start something that she didn't think he was capable of finishing, despite his interest. They had a potential contract killer to find and a cold case to solve.

She peeled his arm from around her waist, trying not to

wake him until she could get further away. He stirred and shifted, his erection tucking tighter into her ass. His body stiffened, and she turned her head in time to see his eyes snap open.

He rolled away and stood, trying to adjust himself inconspicuously, which only made the move more conspicuous.

"I didn't—" Finn visibly struggled for words.

Maria raised her brows when he cut himself off. *I'd like to see you explain this.*

Red infused his cheeks, and she didn't think she'd ever seen him quite so embarrassed before.

"I mean—" He gestured between them as if that conveyed what he wanted to say. Fun fact... It didn't. "You know."

Maria could have let him off easy and could have pictured a time with the task force not too long ago when she would have. But that was the old her. The her before she'd been shot. The her when he'd apparently pretended he wasn't interested in her. Now? She didn't have the time or the patience for that.

Finn took a deep breath and cleared his throat, the calm, cool, collected special agent taking over for the flustered one.

"My apologies. I didn't intend for that to happen."

"Trust me. No one was more surprised to feel your dick pressed against my ass than I was."

And just like that, flustered Finn returned, crimson flashing up his neck.

Before he could apologize again and make a bigger deal out of it than it was, Maria decided to go easy on him. "I worked undercover as a sex worker, Finn. I've had plenty of dicks pressed up against me."

That line re-formed between his brows, the line he always got when he had to fight hard to keep his temper in check.

"Why did you let—"

Oh, no. He didn't get to say that to her.

"I didn't *let*, asshole. But it still happened. It's hard to sell yourself as a sex worker if you never let people put their hands —and other things—on you. And you might want to check yourself before you *let* any more words drop out of your mouth without thought."

Then she took a piece of her own advice and checked herself before *she* said something she couldn't take back. Before saying something that might give him too good of an idea of what working undercover as a sex worker had been like.

He stretched a kink out of his neck, but Maria didn't allow his apparent new, calm demeanor fool her. She'd seen the way his eyes narrowed. And it reminded her of the ass chewings she'd received early on in her career when she'd joined the task force, deserved as they were.

"I don't recall seeing any reports of sexual contact crossing my desk."

Mierda. Her and her big mouth. Her mother always said she never knew when to keep quiet.

Sometimes speaking your mind wasn't such a good quality.

Maria tried to minimize what she'd revealed. "There wasn't much to report."

And really, what she'd endured was all in a day's work. "It's not like I had sex with any of the johns," she carefully qualified.

She didn't want to talk about it anymore. Not that she'd been traumatized, but because... because...

Because you don't want him thinking bad about you? Think bad about you for doing your job?

She brushed past him, snagging her shoes off the floor as she went to take her seat.

With a mental shove, she pushed her negative thoughts aside. She didn't need to slut shame herself for doing her job— and a damn good job at that.

And if Finn were the type of man to slut shame her for that, then he wasn't the man she thought he was.

Finn followed her to the seats and buckled in across from her, quiet as he took her advice and carefully considered what he would say next.

"Why wasn't this brought to my attention?"

"Because no one would have taken me seriously if I dissolved into a pool of tears every time someone grabbed my tits, ass, or rubbed their junk up against me."

"That was never part of the scope of work."

Maria let out a bitter laugh as the plane banked on its approach to the airfield. "Tell that to the brass. Those men have no idea what it entails to stand out on a street corner late at night and pretend you're a sex worker. At least if you want to make your cover believable."

She didn't give him a chance to speak now that she was on a roll. "We never would have gotten where we did on that sex-trafficking case if I hadn't been out there. You know it. I know it. And I hope to hell the brass knows it."

She stared out the window as they dipped below the clouds and D.C. came into view. Her chin came up, and her eyes narrowed at him when she turned back to him and said, "I'm not ashamed of the work I've done. The same way I'm not ashamed to admit I liked waking up to you curled up behind me."

Setting her jaw, she almost dared him to contradict her.

"I liked it, too."

Maria's jaw almost dropped into her lap. Finn looked startled at the admission. She didn't know which one of them was more surprised.

The landing gear clunked and locked into place. Finn cleared his throat. "About the undercover work... as much as I hate that that happened, as much as I wish you would have reported it to me, we would still be trying to close that case if you hadn't done what you did. I'm proud of you and what you accomplished. I wish there had been a better way."

His voice dropped with his last declaration, and Maria felt a buzz in her belly as warmth spread through her chest.

"I wish I could have protected you from that," he said.

Though she appreciated his words, she wasn't his to protect. She could damn well take care of herself.

If you were his, would you even let him?

Honestly, she didn't know. She'd grown up pretty much having to stick up for herself from day one. So much that she had a hard time visualizing what being protected would look like. Would she feel supported or smothered?

The plane landed with a bark of the tires on the concrete. The flaps on the wings flipped up, slowing their speed. She let her end of the conversation drop, not knowing what to add after he'd admitted he'd liked to wake up beside her as much as she'd liked him being there.

But him being man enough to admit it, even knowing he didn't want to pursue anything with her because of his perceived notion of impropriety if they became involved, went far in her book.

Maybe inside the rule-follower was a rebel fighting his way out.

<hr>

THEY STEPPED off the plane into pissing rain, of course. Finn couldn't have expected the weather to hold out and make the trip less miserable.

Between packing up their gear, getting their luggage off the plane, and picking up the keys for the car he'd asked to be dropped off and waiting at the municipal airport, Finn had been able to set aside the realization that he'd revealed way too much of his interest in Maria than he'd ever wanted her to know.

It was hard enough ignoring that interested part of him

when she hadn't known, but now he worried he had one less thing holding him back. He didn't need this complication in his life right now. Not when he needed to focus on his sister's case to ensure that another opportunity to find her killer didn't fall through his fingers.

He hung up his rain-splattered suit coat on a hanger behind the driver seat, got behind the wheel, and plugged Congressman Fitzhugh's address into the map app on his phone.

Maria glanced at her phone when it pinged with an incoming text. She answered it. "That was Wyatt. I'd let him know we landed. He wants me to keep him in the loop as much as possible. He said Massey offered support if you need it while we're here, though, with their stakeout situation, he may not always be able to get the information we need promptly."

"Any little bit of help we can get, I appreciate. Though I'm not sure there's anything pressing we need from him. Right now, we need to see what information we can get from the agents on the scene if they're willing to talk to me."

"You think they're still processing the scene? It's been what, two days since he died? You don't think they would have finished already?"

"Most likely," Finn said as he started the engine and pulled out of the airport parking lot. "But with it being a congressman, a congressman on the house appropriations committee, I'm hoping that they're being extra careful and processing every last cat hair, mouse turd, and minuscule sliver of evidence they can find. If it turns out to be an accidental death or a suicide, then all that effort may seem like overkill, but it's hard to go back to a scene and get clean, usable evidence after it has been released back to the family."

They fought their way through lunch hour traffic in the heart of D.C. to get to the congressman's house. Finn sighed with relief when he'd had to show his credentials to the uniformed officer at the gate and sign himself and Maria in. The crime scene truck in the circular drive in front of the congressman's house was a welcome sign. If he were lucky, he might be able to sweet-talk whoever was in charge of the investigation into letting him and Maria inside.

The congressman lived in a neighborhood without sidewalks. The high walls and imposing gates around the properties told the people on the outside that only the privileged were allowed in.

The house was some sort of bastardized version of colonial style. Finn couldn't tell if it was really old and had been fixed up or if it was a new construction made to look like it had been there since before the signing of the Declaration of Independence.

Like at the front gate, a uniformed officer stood outside the front door. At a crime scene, you didn't want every swinging dick walking through the door and potentially contaminating your crime scene.

He flashed his badge to the officer, even though he wasn't there on official FBI business. But he'd hoped to gloss over that part until he could get to the agent in charge of the case.

"I'm special agent Oscar Finn, and this is..." His words trailed off as he turned to Soto, the realization hitting him that she no longer had a badge.

"Maria Soto," she said with a disarming smile as she reached out a hand for the officer to shake. She didn't bother to say what part of the federal or local alphabet soup of agencies she belonged to since she couldn't do that without flat out lying and misrepresenting herself.

Ronan might be giving Finn some leeway, but he'd come unglued if Finn tried to pass Soto off in any official capacity. As it was, Finn was on the edge of a very thin line.

The door opened behind the officer, and a woman and two

haggard men in rumpled suits stepped through the door. The men he'd never seen before.

The woman was another story.

She was a petite, vivacious woman who'd taught him the tough lesson that office romances could be disastrous. Besides having a history that went way back, Finn would rather square off with a heavyweight MMA fighter than Anita Quan, any day.

What she lacked in stature, she more than made up for in shrewd intelligence and dogged determination. She drew up short at the sight of Finn standing in front of her.

The two men nearly bumped into her.

The scowl on Quan's face only deepened. "Finn. What the fuck rock did you crawl out from under?"

She pushed past Finn. The men behind her veered off and got into the same car while Quan headed for a black, departmental SUV.

"Anita, can you hold up a minute?"

Anita Quan spun on a heel, the expression on her face nothing short of murderous. If Finn weren't careful, Quan would make more evidence for the crime scene technicians to collect, and Finn wouldn't have to wonder anymore if he dared try to start anything with Soto.

"What do you want?" Anita reached down and removed the booties she'd worn over her shoes to prevent contaminating the crime scene.

If Finn could have picked the worst agent for him to have to deal with, it would have been Quan. They'd managed to avoid each other ever since they'd both left the white-collar crime unit in New York, where they'd been assigned shortly after they'd both left the academy.

You mean since she came to her senses and dumped your ass before you could ruin both of your promising careers?

Before he could answer, her complexion almost turned

green when a realization hit. "Please don't tell me you've been assigned to this case."

"No."

The relief on her face would have been comical if the case weren't so serious. He decided that the only way to get Quan to help him out was by being one hundred percent transparent. Anything short of that, and Quan would kick him to the curb faster than she had all those years ago.

"I'm here for more personal reasons," Finn said.

His response knocked her back on her heels for a second. He watched as the sympathy rolled across her features before it solidified into something more neutral. "Don't tell me you're still chasing a ghost."

"The person who killed my sister isn't a ghost. They're out there. Still. I think there could be a connection between Fitzhugh and my sister's murder."

"Her death was ruled an accident."

He lowered his voice to keep from raising it. "You and I both know that's bullshit."

Quan's eyes shifted to Soto. "Who's this?"

Soto offered her hand. "Maria Soto. Finn and I worked together on a joint task force."

Quan shook her hand, but her gaze flicked back and forth between the two of them before landing on Finn again. "You banging her, too?"

Soto broke out with a laugh as if the accusation were preposterous. "Yeah. No."

Maria sounded believable. She sounded like she hadn't recently admitted she'd liked having her ample ass snugged against his crotch. "I'm just here to help."

Quan leaned against her SUV, balled the dirty booties up, and shoved them into her pocket. "You're not going to leave me alone until you get inside the crime scene, are you?"

While Quan could come off as a hardass, deep down, beneath all that bluster was a compassionate woman. At least she had been. And puffing out his chest and going toe to toe with her wouldn't get him anywhere. If he wanted to get her on board, he had to appeal to her sense of decency and justice. "I'm asking for your help. But if you want me to leave, all you have to do is say so."

Of the three people who'd seen the files he'd accumulated on his sister's death, Quan was one of them. Ronan and now Soto being the other two.

Her eyes went to Soto again. "He can be awful hard to say no to."

"Tell me about it," Soto said.

Quan checked her watch. "You've got twenty minutes. Then I have to leave for a presser with the mayor. They want this thing solved in an hour, less commercials. It's hard to explain to the public this isn't an episode of CSI."

Quan stepped forward, and Finn and Soto followed behind. Finn caught up with her with some effort. What she lacked in stride length, she more than made up in sheer speed.

"Let me guess," Quan said, "You're here because of the backward bathing suit, aren't you?"

Finn glanced over at Soto. She gave him one of those looks that said Quan had impressed her.

Quan turned around, walking backward when she said, "I don't even want to know how you found out that detail. That information hasn't been released to the public. Do I have an internal problem I need to be concerned about?"

Quan turned back around as they approached the front door. She had Finn and Soto sign in with the officer standing guard. Right inside the door, a table had been set up with booties and gloves. They covered their feet and hands and followed Quan through the foyer, the spacious den, and out the open sliding doors to the outdoor entertainment and pool area beyond.

When Finn was sure no one was within earshot, he answered Quan's question. While he didn't know how Massey had gotten the information about the congressman's swimsuit being found on backward, he had the sense that it wasn't information that Quan had to worry about leaking to the general public.

Massey wasn't that kind of guy, and Finn didn't think he would align himself with someone who had plans to compromise the investigation.

"I don't think you have anything to worry about that information being leaked. I can almost guarantee that."

At least he hoped he could. Maybe he needed to have a word with Massey and make sure.

She led him around the pool to the deep end. "The housekeeper found him at the bottom of the pool. She jumped in, dragged him to the shallow end, and called 911. He wasn't breathing, and she couldn't find a pulse. Paramedics got him out of the pool and administered CPR, but it sounds like it was already too late."

"What did you think about the bathing suit?" Soto asked.

"Honestly," Quan said, her attention turning to Finn, "I thought about your sister. But seriously, what are the odds? It's been what, over twenty years?"

"Twenty-five years and two months." Finn didn't even have to do the mental math. His subconscious kept track of the time since it never took a break from working on the case. He frequently had dreams about the case. All these years, he'd waited for a midnight epiphany that, so far, had never come.

"I would think a contract killer would go out of his way not to leave identifying or signature clues behind," Quan said.

"What about drugs in his system? Anything from the medical examiner yet?"

"She put a rush on the tox screen, but nothing has come back. We don't know if he had drugs in his system when he drowned. Hopefully, we'll know something soon. The governor is on the mayor's ass, and now the mayor is on mine. I've worked high profile cases before, but the pressure on this one is magnified, especially since that article came out in the New York Times yesterday."

Finn glanced over at Soto. "Did you read the article?"

Soto shook her head. "No. But that was about the time you came to the facility and interrupted my workout."

The image of Soto all sweaty in her spandex shorts and sports bra popped into his head, and he had to shove it aside so he didn't get distracted.

"What article?" Finn asked, hating that he might have missed something vital.

Quan rolled her eyes. "Something to do with that cryptocurrency betting site. Dead something or other. Conspiracy theories, you know the sort of thing."

"The betting site is called DeadMoney. And I have a credible source that believes it's all too real."

Quan sent him a look that said, *Oh, no. Not you, too.* As if he'd unwittingly drank the Kool-Aid. "Maybe I should call the brass and get them to transfer you out of the bumfuck sticks before the smell of manure and hay completely rots your brain."

Ignoring the jab at his career out of the limelight of the big cities like New York and D.C., he said, "DeadMoney is a legitimate threat. If the bureau doesn't start taking it seriously, we're going to get caught with our pants down, and it will make us look like an ass."

Finn used the be in the same boat as his brothers and sisters at the bureau as far as his opinion on DeadMoney went, but after talking to Massey, he'd come to believe the DeadMoney theories were true. That somewhere out there, people were cashing in on other people's deaths. What better way to order a hit on someone than through an anonymous dark website with a cryptocurrency that is near impossible to trace?

With Fitzhugh's body long gone, there wasn't much to see by the poolside, though he did like being able to see the crime scene to put everything into perspective. And yes, Finn considered it a crime scene. If it were ruled an accident or suicide, Finn would eat his hat and save the leftovers for lunch the next day.

Finn glanced around when he realized Soto wasn't standing beside him anymore. He found her walking up and down the backside of the house. She climbed up on the side of a planter with a large tree-like shrub near one of the downspouts.

Quan slipped past him to see what Soto was up to. "What did you find?"

Soto popped her head out of the bush. "I found a camera."

She parted the branches on the bush, exposing a camera.

"Let me see," Quan said. Soto moved out of the way, and Quan climbed up on the brick wall of the planter, putting one foot on the lower sturdier branches to keep her balance. "It's wireless. All of the other security cameras are hardwired into the soffits of the house. I'll have a tech crew come out and see if they can tap into the feed." She turned to Soto, respect in her voice when she said, "Nice catch."

"I saw the sunlight flash off the lens through the gap in the branches." Soto glanced back at the pool. "It has a direct line of sight to the diving board and those lounge chairs near it. Maybe it caught something the main security cameras didn't."

"I don't understand what he thought he might catch with this one that the others wouldn't," Finn said.

"An affair, maybe." Soto shrugged. "Wasn't he the one pressuring interns for sex?"

"*Allegedly*," Quan said as she hopped off the planter. "From what the tech guys told me, someone had manually shut off the security cameras sometime before he died."

"Was he meeting someone he didn't want caught on camera?" With Fitzhugh's reputation of sex scandals and shady, backroom deals, Finn wouldn't put it past him. "Question is, did he know about the hidden camera? Or did his wife put it there without him knowing?"

"Future ex-wife," Quan said. "They're legally separated. But she's living in the house until the divorce is final."

"If she was living in the house, where was he living?" Soto asked.

Quan bumped her chin toward what looked like an old carriage house. "He was living there, according to the wife."

After a quick check of her watch, Quan added, "Time's up, Finn. You're already going to make me late."

She headed for the back door. Finn and Soto had little choice but to follow. They signed out with the officer at the front door and walked Quan to her truck.

"I appreciate you letting us in," Finn said, even though he didn't have much more information than he had when he'd arrived, though Soto's discovery of the hidden camera may turn up some leads. "I'd appreciate it if you kept me in the loop on the investigation."

"Finn," Quan said as she climbed into her black SUV, "I can't do that. I shouldn't have even let you in. You know that. If you want updates, you're going to have to watch the press conferences like everyone else in D.C."

8

Soto and Finn climbed into the rental and buckled in.

"So... you and Quan?" Soto asked as he pulled away from the curb.

As soon as the words left Maria's mouth, she wanted them back. It wasn't any of her business who Finn had been with. But it was hard to picture them together, mostly because they seemed too much alike. Two peas in the same government-issued pod.

"It was a long time ago," Finn allowed. "Jealous?"

"No." There was no way she would be jealous of a relationship that had long since run its course. "But you had to have been close for her to know about your sister's case. I'm glad you had someone to share it with back then."

Finn did a double-take.

"What?" Maria said.

"You're telling the truth."

"Why wouldn't I be? She's not a threat to me. I already told you that I was into you. What you choose to do with that information is up to you. If you want her or someone else, great. I made the first move here. I'm not chasing after you like a lost puppy. If you want me, I'm counting on you to let me know."

"I already said I was interested."

She pivoted in the seat to look at him, and he took his eyes off the road for a split second.

"Your lips moved," she said. "The words came out of your mouth, but if I walked away now, you wouldn't come after me. I've lived my life feeling like I was in the way, that I was an afterthought. For once, I want to be someone's priority."

He opened his mouth, and before he could say anything else, she added, "And I know your sister's case comes first. I know that's your priority. I'm okay with that—"

"*Maria.*"

The way her name fell from his lips, with that deep, chiding tone, the low, intimate register as if the word were meant for her ears only…

That word made her want to hear him whisper her name like that when she was lying beneath him, with Finn balls-deep inside her. It made what she had to say next even harder.

"Kissing you was a mistake. I'd take it back if I could."

"You're lying." He didn't have any heat behind the words. If anything, he had a bit of a self-satisfied smirk.

"Why? Because you think you're such a good kisser?"

"No. Because we've worked together for a long time, I can tell when you lie."

"If it were easy to tell that I'm lying, I wouldn't have made such a good undercover agent."

Finn grinned. And to see a serious man like him with a genuine smile on his face made Maria want to see it that much more. "I didn't say it was *easy*. I said that I could *tell*."

A few lights up ahead, Finn hooked a left into the turn lane at the last second, making it through the light as it turned from yellow to red.

Maria grabbed onto the handhold on the dash in front of her. "What the—"

Finn made an immediate right into the next parking lot and pulled into one of the empty spaces facing the building. He placed the car into park but kept the engine running as he stared out the windshield.

The name on the front of the building said *Franklin Public Library.*

She'd seen that name before. "This is where your sister worked."

He blew out a breath and, after a long second, said, "Yes."

Maria popped the buckle on her seatbelt and the latch on her car door.

"Where are you going?"

"Inside?" It came out as a question because why else would they be there?

"I've crawled all over that library. There's nothing there that can help us."

"Your unpopular conspiracy theory is that your sister was involved with the government. The old rumor is that there's a tunnel under the building leading to the CIA building. I want to look around."

She didn't wait for him to answer. Sometimes it was better to keep pushing than to allow Finn to try to talk her out of something. Usually, it saved time.

Maria got out of the car and closed the door, leaving a disgruntled Finn to follow after her.

Finally, he caught up with her. "I've been all over this building. There's nothing here."

"Great. Then it won't take us long. We came a long way only to have Quan shut us down. We might as well make the most of the trip."

At the front of the library, Finn stepped ahead of her and

held the door for another woman heading inside and waited for Maria to proceed him. She immediately went to the library directory near the circulation desk and looked at the building map.

Archives were in the basement.

"Microfiche, here we come," she said.

She pushed through the door to the stairwell, the heavy fire door slamming closed behind them, their footsteps echoing on the concrete steps as they hurried down.

"How many times have you been down here?" Maria asked.

"Enough," Finn said. "It's the obvious place for a tunnel to start."

As they entered the basement, that dank, moist scent hit their noses as well as the industrial-grade air freshener the janitorial staff used to try to hide it.

One wall had a string of microfiche machines, computer terminals for searches, printers, and multiple coin-operated copy machines.

On another wall, perpendicular to the room, they had bookcases of bound documents, old periodicals, and of course, the microfiche storage.

In the center, they had some tables and chairs to work in, but the flickering florescent lighting, the buzz of the light ballasts, and the lack of natural light made Maria claustrophobic, even with the basement being two to three thousand square feet.

Since no one else was down there, they didn't have to pretend they were doing anything other than what they were— walking the perimeter in search of doors that might lead to a secret tunnel.

"See," Finn said as they made it three-quarters of the way around the perimeter with nothing but solid walls or eight-foot bookshelves to show for it. "There's nothing here. And if there were an entrance to a secret tunnel still in use, they wouldn't hide it behind an overstuffed bookshelf."

"Maybe it's one of those super sophisticated secret doors like they have in all the spy movies that when you push a button, the shelves open soundlessly to reveal a hermetically sealed secret hall or room behind it." Maria was kidding, but only by half.

"Now, who's the one with the crazy conspiracy theories? We're not in a James Bond remake. This is real life. It would be much less sophisticated than that."

"You don't have to spoil all my fun." Maria smiled. "I think I would make an excellent James Bond girl. I know all the cool fight scene moves, even if I don't have the long legs. I think the world is ready for a curvy, Latina love interest."

There it was again. That smile. *Fuck.* Finn didn't need to carry a weapon, not with a killer smile like that. "I'm sure it is."

Along the last wall was a short hallway leading to the restrooms and a water fountain with an out-of-order sign. Maria opened one of the doors, only to find what she'd expected, a five-by-five janitor's closet with nothing but a dried and dusty mop, a dustpan without a matching broom, and an empty box of trash bags.

"This building is old. They could have covered it in a later renovation. So the rumors could be true, but the tunnel is no longer functional. It's a long shot that your sister was involved in anything governmental."

"You're not telling me anything I haven't already told myself a hundred times before."

"I'm sure. Why do you think she might have been working with one of the agencies?"

"She'd always drive out of the city on the weekends and come home to Sunday dinner at the house. But there were times when we wouldn't see her for a while. My father said her work kept her busy, but sometimes we wouldn't see her for months."

"She was young. Maybe she preferred staying in the city with her friends. Wouldn't be the first time someone lied to their parents when they didn't want to come home."

Finn's face scrunched as if he didn't like that implication. "She and I were close. As close as siblings could be, considering our difference in ages. I never got the feeling she came home to visit our parents. I'd always thought she came to see me. At least, that's what I let myself believe. I don't think she would not have come home for that long if she'd had a choice."

"But you don't know that." It wasn't a question. She could hear the truth of it in his voice.

"No. There's a lot I don't know. Not really. So many things I look at through the lens of that kid without the perspective of an adult."

"What did your parents say about it?"

He cut his eyes to her and leaned against the wall. "They refuse to talk about it. Hell, they'll hardly even say her name. After Ali died, my mother took her photos off the wall and stored them away, as if she never existed. They didn't want to talk about her. Ronan was the only person I could talk to about her, but he had been a kid as well."

Maria swallowed down the stricture in her throat. "That had to be hard."

Finn stared off into the distance, even though the opposite wall was only a few feet in front of him, then refocused on her. "You have no idea."

She took a tentative step closer, wanting to offer comfort, but she didn't know if he'd welcome it. "I'm really sorry about your sister, Finn."

He reached out, snaking an arm around her shoulders, and pulling her into him. "*Christ,*" he muttered, his voice thick as he held on tight.

She looped her arms around his waist and stood there with

him as he felt his feelings. As much as he'd kept the team away from his personal life, about his sister's death and even his divorce, it said something that he hadn't pushed her away.

Even if nothing ever came from their kiss, she liked that at least now he'd lowered his walls enough for her to have a peek at the man on the other side. She may not be able to fix anything, but at least he knew that he wasn't in this thing entirely alone.

They stood there for a few minutes until the elevator pinged, and a college-aged kid with a backpack over one shoulder stepped out, heading for one of the computers.

She stepped away, squeezing Finn's hand as she did.

"You ready to get out of here?" he asked.

Hitching her thumb over her shoulder, she said, "I'm going to run into the little girls' room first. If you want to meet me out—"

"I'll wait."

Maria pushed through the door to the women's restroom. There were three stalls on her right. The last one had a sign that said out of order, similar to the water fountain. Across from the stalls were a couple of sinks, as expected.

She did her business, then washed her hands, looking at herself in the mirror wondering if anyone could tell that even though she'd said that kissing Finn had been a mistake, seeing the softer side of Finn was only making her fall for him harder and faster.

As she reached for the paper towels, she noticed a detail in the reflection of the shiny metal paper towel dispenser. She spun around, her hands still dripping water, and saw the upper left corner of a door on what should have been the back wall of the stall.

She took a moment before she got down on her knees to look under the door, trying not to get her hopes up.

"No fucking way," she said to no one as she stared at the door in front of her.

The steel fire door.

It could be another utility closet, but why hide it behind a bathroom stall door that said out of order? Of course, it was out of order. It didn't even have a toilet installed.

Besides, what utility closet needed you to scan a security card to open it?

Finn waited across from the ladies' restroom and scrubbed his hands down his face. It had been a long time since he'd been to the library. There were only so many times he could search the basement for a door that wasn't there.

He also hadn't expected it to be as emotional for him to be back. This trip had brought back all the expectant excitement as well as the crushing disappointment.

He needed to get out of there. Get some fresh air. Maybe some lunch.

What was taking Soto so long?

He raised his hand to knock on the door to make sure she was okay when the door opened. He had to stop the door with his hand to keep it from slamming into him.

"What's wrong," he said as soon as he saw Soto's flushed face.

Instead of answering, she said, "On your other trips here before, did you ever go into the restrooms?"

He thought back. "Once, I think."

"The men's *and* the women's?"

"I'm not going in the women's restroom."

She rolled her eyes. "You're such a rule follower."

Taking his hand, she opened the door wider. He dug his

heels in and risked a guilty look over his shoulder to make sure no one was watching and hissed, "I'm not going in there."

"Don't be so hard-headed."

"Fine." He shook off her hand. He didn't need her leading him in there like some errant toddler. "If someone catches me in there—"

Finn raised a brow when Maria got on her hands and knees in front of the third stall. Did she seriously want him to look under the door?

"Get down here."

There was his answer.

He got on all fours, his ass in the air as he looked under the stall door. The first thought that ran through his head was, *You've got to be fucking kidding me.*

He stood and leaned a shoulder against the stall divider. Soto stood beside him with her arms crossed over her chest and a self-satisfied smile on her face.

"You think this could be it?" He almost didn't trust himself. Worried that he'd read too much into a stupid door that probably led to a supply closet because he wanted so much to believe he'd been right.

But who put a stall door in front of a supply closet?

"I don't think they would spend the money to have a security card reader installed to keep people from stealing a worn-out mop and a bottle of bleach."

They heard mumbled voices, getting louder as they drew closer. They weren't coming from the hall behind them. They were coming from behind the door. Finn grabbed Soto's arm and dragged her into the second stall, closing and locking the door as the secret door in question opened.

He pressed Soto against the wall in front of him, their bodies touching from chest to hip, but he didn't dare move.

"... all I'm saying," a woman's voice said, her high heels

echoing in the tiny space as she opened the stall door, "is that Cramer should consider Erickson's men a domestic terrorist group. Just because their leader is young doesn't mean he's not a lethal threat."

A man's voice replied, "There's only what? Ten of them?"

The man closed and relocked the stall door. The two opened the door to the restroom, their voices fading as the woman said, "Ten that they've identified, but…"

Soto blew out a breath, and Finn took a step back.

"Holy shit," she mouthed as if still afraid to be overheard to speak any louder.

"You can say that again."

"Where do you think it goes?"

"I don't know, but I'd love to find out."

He unlocked their stall door, and Soto stuck her head out into the hall and looked both ways before she said, "It's clear."

They hurried out of the restroom and made a beeline for the stairs and their car. He didn't want to say anything inside the library that someone might overhear.

Climbing into the rental, they both closed their doors and sat back without saying a word.

"Honestly," Finn said at last, "I don't know what to think about that."

"And finding some secret door in the basement of the Franklin Library doesn't mean that your sister had any involvement with any federal agencies."

"It doesn't," Finn allowed. His heart still hammered as he turned the key. The engine rolled over as he tried making sense of everything that had just happened.

The tunnel's existence, but that didn't mean he could let his mind run away with all the possibilities. His stomach grumbled, and he realized they hadn't had anything to eat since the soggy sausage biscuit on the plane. "You want to get some lunch?"

"I could eat."

Finn pulled out into traffic, and Soto pointed to the nearest fast-food restaurant. "Let's stop here. We can eat in the car and talk and not have to worry about anyone overhearing our conversation."

They ordered and picked up their food, and Finn fought the traffic for a few blocks before turning into a nearby park.

Having grown up around D.C., he'd been there many times before. Normally, it was full of people during the day, but with the cloud-cover and intermittent rain, few people braved the weather except a few dedicated runners.

He pulled into a parking spot and cut the engine. Soto handed him a paper-wrapped burger and a box of fries that had already gone limp.

"What did you say your father did, again?"

"He retired about five years ago now, but he worked with the State Department."

"Doing what?"

"Started as an accountant, I think. Worked his way to upper management. Low profile, though. It wasn't like he reported to the President or anything." Finn took a bite of his burger and swallowed it down. "I don't know all the specifics. He never talked about it much."

She started in on her fries, but her mind wasn't idle. He could practically hear the gears churning and grinding as she filtered her thoughts and considered ideas.

"Have you ever considered..." She let her words trail off and dived in for another fry. "Never mind."

"No. I want to hear it even if you think it might be off base. That's one of the benefits of a fresh pair of eyes looking at the case."

"Okay." She finished off her remaining fries and started in on his. He passed them over to her, and she gave him her untouched hamburger. "What if your sister wasn't involved with the government. Maybe she was just a librarian, and the secret tunnel is the red herring in your case."

He didn't know where Soto was heading with this, but he was curious to hear her thoughts. "Go on."

She sucked down half of her soda before continuing. "What if your sister wasn't killed because of something she knew or was involved with. Maybe she was killed because of something your father was."

9

———

hat if your sister wasn't killed because of something she knew or was involved with. Maybe she was killed because of something your father was.

Finn sat back, blood buzzing behind his ears.

What if...

"I never..." With so many thoughts swirling around in his head, he didn't even know what he wanted to say. "How could I have not considered this?"

"Because you were what, twelve when it all happened?" Soto said.

"Yeah."

"Still a kid."

He pushed his half-eaten burger away. "I'm not anymore, though."

"No. But look at it this way, it's like that song you hear as a kid and get the lyrics wrong, but you don't know it, and you grow up never questioning it because, in your mind, it's correct until someone points it out. This is similar."

"I don't know."

"I do. And from the sound of it, your parents weren't willing to talk about your sister's death. And even if they were, it's not like they're going to tell you that her death had been related to your father's work."

"But he didn't do much for the State Department. At least nothing that would have made him a target for bad actors."

"If he had been, it's not like your parents would have told you."

Jesus fucking Christ.

The burger in his belly soured, and he tasted bile at the back of his throat. Not even Ronan had considered this, but then again, they'd both been kids at the time.

Maybe Soto had a point.

He pointed to her half-eaten second container of fries. "You finished with that?" he asked as she munched on a handful of three.

"What do you have in mind?"

"I think it's time I had a heart-to-heart with my parents."

She dumped the remaining fries into the bag and disposed of the rest of Finn's burger before stuffing it all on the floor at her feet. She took a long sip of her drink then rubbed her hands as if excited to get going.

"Sounds like a plan," she said. "Where do your parents live?"

Finn stretched his neck from side to side. There was only one way to get the answers he needed. That's *if* he could even get his parents to talk.

"It's about an hour and a half outside the city if the traffic cooperates. Two hours or more if the traffic backs up."

"An hour and a half? And your dad drove in that traffic every day to and from work? That's a hell of a commute."

"Well," Finn said, "the helo helped some with that."

"*Helo?* As in helicopter? Your father took a helicopter to work?"

"Mostly."

"And when he didn't?"

"He had a driver."

"Of course he did," Soto laughed, shocking Finn that she didn't have any disdain in her voice. "I can't even imagine."

"Money can't buy happiness. There's no lie in that statement."

"Maybe not, but it would make me happy to take a helo to work to avoid D.C. traffic."

"It's not without its benefits."

As he wove in and out of traffic on their way out of the city, his thoughts turned inward. Soto must have been up in her head or, if nothing else, giving him the space to process what they were about to do because she didn't say anything either.

It wasn't like he hadn't tried to have conversations about Ali with his parents in the past. It was that those conversations had been an exercise in futility, shortening his long fuse immeasurably. There were only so many ways he could ask a question and get rebuffed and still maintain his sanity.

The closer they got to his parents' house, the more he noticed the tension headache brewing. He could have put his head in a vise and turned the crank, and it wouldn't have felt any worse.

"You okay," Soto asked after he turned on Potomac Way— the several miles long, curvy two-lane road leading to his childhood home.

It's where he'd taken up jogging, his feet slapping on the pavement mile after mile as he ran up and down and up again. It got him out of the house when he'd needed fresh air to breathe and a way to relieve stress. To say that did not affect how well he ran cross country in high school would've been a lie.

"I'm fine. Why?"

"Because if you grip that steering wheel any tighter, you're going to lose all sensation in your fingers."

"It's been a while since I've been home."

Understatement.

That was about as much as he wanted to get into it before he had to step foot in his father's house again.

"Should we have called before we came?"

Finn glanced over at her. Calling ahead would have been considerate if his relationship with his parents had been more... *normal.* "This way, they can't make up an excuse for why they don't want me stopping by."

"They would seriously do that?"

"You obviously haven't been around the Finn family household. Otherwise, you wouldn't have to ask that."

"Should I wait in the car?"

He pulled into the driveway of his parents' estate and stopped at the towering wrought-iron front gate, almost embarrassed for her to see how he'd lived growing up.

He'd grown up with more privilege than any one person had a right to, but that didn't mean his life had been all sunshine and unicorns.

And as much as he wanted to spare Soto the shit show that could be his parents, he liked the idea of having her there not only to pick up on things that he might not notice but also to act as a buffer.

Sad, but true.

"Honestly, I'd appreciate it if you would come inside. Besides, there's no telling how long this is going to take."

"Whatever you need."

He lowered the window and punched in his entry code, mildly surprised that his father hadn't changed it since the last time he'd shown up unannounced.

The ornate gate started to open. Though he might not have called ahead to tell his parents he was coming, as soon as he'd punched that number into the keypad, they'd get an alert.

Not the complete surprise he'd wanted, but enough of one to maybe put them on the defensive. Which, in Finn's experience, had never been an easy thing to do.

The gates opened, but he took the time to really look at her. "You mean that, don't you?"

The gates started to close, and Finn pulled forward, breaking the infrared beam with the car's front end, and the heavy gates started opening again.

She looked at him as if he'd grown another head or at least lost the commonsense God gave a goose. Her head tilted. "Why wouldn't I mean that?"

Finn didn't have much of an answer. He'd been going at it alone for so long, he'd forgotten what it felt like to have someone there for him in not a strictly professional capacity. "I don't know. I appreciate it, though."

Soto smiled. It was one of those smiles that more poetic men than him wrote sonnets about. The kind of smile that did funny things to his insides and made him want to find a way to make her smile at him like that time after time.

He could get used to that.

Winding their way up the long drive, the branches of the massive American elm trees blew in the mild breeze. Not a single leaf marred the perfectly manicured lawn. They wouldn't dare.

As soon as they opened their car door, the briny scent of the Chesapeake hit his nose. He'd forgotten how much he'd missed the smell of the bay living land-locked near the Rockies for so long. He filled his lungs, then met Soto at the front of the car.

"You ready?" he asked, even though she had no clue what she was about to walk into. At least before a task force raid, they had a proper briefing beforehand and didn't have to go into a situation blind. He should have spent more time preparing her on the drive over. It would have been the considerate thing to do.

Then again, he wouldn't have wanted her to jump out of the moving vehicle when the reality hit.

A bit of an exaggeration?

Maybe.

Maybe not.

"Now you're starting to scare me," she said, even though she sounded more determined than deterred

"All I can say is that I apologize for whatever happens next."

FINN STRAIGHTENED HIS TIE, tugged at the cuffs of his suit coat, and knocked on his father's front door—a double-wide monstrosity that might have been pillaged from the entrance to a medieval castle back in the day and shipped over on the Mayflower.

Maria pictured a tuxedoed butler with his clothes pressed within an inch of his life coming to answer the door, so when who she assumed was Finn's father opened the door, it came unexpectedly.

"You should have called first," his father said by way of greeting.

Ignoring the comment, Finn said, "This is Maria Soto, a colleague of mine. Maria, this is my father, Walter Finn."

She stuck out her hand. "Nice to meet you, sir."

After a long pause, his father shook her hand, but by the thinly veiled look of disgust on his face, he would have wiped his hand on his trousers if he hadn't feared soiling them.

"May we come in?" Finn finally asked after a drawn-out silence.

For a beat or two, Maria thought Walter would refuse. Then he opened the door and stepped back to allow them through.

Finn put his hand on the small of Maria's back and ushered

her into the foyer ahead of him. The fries sat heavy in Maria's gut even though they should have been digested by now.

What had she agreed to?

"Where's Mother?" Finn asked as Walter followed them down the hall. "I want to talk to both of you."

The open foyer must have soared for three stories. But Maria couldn't take in the opulence when all she could think about was if that massive chandelier fell, all three of them would be crushed.

She stuck close to Finn. If she made a wrong turn, there was no telling when she'd be found. Maybe she should have kept the hamburger buns and used them to leave a trail of breadcrumbs.

In her house growing up, she had to worry about not being able to get away from everyone. Her house hadn't been so enormous that she required a GPS and a personal, dedicated satellite to navigate from one room to the next.

Finn took her by the elbow and pulled her into a room on their left. It was some sort of sitting room or den. A large mahogany desk occupied the space in front of a massive picture window, so maybe this was his father's office, though there wasn't anything useful on the desk like a computer or stacks of files.

Maybe it was there for decoration.

Finn leaned in and under his breath said, "Mother should be in shortly. Her tennis lesson is nearly over."

Maria must have missed that part of Finn's conversation with his father.

Walter walked directly to the drinks cart and pulled the top off of a crystal decanter that looked old enough that Maria feared they'd all get lead poisoning, even though it didn't look like it had hurt Walter any.

In reality, Finn's father looked about ten years younger than he probably was. Whether that was through clean living, good genetics, or a plastic surgeon's knife, she couldn't be sure.

"Oscar?" Walter said as he held up the decanter, asking his son if he wanted a drink. If Finn hadn't nodded, Maria would have insisted. If anyone could use a drink, it would be the special agent beside her.

Maria declined a drink when offered. She needed to keep her wits about her in a situation like this. No, she wasn't worried about being ambushed—at least not from bad guys with guns and knives. Though she had the feeling, Walter's words could be equally deadly.

The door to the hallway opened, and a woman in a bright white tennis outfit strode in. Every hair remained in perfect place, and no beads of sweat dared soak her skin.

"Really, Oscar," his mother said as she accepted the drink her husband had poured for her. Some sort of whiskey with one of those big balls of ice from a dedicated special ice maker, because of course. "You know Sundays are not good days to visit."

"I wouldn't have come here if it weren't important."

His mother sniffed and looked Maria up and down a critical few seconds. "And you are?"

"Maria Soto," Maria said. "A colleague."

His mother returned her attention to Finn. "That's a relief. I thought you were here to tell us you were getting married."

Maria's mouth dropped open. Before she could ask what the hell that meant, she caught the tiny shake of Finn's head. This wasn't about her. And as much as she'd never had someone dislike her so fast, she'd hold her tongue... for now.

For Finn.

"This is my mother, Vivian," Finn supplied since it seemed his mother wouldn't.

"Nice to meet you," Maria said, though she doubted the feeling was mutual.

His mother sat in a floral wingback chair while his father stood beside her, drink in hand.

"Have a seat," Finn offered Maria. She sat on the couch across from his parents, patently aware that she was way under-dressed for the situation. If she'd known, she would have tried to clean herself up before they'd arrived, but in truth, she didn't think there was a level of dress that his mother would have approved of.

Mainly because it wasn't so much the clothes they didn't approve of, but the woman wearing them.

"Is that how you dress these days, Oscar? No wonder Ronan is now your boss. You can't expect to get anywhere in life dressed—"

"*Mother*." Finn swallowed back his drink and went for a refill. "I'm not here to talk about how I dress, and even if I were, I can assure you that Ronan didn't get promoted over me because I have a few wrinkles in my suit."

With his glass refilled, he returned to stand near Maria.

Finn paced to the window and back again as if he didn't know where to start. Maria considered jumping in but decided the less she said, probably the better.

"Sit down. It's rude to pace," Vivian said. "We taught you better than that."

A muscle twitched at the corner of Finn's jaw, and if he were any man other than the one he was, Maria knew he would have fired back a retort. But that wasn't Finn's style. Whether he'd learned that from his parents or despite them, Maria couldn't be certain.

Finn sat beside Maria and finished off his drink. The deep breath he took told Maria of his difficulty finding his words. This conversation wouldn't be easy for him. Then again, how could it be?

After setting his empty glass down on the glass coffee table, Finn clasped his hands in front of him, his elbows on his knees, his demeanor somber.

Vivian sat up straighter, thinly veiled disdain on her face. "You got her pregnant, didn't you?"

Maria huffed out a laugh, even though no one else so much as chuckled. They would have to have done more than kiss once, and Finn rub up against her at forty-one thousand feet for her to get pregnant.

"Vivian. Let the boy talk," Walter said as if Finn were still a schoolboy.

"Christ, Mother. No. She's not pregnant." He shifted his gaze to his father, and Maria watched closely to see his father's reaction to what Finn had to say next. "But we did find the tunnel entrance."

Walter stiffened, his face blank of emotion. He tossed back his whiskey and swallowed it down with a grimace. Whether the grimace was from the burn of the liquor as it slid down or the bitter taste of Finn's words, Maria couldn't determine.

"I'm sure your father has no idea what you're talking about."

Finn sat up straighter. "I think he knows exactly what I'm talking about, Mother."

Maria had to admire the way Finn refused to break his father's gaze, impressed how he hadn't come at his father with a question he could deny, but a truth he couldn't.

"What do you know?" his father asked as he took a seat in the wingback on the other side of a small side table from his mother, not giving anything away.

"Not much of anything," Finn allowed. "But obviously, you know."

"I'm not sure if this is the time to—"

"It's past time. It's past time you told me everything. Past time that you and Mother stop pretending Ali never existed. Past time you tell me what you know about her murder so I can find her killer once and for all."

His mother didn't even pale at the mention of her daughter's murder. It wasn't any news to her that her daughter's death hadn't been an accidental drowning.

The red ran up Finn's face, the pulse at the base of his neck beating a rapid tattoo, yet when he spoke, his voice came out calm and without the waver Maria's would have had. She wanted to squeeze his hand. Wanted him to know that she was there for him, but any effort on her part would only be an unwelcome distraction, at least where his mother was concerned.

So, she sat there beside him and watched as he confronted his parents.

"You'll never find him. He's a ghost," Walter said. "Let your sister rest in peace."

"You've got to be fucking kidding me." Finn delivered the words evenly, but his mother stiffened at the language.

If you asked Maria, they were strong but long overdue. She couldn't imagine the rage Finn must be feeling to find out that his parents had been keeping him in the dark about his sister's death all those years and had only allowed a crack in the concrete veneer when directly confronted. "Ali deserves justice. And that man is still out there. Still killing."

"Greg Fitzhugh." Walter nodded as if the words made a connection in his head. "You think the same person who killed your sister killed the congressman."

Maria had to hand it to Finn, he didn't say *duh*, but he did allow his father time to process his thoughts without interruption.

"Why?" his mother asked, the imperious tone Maria had heard up until then came out barely a whisper. She cleared her throat. "Why do you think it was the same person?"

"Do you want to tell her, Father, or do you want me to?"

10

———

Finn's father didn't answer.

Finn shifted on the couch. The slight movement brought his hips and thighs into light contact with Soto's.

It was less than he wanted, but more than he should allow himself with his parents—*his mother*—in the room. He didn't want to give his mother another reason to be more... more... *herself.*

He could handle it, but he didn't want Soto exposed to any more of it than humanly possible.

Exactly how have you handled it? You call hiding out halfway across the country handling it?

Maybe not so much *handled* as out of sight, out of mind.

And if it hadn't been for Ali's case requiring the visit, he wouldn't have come.

There were so many questions he wanted to ask at once, but now that he felt like he had his father on the defensive and talking, he wanted to ask the big questions first in case his father decided he didn't want to talk anymore.

It was a gamble going with the big ones first, but it was a gamble he willingly took.

"Was Ali's murder connected to something in her life or something in yours?"

His mother stood abruptly. "I can't listen to this."

"It's time the boy learned the truth."

Finn let *the boy* comment go even though he'd been a grown-ass man for a very long time. In the grand scheme of things, it was a little thing to endure.

Finn's father reached for Vivian's hand, but she shook him off. "You already got our daughter killed. I'm not going to sit here and watch you do the same with our son."

His mother walked out without so much as a nod in Finn and Soto's direction.

She must have some affection for me if she doesn't want to see me get killed.

Then that cynical part of Finn kicked in. *She's probably more concerned that if you die too, it will take her out of the running for mother of the year.*

Finn's father finally met his gaze. "Sorry. You know how sensitive your mother is."

No. No, Finn didn't. He'd known his mother to be many things, but *sensitive* wasn't one of them. If Vivian Finn possessed a sensitive side, she'd buried it under layers of caked-on superiority, narcissism, and manipulation.

"Tell me," Finn said. "Tell me everything."

His father took one look at Soto as if he were going to ask her to leave. Finn took her hand like he did that every day, laying their joined hands on his thigh. He didn't realize how much he'd needed that touch—that connection—until her fingers interlocked with his.

"She stays." Finn kept his voice even but used that tone he

sometimes had to use in the task force briefings. The tone that said the issue wasn't up for debate.

"Ali was CIA," his father said. "Your mother blames me for bringing her into the business."

Finn thought the relief would have washed over him, having heard those words. He'd suspected for years Ali had some ties to the organization, but even with his FBI clearance, he'd never been able to substantiate his theory.

Hearing the confirmation didn't make him feel better or even vindicated. He only felt Soto's—*Maria's*—hand in his, giving it a reassuring squeeze.

The only way his father would know... "So are you."

"Not anymore," his father said. "It's a younger, more idealistic man's game."

"Why didn't you tell me? All these years, I've been searching for Ali's killer. If I had known, I could have—"

"Could have what, Oscar? The man is a ghost. He's been operating against United States assets for too many years. He doesn't make mistakes."

Maria broke her long-held silence because what Finn's father said simply wasn't true. "Everyone makes mistakes."

"The backward swimsuit for one," Finn pointed out.

"The backward swimsuit isn't a mistake. It's a fuck you," Soto said. The hand squeeze and sympathetic smile told Finn that she'd hated to say it.

Finn's father gave Soto the briefest smile and an almost imperceptible nod, which would probably be Walter's only outward expression of approval. Not that Finn needed his father's approval or even acceptance where Soto was concerned.

Walter's expression softened a fraction. "Well said."

"That may be true," Finn said, "but without the bathing suits turned around, it would have made it harder to link the two deaths. The question is, why the congressman? Why now? And why does his killer—this *ghost*—not care that the two deaths could be linked?"

The subtle shift in his father's eyes told Finn he might have an answer to that question. Finn waited him out. Walter Finn wouldn't disclose any information he didn't want to. Finn applying pressure wouldn't change that.

The silence dragged on. The house remained quiet except for the buzz of a leaf blower from one of the landscapers outside.

"Fitzhugh had been your sister's handler back in the day," his father finally said.

Walter could have said the sky was green or that there really were aliens at Area 51, and Finn couldn't have been any more surprised.

Soto's brows rose, and her grip tightened in his hand, the unasked question in her eyes—*What are we getting ourselves into?*

At that point, Finn had no clue. He had to bite back the bark of derisive laughter and swallow his incredulity.

"Fitzhugh was CIA?"

"Briefly," his father said. "Before your sister died and the sparkly lights of politics caught his eye. He wasn't any better as a handler than as a politician. But at least as a politician, he wouldn't be getting anyone else killed.

Finn must have had a funny expression on his face—and who could blame him after everything that his father had revealed?

His father asked Finn, "What's that look?"

So many thoughts swirled through his head he didn't know where to start. Soto's gentle squeeze brought him back to the conversation.

Having his long-held suspicions about his sister confirmed had thrown him for a loop.

He returned his attention to his father. "I'm having a hard

time processing the knowledge that you've lied to me all these years."

His father leaned forward. The vein in his forehead that had always been an infallible barometer of his heightened emotions pulsed.

"I was trying to protect you. If the ghost could get to your sister, he could get to you, too."

His father's voice cracked at the end, and it was the most emotion Finn had seen from his father besides anger and perhaps, disappointment in years.

Finn blew out a breath, releasing his pent-up fury and frustration. "I'm not a kid anymore. I find bad guys. *This* is what I do. *This* is what I'm good at."

The pulsing vein disappeared. His father ducked his head, his voice dropping when he said, "No, you're not a kid anymore, but you're still my son."

"I get that. I do." And for the first time since Finn could remember, he felt something other than judgment from his father. "But I need your help. Help me... Dad."

Dad. From the astonished expression on his father's face, his father was as surprised to hear the word come out of Finn's mouth as much as Finn had been saying it.

"Help me find this guy. Help me find justice for Ali."

<hr>

IF FINN HADN'T HAD SUCH a tight grip on Maria's hand, she might have stood and given him and his father some time alone, but clearly, that was the opposite of what Finn wanted.

She'd stayed beside him on his father's sofa, mostly quiet while Finn and Walter verbally danced around each other. But now that some of the truth had been revealed, was Walter ready to talk, or would they have to pull information from him piece by sorted, dirty piece?

Only one way to find out…

Maria cleared her throat. "I don't believe for a minute that whoever wanted Ali dead and could find her didn't also know who her handler was. So they killed her but let Fitzhugh live? There has to be a reason for sparing him back then. What changed?" Why kill him now.

"What changed," Walter said, taking her interjection into the conversation more seamlessly than she'd imagined he would, "was that Fitzhugh had been served a subpoena to testify in front of Congress when classified documents to a related case of your sister's got leaked to the press.

Finn sat back. "The Harding case?"

Walter held Finn's gaze for a long second before breaking it. Maria wondered if the next words out of Walter's mouth would be a lie.

The Harding case had made all the headlines after the document breach, defying the twenty-four-hour news cycle by refusing to die.

"No," Walter said after the long-drawn-out silence that only made Finn's grip tighter. Was Finn expecting his father to lie as well? "The Marcus Wright fiasco."

Finn's grip eased, and blood rushed back into Maria's fingers, the thump of her heart drumming a staccato tattoo in her fingertips. "Never heard of it."

"The Harding case is smoke and mirrors. Sure, it's sensational, even criminal, but if I were a betting man, I'd say the CIA is fueling the leaks behind the scenes to keep everyone distracted. To make them focus on this shiny thing to keep anyone from noticing that the CIA killed one of their own."

Maria managed to keep the *What the fuck* from slipping past her lips—just. But a whoosh of air escaped her lungs at the same time Finn said, "Come again?"

Walter stood and went to a wall safe behind a replica of some famous painting Maria couldn't remember the name of. She'd used the darkened rooms during her art history class in college to catch up on her much-needed sleep.

Then again, with what she was learning of Finn's family, it wouldn't surprise her if the painting were an original.

From where she sat, she didn't have a direct view into the safe. She wouldn't have known what to expect if she had. Stacks of banded cash? Bars of gold and silver? The crown jewels?

Hell, the only thing she'd had as a kid that locked was a diary with a lock on it that she'd promptly lost the key to before she could use it.

Walter returned with a flash drive and handed it to Finn.

Finn took it. "What's this?"

"Nearly illegible redacted reports. But it talks about your sister in there, and I suspect a whole lot more."

"Why are you giving this to me?"

"Giving what to you?"

So it was going to be like that, was it? Walter would deny it if Finn ever divulged where he'd gotten his information.

Finn gave Walter a curt nod of understanding, then Walter's eyes dropped to their joined hands. "So... you two... you're together?"

If Walter held any disdain, he managed to keep it out of his voice. If Vivian had said those same words, Maria doubted she would have been so lucky.

Finn stood, pulling Maria to her feet by their still joined hands. She had no idea how to classify their relationship/non-relationship, so she let Finn answer, curious to hear his reply.

"It's complicated," Finn allowed.

"It always is." Walter's expression became unreadable when he glanced at Maria. "Until it isn't."

A knock came at the door. "Come in," Walter said.

A young man opened the door and stuck his head in. "Dinner is ready."

So much for making an escape and getting back to their hotel early. Would Maria rack up bonus points in heaven for making it through dinner without killing Finn's mother?

11

Finn sat outside his parents' guest house in the darkness, the stars blinking on and off overhead. More stars were visible at his parents' than in the center of D.C, where the light pollution obliterated all but the brightest stars. Still, there were more stars back home—

Home.

While he'd been living and working in Wyoming for years, he'd always considered D.C—or at least this corner of the northeast, home—even if it had never felt like a real one.

Sure, he'd lived here growing up—*existed* here—but now that he thought back on it, he'd never felt like it was a place where he belonged, no matter how hard he'd tried to fit in with his family.

Look at him, thirty-seven years old, and he was still looking for his family's approval.

He chuckled to himself. He was a grown man. It was about time he quit looking to his parents for the approval he'd never get.

"What's so funny?"

Finn glanced over his shoulder as Soto came through the

guest house's sliding glass door. They'd reluctantly decided to stay the night after a tense, awkward dinner with his parents, too exhausted to drive back to the city.

"Life," Finn said, not meaning to sound so cryptic. "It's enlightening being back here, being immersed in the dynamics of my youth, and realizing nothing has changed."

Maria sat down in the chair next to him. She looked tired, and he wanted to tell her to go to bed and get some rest, but selfishly, he wanted the company more.

"Not gonna lie, seeing the dynamic in person explains a lot about you."

The humor in her voice had him cracking a smile instead of taking her words the wrong way. "How's that?"

"Your penchant for rule-following, your perfectionism. You could become the president of the United States, and they'd be asking what took you so long."

Her words hit home, but they weren't anything he hadn't realized years before. Sometimes, you could never live up to expectations, and he'd had to learn to live with that. Still, it didn't mean it didn't suck.

"For better or worse, it made me who I am today."

"Do you ever wonder how things might have been different if your sister hadn't died?"

"Different, how?"

"Would your parents have been more forgiving, more loving, less judgmental?"

Finn thought for a moment. Thought back to a time when he still considered himself part of the family. Had they been better, or had all the bad times overshadowed the good?

Soto waited patiently for the truth he didn't want to admit. Even though it wasn't a reflection on him, it kind of felt like one.

"In many ways, my sister was like me. Driven. A rule

follower. A perfectionist. I could blame it on genetics because my parents are the same, but..."

Finn stopped himself, deciding how much he wanted to reveal. If he stood now and went in for the night, Soto wouldn't push, but she would always wonder.

And as if to prove to his parents, to his ex-wife, to Maria, his therapist, or himself that he had the capacity to let his walls down and be vulnerable in front of the woman he couldn't get out of his head, he said, "This may be who I am, but it's not all that I want to be."

"Growing is a part of life. If you really were all that perfect, how boring would that be?"

The bark of laughter that escaped him knocked a few needed holes in his defenses. He liked that about her, that she made him want to say *fuck it* to his carefully constructed persona and show the world—or at least her—the imperfect man beneath.

He'd never wanted to be that vulnerable before. Luckily, his ex-wife leaving and her subsequent grace in building a friendship in the aftermath of their divorce had taught him something valuable. It taught him that if he ever wanted another significant relationship in his life, he'd have to be willing to reveal all his scars and imperfections.

And he'd have to be willing to watch the other person walk away if it were all too much for them to handle.

It had taken Soto walking through his door the night before for him to realize she might be the one brave enough to stay.

Soto? You sticking with the last name thing? Still trying to keep her at a distance because you know you'd rather pull her closer?

"I expected to come out here and find your nose buried in your computer combing through those files your father gave you."

Finn gestured at his closed laptop on the side table. "I almost did, but..."

He didn't quite know how to explain his hesitancy in pouring over the files. In the past, he'd jumped on every shred of new evidence that might help him find his sister's killer, but for once, he needed to take a moment before he lost himself in the documents, the facts, the theories, the suppositions.

Ali would understand.

It didn't mean his determination had wavered.

"But what?" Soto—*Maria* prompted.

"I needed to come up for air."

Maria held out her hand. "Come inside. Take a breath. Go to bed without falling asleep in your files for once."

He tucked his laptop under his arm and took her hand. The bemused smile playing on her lips told him she hadn't expected him to do that. And he liked that he'd surprised her a little too much.

Once inside, he said, "Why don't you hit the shower first. I'll make sure there are sheets on the beds."

FINN HAD DISAPPEARED behind the second bedroom's closed door by the time she exited the bathroom in her super-soft, polar bear print shorty pajama set.

She heard him moving around behind the door as she passed, the soft words he'd said to his father about the two of them rattling around in her head—*It's complicated.*

In reality, it wasn't. Nothing prevented them from getting together for a night, a week, a month, or longer.

Nothing but themselves.

She'd made her interest in him clear. It was up to Finn to do with that information what he would. She liked the guy—okay, more than liked for much longer than she'd like to admit—but desperate, she wasn't.

And she had her fair share of self-respect.

She turned on the bedside lamp and climbed onto the tall queen bed, the luxurious mattress probably something the Queen or the Pope slept on. The five-hundred thread count sheets felt cool and super soft against her skin and didn't disappoint.

She fired off a quick update to Wyatt, not expecting to hear from him until the morning. With her laptop on her lap, she propped a pillow against the sleigh bed's headboard and tapped into the guest's wifi using the password provided in the decorative frame on the nightstand.

Clicking on the bedside lamp, she logged into her streaming service and pulled up the second season of a new sitcom that was all the rage. What this day needed most was a bit of levity.

The shower in Finn's room ran for a long time before shutting off. She laughed at the sitcom, unable to keep from snorting a bubble of laughter, then laughed out loud at the last line as the closing credits started to roll.

Her abdominal muscles hurt from laughing. She swiped at the tears on her cheeks and caught movement out of the corner of her eye.

Finn.

He stood in her partially open door, a pair of long pajama pants slung low on his hips, his chest bare, and a dark, thin treasure trail disappearing beneath his waistband.

She wanted to follow that trail down and watch Finn lose some of his tightly held control.

He brushed a hand through his damp hair. "What's so funny?"

Finn stood there at the threshold like the little kid desperately wanting the other kids to invite him to play but was too afraid to ask.

"A new show I was watching."

Finn nodded, not saying anything. When he went to step back and turn away, she said, "Come watch with me."

His eyes darted to her computer then to the vacant side of the bed before looking at her.

He stuffed his hands into the pockets of his pajamas. "I shouldn't."

Maria rolled her eyes. Then she lifted her chin up a notch. "Says who?"

His head dropped, and he scoffed, shaking his head to himself.

"It's not a rhetorical question," Maria said. "It's you and me and a sitcom. There's no *should* or *shouldn't*. There's only do you want to?"

Frankly, she didn't know why she'd asked. Finn was stuck in his ways. Despite having the self-awareness to know that many of his internalized beliefs had come from his parents' skewed morals and were not his own.

He turned off the overhead light, and in a move that had Maria's heart stumbling into higher gear, Finn stepped into the room. Quickly, she scooted over, making room for Finn.

He climbed in beside her, an adorable red flush rushing up the back of his neck.

Such a contrast to the man who'd trapped her against the bulkhead of the private jet that morning. Confident Finn turned her crank, but shy Finn did a number on her, too.

They scooched and scooted until they'd both settled close enough that they could both see the screen. Finn had one leg beneath the covers and the other out as if he couldn't decide whether to stay or to run.

Their thighs touching, Maria laid the laptop on both of their legs and hit play.

She leaned her shoulder against Finn's, angling her head to see the screen better. She glanced up at him. "This okay?"

"Yeah, sure."

Somewhere between the first and second episode, Finn had shifted, and his arm ended up around her shoulders, her head resting on his bare chest. She loved the clean, masculine scent of him.

Her eyes drifted closed, and Finn's warm chuckle shook her awake. She straightened, stifling a yawn.

"I think I'd better let you get to bed," Finn said as if it were the last thing he wanted to do. But if they were going to be worth anything tomorrow, they'd be less likely to miss something vital if they weren't exhausted.

She hated to let him go. She liked having him close, but more importantly, she liked that he'd let his guard down enough to slow down and let himself just *be*.

She reached for the laptop, the corner jabbing into the meat of her hand where the rope burn was the worst.

"Ouch," she said, sucking in a quick breath and grabbing her hand. The laptop tumbled backward, the lid closing as it flopped upside down on the edge of the bed.

"You okay?" Finn took her hand and gently straightened her fingers, his touch so gentle it made her stomach impervious to gravity.

She had scabs on the palm of her hand, broken where the creases cut across them. At least they weren't hamburger raw anymore. He lifted her palm to his lips and kissed it as if that would make it better.

No kiss had ever healed a flesh wound in the history of ever, but she had to admit his lips on her palm made her forget about the pain.

He lifted her other hand and did the same to it. She had no clue what he wanted to happen or not happen between the two of them. Nothing in his soft touch conveyed anything but caring and concern.

His eyes went wide as if he'd suddenly had an epiphany, his soft expression morphing into concern. "I'm sorry. It must have hurt like hell, me squeezing your hand when we were talking with my father."

She shrugged because she didn't want to admit it had hurt. The discomfort had been temporary, and she appreciated that he'd allowed himself to lean on her when he'd needed the support.

Besides, she'd been through a lot worse in the few months since she'd been shot. "It's okay. I didn't mind taking one for the team."

He chuckled like she hoped he would. Instead of releasing her hand, he rubbed his thumb over the pulse point on the underside of her wrist. She hoped he couldn't detect the bump in her pulse rate from his touch.

If he looked close enough at her face, though, he might see the flush of arousal creeping up to her cheeks.

The smile slowly faded from his lips, and he met her gaze. The bedside lamp cast his face in shadows, all but obscuring his raw concern. "You do that a lot."

Confused, she scrunched up her nose. "Do what a lot?"

"Take one for the team." He bobbed his chin at her injured leg.

Maria glanced at her thigh and pulled down the hem of her pajama shorts, covering her healing scars. She wasn't ashamed of how her leg looked, but besides her and her doctor, no one else had seen them. She hadn't realized how vulnerable that would make her feel.

She gave him an exaggerated roll of her eyes, trying to add

levity because the vibe in the room had turned too heavy too quick.

So, it's okay for you to expect Finn to be vulnerable and allow you a glimpse on the other side of his sturdy wall and for you to duck back behind yours when things get uncomfortable?

Well, no. But this was different.

Bullshit.

"It wasn't like I volunteered to get shot." She forced a huff of a laugh into her words, trying to lighten the mood.

Finn's flash of a smile came and went, a brief acknowledgment of her efforts, but he clearly had something he needed to say. "No. But you saved civilian lives. No telling what would have happened to those women under their control if you hadn't acted when you did."

"I know the brass came down hard on you and Ronan when my cover was blown, and almost a year's worth of investigation went up in smoke. Because of me. Not to mention two men are dead."

"Are you sorry about that?" he almost sounded incredulous.

But she was still directly responsible for one of the men's death.

"No." Saying it out loud didn't make her feel worse, but it didn't make her feel any better either. "I know that's not what people want to hear. Or what I should admit. But it's the truth. They weren't good men. They were men who didn't care who they hurt or who lived or died as long as they made money in the process."

"If you hadn't killed Billy, he would have killed you, potentially putting other women in danger as well. It was self-defense. And you were cleared. It was a good shoot."

And she'd survived.

She had to admit that there had been a few days there when she wasn't sure that she would.

Which, on some fundamental level, had changed her, and she was still discovering all the ways it had.

"Can I see your leg?" he dropped her hand, and his eyes fell away. "Wait. Forget I asked that. That was insensitive and way out of line."

He shook his head, and she waited him out instead of responding because he seemed like he hadn't finished.

"I just…" He met her gaze. "I just want to know that you're as okay as you pretend to be."

Perceptive. When she'd first been released from the hospital, it had been a fake-it-until-you-make-it sort of thing for her. Until, finally, she'd made it to the other side, mostly intact.

But she could understand where he was coming from. He wanted proof that she was okay.

He wanted to see it with his own eyes.

Moving her hand off her thigh, she said, "You can look."

Shifting on the bed so that his body no longer blocked the light from the bedside lamp, he reached for the hem of her shorts, stopping shy of it.

"May I?"

His hesitancy was as endearing as it was classic Finn. He didn't want to cross any lines, which she appreciated on some levels but wished he'd forget all decency on a baser level when he looked at her like that.

He looked at her like he wanted to start at her thighs and work his way up and down her body until they were both sweaty and oh, so satisfied.

Her *yes* came out mangled and embarrassingly breathy, but it was out there, and she couldn't take it back.

Not only was Finn a perfectionist, but he was also perceptive. The flash of heat in his eyes expressed that he loved what his near touch had done to her.

She half expected him to pull away, to catch himself and

make up some bullshit excuse about impropriety. Her breath caught as his fingers brushed against the soft fabric, and she didn't try to hide the small smile that tipped up the corners of her lips.

He didn't shove the material up her leg. Instead, he eased it up, only exposing enough of her leg for him to see the wound. His fingers brushed across her imperfections, and a rash of goosebumps covered her body.

Shifting, he laid on his side, her legs falling in that space beneath his arm and chest as he rested his head on his upturned hand.

She was too busy watching the fingers of his free hand on her leg to watch his reaction to seeing her scars. He skimmed the fingertip of his forefinger along the raised goosebumps on her skin.

"Are you cold?"

Could he be that clueless as to what his touch did to her?

She glanced at him, doing a double-take when her brain finally registered the playful, devilish grin on his face. Yeah, he knew *exactly* what he was doing to her and apparently loved every damn minute of it.

To say that seeing this unexpected roguish side of him didn't do unspeakable things to her lady bits would be a blatant lie.

She opened her mouth and closed it again, not sure how to respond, which only made his grin wider and that much deadlier.

He dropped his attention to her leg. That same light touch ghosted over the jagged exit wound scar then down the long line on her inner thigh—that scar from the surgeon's knife where they'd gone in to repair as much of the damage as they could.

Despite their efforts, she'd lost a good chunk of muscle. Finn's finger dipped into the divot beneath the flesh. She'd never considered her wound could be an erogenous zone.

Then again, she'd never imagined what Finn's gentle, reverent touch would do to her.

"Does it still hurt?" Finn asked as he traced the scars like they were something to celebrate, not something to hide.

"Sometimes," she hated to admit. "Usually only when I push myself too hard. I want to get back to where I was physically so badly that I don't give myself credit for how far I've come in so little time."

"Shocking," Finn said with so much uncharacteristic sarcasm it made Maria laugh.

"What do you mean?"

His smile fell, and his teasing tone turned more serious. "I mean, I don't know anybody who puts as much pressure on themselves as you do."

For a man who seemed so self-aware, he had a huge blind spot for the undue pressure he put on himself as if the proof of his investigative obsession weren't stacked on his kitchen table as they spoke.

She raised a brow at his obtuseness. "Seriously? Not another person comes to mind?"

He blew out a laugh and shook his head when he caught her meaning, his eyes dropping to his fingers and the soft circles he was tracing on her leg. "It's not the same thing."

If it hadn't been so quiet in the room, she wouldn't have heard him. It didn't sound like he wanted to disagree. It sounded like the words had tripped out all on their own, and he was doing his best to hide them.

It was late, they were tired, and she let the conversation drop and her head fall back against the headboard with a soft thunk, his fingers tracing those circles, as she let herself just *feel*.

12

───────

Inwardly, Finn sighed when Maria let the conversation die a natural death. Tonight, he didn't want to think about his inadequacies. Not when he could be giving his full attention to the incredible woman beneath him.

Well, not *beneath* him, beneath him.

They both had their clothes on, his torso laid across her legs as he massaged her injured leg. But he never thought he would have allowed himself this much intimacy, so he wasn't upset that they weren't both naked with him between her warm, imperfectly perfect thighs.

He'd tried to bury his alarm when he'd exposed her scars. There were hard lines and ridges of pink scar tissue that hadn't had time to fade to silver. But it wasn't the scars themselves that had alarmed him, at least not the sight of them.

No, what truly frightened him was how close that bullet had come to doing even worse, potentially deadly damage. Shifting so that he could get a better look at the entrance wound on the outside of her thigh, he traced a finger across that smaller imperfection.

"You got lucky." He pictured the trajectory of the bullet. It had entered on the outside of her thigh, exiting her inner thigh behind the midline. "Nine mil full metal jacket?"

She opened her eyes but rested her head on the headboard. "That's what the casings were. Nine-millimeter. And if it had been a hollow point instead, I think it would have destroyed my femur and probably would have gotten my femoral artery as well."

She said it like it was no big deal, like the thought of bleeding out in a couple of minutes from a catastrophic injury to a major blood vessel was just a normal day. Like it hadn't affected her in some sort of way.

He scooted closer, propping himself on his hand beside her hip, and brushed the loose hair behind her ear. Her heavy lids opened wider. "I'm really glad that didn't happen."

As soon as those words left his mouth, he wanted them back. Not because they weren't true, but because that really wasn't what he'd meant. What he'd meant was harder to admit. "What I meant to say was, I'm glad you're here."

Her eyes skimmed his features, catching his gaze and letting his words sink in. He could tell she knew he meant he was glad that she was alive, not from a professional standpoint, but a personal one. Her gaze dropped to his lips, long enough to send a zap to his dick.

Finn reached for the pillow propped against the headboard next to her and dropped it over his lap. When his mother had bought the extra fluffy designer pillows, she'd probably never imagined that her son would need them to hide his growing erection.

He quickly shoved all thoughts of his mother out of his mind. She definitely was the last person he wanted to be thinking about.

Maria lifted her head, the spark in her eyes meeting his then flicked to his lips and back again. "You going to kiss me or what?"

The words held no judgment, but he didn't miss the hint of a challenge in her tone.

Although some discomfort remained about blurring the professional and personal lines if she was good with it, why couldn't he be?

"Get out of your head," she said. "Kiss me if you want to, or don't if you don't. But don't you dare let some preconceived notions of propriety stop you when I've already made it clear I'm into you."

He smiled up at her because how could he not? And all he could think was *fuck it.*

Reaching up, he cupped the back of her neck, his thumb sketching the outline of her strong, stubborn jawline. She met him halfway, her hand going to the back of his head as their lips touched.

A soft *oof* escaped his lips at the gentle impact, and Maria let loose with a sage chuckle. One that said she'd known what the kiss would do to him and wasn't afraid that he knew it.

She tasted like the soda they'd shared while watching the sitcom. He deepened the kiss, her mouth opening and inviting him in. Maria's hand drifted to the back of his thigh, her slight tug encouraging him to move closer.

Finn broke the kiss. "The only way I can get closer is if I straddle your legs. I don't want to hurt—"

She shut him up with a kiss, then pulled away when she had his full attention. "You're not going to hurt me. I'm healed enough for a little grinding."

His forehead dropped to hers, his words tight and hoarse when he spoke. "*Jesusfuckingchrist.*"

"I love how you lose a bit of that tight control when you're turned on."

"Oh, yeah?" he said as he changed position. Even though she claimed he wouldn't hurt her, he was careful not to drop his full weight onto her legs when he straddled her.

She pulled him in for another kiss, her tongue sparring with his. Her hands went to the small of his back, then slipped under the waistband of his pajama bottoms, pulling him closer.

The front of his pajamas already had a wet spot from precum. He reached down to adjust himself. Her hips pressed up into him, her heat no match for the two thin layers of material between them.

Breaking away, he kissed a line down the column of her throat from the delicate spot beneath the corner of her jaw to the pounding pulse at the base of her neck.

Maria may have been small, but she was in no way delicate. She had lean muscle definition in her neck and shoulders from her many workouts. His finger trailed down her chest, dropped into her cleavage, and stopped at the first button of her pajama top.

He moved one edge of the fabric to the side, pressing a kiss to the top of her breast. She ground up against him again. The soft grunt and purr of her exhale only made him harder.

He wanted more.

He wanted it all.

Where they'd go from there afterward, he had no clue. They might fumble their way through it, but they'd find a way to navigate that space. An awkward morning after would be a small price to pay for the promise of the woman before him.

ALL MARIA WANTED WAS Finn naked.

And then they'd get to the good stuff. She slipped a finger

into the waistband of his pajamas, her finger skimming over the slick head of his dick.

The reverent breath he sucked in with the muffed *fuuck* made her grin. For a reserved man in the outside world, she loved how responsive he was. How her touch alone could make his breath catch, his body shiver, and obscenities fall from his lips.

"Ditch these," she said, tugging at the waistband.

Still fully clothed herself, she saw the question in his eyes, the one that asked what about hers. But he let it go, stripping the material down his legs and kicking them to the floor.

He straddled her again, his finger tracing the V of her neckline, his heavy cock, and balls resting in her lap. Her nipples pebbled beneath the soft fabric, and she wanted his warm, wet mouth there more than anything.

Well, almost anything.

"Raise a bit," she said, more of an order than a request, but Finn didn't seem to mind.

When he rose, she shimmied down the bed until she laid flat on the mattress, his junk hanging heavy above her. He held onto the top of the curved headboard and looked down the length of his body at her.

He had one of those long, lean, runner's bodies, and she couldn't keep from running her hands up the back of his straining hamstrings.

"What are you doing?" He managed to sound curious, amused, and turned the fuck on all at the same time.

She slid even farther down between his legs. "You'll see."

13

There were so many things Finn should have been doing besides watching Maria scoot farther down the bed beneath him, her dark hair fanning out on the pillow behind her.

But fuck if he could think what they were.

He'd never been with a woman who wasn't afraid to go after exactly what she wanted the way Maria did.

And it turned him on.

She peeked up at him with a devilish light in her big, beautiful, brown eyes a second before her hands encircled his thighs and pulled him closer.

That wicked tongue of hers licked a scorching path from his taint and up the backside of his balls. He sucked in a broken breath, and his eyes fluttered closed. His free hand automatically threaded through Maria's silky strands of hair as he cupped the crown of her head.

"That feels so fucking good," Finn said, hardly recognizing the feral growl in his voice. Who was he? Where had the calm, cool, collected version of himself gone?

Her tongue teased the underside of his sac and precum gathering at the tip of his straining dick. He no longer cared about the answer to that question.

Maria chuckled. The vibrations coursed through his balls, making them even heavier. Her warm, wet tongue caressed his balls a second before she gently sucked one into her mouth.

A shiver swept up his spine, and he drew in a jagged, ragged breath. Her talented tongue could have made him come, and she hadn't even touched his dick.

When was the last time he'd been that hard?

As much as he loved every lick and every lash of that talented tongue, there was something he craved even more. "I want to touch you," he ground out between harsh pants, the precum leaking freely and slide down the underside of his dick.

She pulled off him long enough to say, "Patience."

He was fuck all out of patience, but before he could change their positions, she licked up his precum. A moan coiled low in his belly as she toyed with what little remained of his self-control.

For the first time in a long time—or maybe ever—Finn surrendered. Surrendered to the sensations. Surrendered to the building emotions that welled up unbidden and unwanted.

Then Maria shifted, her tongue lashing his sensitive tip a split second before she swallowed him to the back of her throat.

A groan ripped through him. The tingling at the base of his spine warned of his impending orgasm and fireworks to come.

Not those cheap ass fireworks you get ten for a dollar that peter out as soon as the fuse was lit, but one of those mega, professional packs that the city buys for the big Fourth of July finale.

He recognized, too late, the moment Maria shot him past the point of no return. The point of orgasmic inevitability where it didn't matter what he did, he couldn't stop from coming.

"I'm—*fuck*—I'm—"

He went to move off her, but she only tightened her grip around his thighs.

Sweat beaded at his temples. His breath caught as Maria took him to the back of her throat again and ever so slowly—deliciously, painfully, slowly—let him slide out to the tip.

The first pulses of his climax slammed into him, and he mangled her name as he cried out, emptying himself into her mouth.

He hung onto the headboard like a sailor hangs onto a life ring after the ship goes down. Maria pulled off before he became too sensitive and loosened her grip around his legs.

Spent, he flopped down onto the bed, wrapping his arm around her neck and hauling her up against him as he fell back to catch his breath. The sheets lay crumpled in a pile at the bottom of the bed, the ceiling fan overhead turning lazily, barely moving any air.

He pulled her in tighter, pressing a kiss to the top of her head, but it wasn't nearly enough. "Give me a second," he said, "and I'll return the favor."

She pulled back, far enough to see his face. "This isn't a tit-for-tat. I didn't—" Maria closed her eyes as if gathering patience before speaking again. "No one is keeping score."

For some reason, she glanced away. He hooked a finger under her chin until she finally looked him in the eye, the flush of embarrassment on her cheeks. What was that all about? Did she think he felt *obligated* instead of honored?

Did she think for one second he didn't want her?

Did she think she wasn't worthy of receiving the same kind of mind-bending pleasure?

For someone so open, so confident, the sharp contrast of her vulnerability knocked a few bricks out that wall that he'd built around his own heart. "Look at me."

She took a deep breath and blew it out. "What?"

The underlying defiance in that whispered word made him smile. Yeah, Maria Soto was tough as hell, but for a second there, she'd let him see the truth—that she wasn't invincible. That she had a harder time protecting her heart than she wanted anyone to know.

"Do you think I don't want you? Do you think that I don't want to touch you, to taste you, to bring you as much pleasure as you brought me?"

She glanced away again, only looking back when he gave her chin an almost imperceptible shake.

"Whatever you're thinking, stop."

A playful spark lit her eyes, deflecting from the seriousness of the conversation. "Is that an order, Special Agent?"

"Yes," he said without hesitation.

Finn leaned in and kissed her, still tasting his saltiness on her tongue. It was hot as hell, and his dick started to stir. He wanted her any way he could have her. And after that mind-blowing orgasm, she deserved some of the same.

"Now," he said, "about returning that favor..."

FOR AN EXCRUCIATING SECOND, Maria thought Finn might have been humoring her about wanting to go down on her. After all, Finn was a thoughtful, conscientious guy. He wouldn't be one to leave a girl hanging.

But then she saw the thirst in his eyes. The raw hunger. The tight-leashed desire. The unrelenting focus.

And she knew he wanted what was coming next as much as she did.

With a gentle hand on her shoulder, he eased her back against the mattress and quickly divested her of her pajamas. He painted small circles with his finger near the ball of her shoulder. He worked his way to her collar bone, then slid that finger between her breasts to her abdomen. His hand spanned her ribcage, his thumb nestled beneath her breast.

He pulled in a breath, nuzzling her ear. The light scrape of his teeth on her earlobe had goosebumps galloping across her skin.

"You don't know how long I've waited to touch you. To have you in my arms..." He leaned back so he could see her face, the naughty light in his eyes made her shiver. "To have you at my mercy."

He rolled over the top of her, catching his weight on his forearms as their pelvises aligned, trapping his growing erection between their bodies. She had to give him credit for the speedy recovery.

Pretty impressive for a man well past his twenties.

For as long as she'd known him, Finn always had a singular focus when he wanted to accomplish a task, and it seemed that pleasuring her proved no exception.

With open mouth kisses, he worked his way down her body, starting at that sensitive point beneath her jaw where he wouldn't miss the way her pulse throbbed beneath her skin as her heart kicked in anticipation of where his mouth would wander next.

He chuckled when she wrapped a hand around the back of his neck and couldn't suppress a shiver. "Your body's so fucking sensitive," he said in that low, throaty register that had her grinding up against him.

A groan escaped him as he took her nipple into his mouth. A flick and a lick of his tongue made her writhe. As much as she liked having him there, there were other places that her body demanded his attention.

That hand she had on the back of his head now went to the

top and gently pressed down, directing him to where she'd previously only fantasized having him.

As a man used to giving the orders, at least in bed, he took direction well. He kissed a line down her abdomen and settled his torso between her legs. His legs kicked up behind him because of the footboard. It had to be uncomfortable, but he didn't let that stop him.

He nuzzled the crease of her thigh with his nose, kissing the inside of her leg, making her wait.

"You trying to make me beg?"

He laughed. "No. But I think I'd like the sound of that."

He nibbled the inside of her other leg, and even without being able to see his face, she sensed his calculating smile. Damn the man. She pulled his head up by his ears, making him grin wider. "Your mouth. On me. Now."

She'd never been one to beg. But she wasn't opposed to demanding.

He shifted his arms beneath her legs and wrapped them around her thighs. "Yes, ma'am."

She let go of his face, opting to let her fingers sift through his short hair, helping to hold him in place as he went down on her.

The first swipe of his flattened tongue through her folds— teasing, not tentative—made her gasp and fist his hair in her hands.

"You like that, baby?"

For a man who rarely called her anything but Soto, the endearment rolled off his tongue, and Maria's heart stuttered for a rapid beat even though she knew he couldn't have meant it the way it sounded. She wasn't his *baby*. She wasn't his *anything*.

All she could do was grunt as he found her clit. A buzz shot through her—a fire-starting surge on an electric wire.

Previous men who'd gone down on her had treated it as a hit and run, not as if they planned to park and stay awhile.

Not Finn.

He settled in, in no apparent rush to do anything but get her off. He sucked and nibbled on her tight bud of nerves, sending her higher and higher.

She ground against him, craving the friction, needing, wanting to be filled. She opened her mouth to tell him what she needed, except a groan escaped instead of words.

Lifting her hips, he worked his way through her folds until he found her center.

She bucked up, her back arching as his tongue plunged in and out. As amazing as that was, she needed...

"More," she managed on a strangled breath.

He'd driven her so close to the edge. That elusive peak barely out of reach. He shifted, replacing his tongue with two fingers. *Finally*. He slid them in, and she shuddered.

Maria's hips raised of their own volition. He used his fingers and his mouth as she chased her orgasm. She matched his rhythm, taking him deep.

"Come on, baby," Finn said, the growl of his muffled words going straight to her clit.

Stars sparked behind her eyes, her body vibrating as she fell over the edge. Finn's fingers slowed but didn't stop, drawing out every last vestige of her orgasm.

Sweat slicked her body, and her breath came in gasping pants as she relaxed into the bone-melting, post-orgasmic afterglow.

"*Jesus Christ*." Finn reclaimed his hand and planted reverent kisses on the inside of her thighs, breathing her in and devoting special attention to her healing scars as if he'd rather never leave.

She'd been afraid men would be turned off by the scars, yet she'd probably found the only man who seemed to revere them.

He wiped his face on the sheets and worked his way up her

sated body, speaking between each kiss. "That. Was. Fucking. Beautiful."

The scent of their sex salted the air. Finn settled on top, taking most of his weight on his forearms and burying his face in her neck. She had to admit she quite liked it.

Loosely, she wrapped her arms around his neck and kissed the side of his head, pleasantly surprised to find Finn liked to cuddle. Not long after, he rolled to the side, one leg still draped over hers. He rested his head in his hand while the other skimmed over her abdomen, the tops of her thighs, and the triangle of hair between her legs.

A touch meant to admire, not to excite.

But no one told her body that.

Before she could take his hand and put it where she craved it, he kissed her temple and gave her stomach a light pat. The kind of pat that told her that whatever had happened between them had ended.

"Wait here," he said.

He got out of bed, his cock still at half-mast as he headed into the hall. After a few minutes, he returned with a cold glass of water and a warm washcloth.

"Drink up," he said as he held the glass out to her.

"I'm fine."

He didn't lower the glass, that slight raise of one eyebrow telling her to drink the damn water.

She took the water to take a sip, if only to appease him, then ended up nearly draining the glass, not realizing how thirsty she was.

He didn't say *I told you so*, but that little smirk he had on his lips before he swallowed down the remaining water said it for him.

Instead of tossing her the cloth so she could clean herself up, Finn sat on the edge of the bed and did it himself with a thorough, gentle affection and appreciation she hadn't expected from someone as no-nonsense as Finn. This soft, tender side of him was something else about him to love.

Love? Who said anything about love?

Crush. Long-term infatuation, maybe. But love?

Nope.

Not even.

Really.

Fuck, she was in trouble.

Why had she let things go this far? She'd only get hurt.

After dropping the washcloth in the bathroom, he retrieved his pajama pants and slipped one leg through.

Maria didn't know what she'd expected to happen after they'd traded orgasms, but for him to dress and walk out hadn't been at the top of the list. And while Maria refused to beg, that didn't mean she couldn't ask for what she wanted.

Not bothering with her pajamas, she rolled to her side and pulled the sheet up to her waist. "You leaving?"

He stilled one leg in, one leg out. "Do you want me to stay?"

Was that hope in his eyes? Or was it panic he couldn't mask?

"I mean—you could—if you want—" Maria shut herself up before Finn thought he'd finger-fucked all the sense out of her.

She took in a deep breath and blew it out, remembering that you don't get a hundred percent of the things you *don't* ask for. "Yes. I want you to stay."

He dropped the pajama bottoms and kicked them aside. He tilted her chin up and then planted a lingering kiss on her lips. "I want to stay, too, but I didn't want to assume."

Reaching over, he clicked off the bedside lamp and walked around to the other side of the bed. It should have been weird to be sleeping with Finn in his parents' poolside guest house, but for the life of her, Maria couldn't drum up the fucks to give.

If that made her a bad person, she could learn to live with that.

The mattress dipped, and Finn scooted in behind her, his front to her back. Despite their height difference, Finn curled his body around hers for the perfect fit. His groin nestled against her ass, and it took all of her considerable inner strength to keep from wiggling her ass and starting something they were both too exhausted to finish.

His arm came around her waist and pulled her in tight. He brushed her hair off her neck and kissed the top of her spine. "Get some sleep. We have a big day ahead of us."

The next morning, Maria woke at first light to find herself alone in the bed. It shouldn't have come as a shock. After all, she knew where his priorities lay. She heard Finn speaking, but only his side of the conversation, so she assumed he was already on the phone though she couldn't imagine with who at such an early hour.

What the hell time had he gotten up? Had he even fallen asleep?

As she gathered her change of clothes and dressed in her pajamas long enough to traipse to the bathroom to shower, she tried to shake off the disappointment of not waking up to Finn warming her bed.

Someday, she would be someone's priority.

Today wasn't that day.

And she couldn't forget that she'd been the one pressing for the intimacy, not him.

It still stung.

14

———

Finn hung up with Anita Quan as Maria came out of the bathroom freshly showered and dressed. She stepped into the room they'd shared and returned, staring at her phone screen with a scowl on her face.

For a second, his mind flashed to the night before when her face held a much different, more exquisite, and satisfied expression. And he felt stupidly proud that he'd been the one to bring her that pleasure.

He stood from the couch where he'd had his laptop set up on the coffee table and went to pour her a coffee. "What's wrong?"

"Do you know anything about this?" She traded her phone for the cup of coffee.

He read the text message from Ronan. "What does he mean the FBI has opened a new investigation into your shooting case?"

After taking a fortifying sip, Maria set the mug on the kitchen counter and pulled her damp hair into a serviceable ponytail. "I don't know. I thought Ronan might have said something to you. He's your boss."

"True. But you don't work for me anymore. Besides, it has to be bullshit. You were cleared in the shooting."

"A man's still dead."

"A man who tried to kill you first."

She shrugged him off. It wasn't like he was wrong. "I'm sure it's nothing to worry about. And it's not like there's anything I can do about it right now. The Office of Professional Responsibility, OPR, is going to do their thing, and there's nothing I can do to stop them."

He watched as she took another sip of her coffee, her gaze out the kitchen window, looking out over the pool and the backside of his parents' house. She had one of those thousand-yard stares, so he wasn't convinced she noticed any of that.

It wasn't like her to take news like this without a few choice words and a call back to Ronan demanding what the fuck was going on.

He took the mug from her hand to get her attention. "Is everything okay?"

It took a moment before she shifted her focus back to him. "Why wouldn't it be?"

She looked him dead in the eye, but he could tell she was lying.

"You tell me." Was her mood because of Ronan's warning text or because of last night? "Did I do something wrong?"

She moved to step away, but he caught her elbow. "Maria, talk to me."

"We're here to do a job, right?" As he tried to puzzle out the problem, she must have taken his silence as agreement because she added, "We don't have much time. It's probably best we keep our focus on the case and remember why we're here."

He'd definitely screwed up somehow. "*Maria*."

She shook her arm free, and he let her go. "Who were you talking to?"

He scrubbed his hand through his hair. Fine. If she didn't want to talk about it right now, he wasn't going to force her, but eventually, she'd have to tell him.

"That was Quan," he said as he stepped over to his computer. He'd been reading through the documents his father had given him, but with the redaction so extensive, he couldn't get a sense of what the documents even were. "Quan said there aren't any significant updates from yesterday. She's expecting a copy of that hidden camera footage you found at the scene from forensics later today. She said she'd call and let us watch the footage with her."

"That's... unexpected."

"Tell me about it."

She met him at the couch and held her hand out. "Mind if I take a look at that?"

He handed her his laptop. If she had any great ideas, he'd be happy to listen to them. She settled in the corner of the couch. Her bare feet tucked beneath her, the laptop balanced atop her legs.

He stood behind the couch, watching over her shoulder as she scrolled through about thirty pages of the document, zooming in on some of them before glancing up at him. "It's been redacted by hand, some of the words aren't completely obscured by the black marker, but this is still nearly useless."

He'd come to the same conclusion, but he'd hoped her take on it would be different. While he was glad that his father had finally entrusted him with the files, a part of Finn wished his father had kept the documents to himself. At least then, Finn wouldn't have gotten his hopes up. *Again.*

She set the laptop on the coffee table. "You should send the file to Massey. Maybe he can strip the redaction out of the document."

"They can do that?" Even as Finn said that, he came around

the side of the couch and sat down beside her. He uploaded the file to Steele-Wolfe's encrypted file-sharing site that Massey had set up for the company.

Maria pulled her phone out of her back pocket, dialed Massey's number, and put it on speaker. It rang and rang. Finn expected to be put through to voice mail when the phone clicked, and a groggy Massey said, "'Lo."

"Who is it?" came an equally sleepy male voice on the other end of the line.

The other person would have to have been close for the phone to pick up his voice. It sounded an awful lot like Isaac, but Finn couldn't be sure. Interesting.

Maria grinned. Maybe she thought it sounded a lot like Isaac as well. "It's Maria. Did I catch you at a bad time?"

"W-what?" Massey cleared his throat. "No. We were—*I* was just waking up."

There was shuffling on the other end of the line as if Massey were extricating himself from the sheets, then he said, louder this time. "What can I do for you?"

"I've got Finn here. He has a technical question." She held the phone out to him.

"I've got a redacted file that my father gave me that is nearly impossible to read. I uploaded it to the Steele-Wolfe file server. Do you think you can strip the manual redaction from the file?"

"I can try. Give me a day, and I'll see what I can do."

"Thanks. I appreciate it. Everything going okay on your end?"

Isaac said something that Finn couldn't pick up. Massey choked on a laugh, his voice shy when he said, "Better than expected."

Why did Finn have the feeling they weren't talking about Massey's case anymore?

They said their goodbyes, and Maria ended the call with a bemused grin. "Do you think they hooked up?"

"What do you think?"

"Maybe?" Then Maria's smile slipped. "Would that be a problem for you?"

"Why would the person Massey sleeps with be a problem for me? It has no bearing on his work product. And if getting laid—whoever that might be with—helps improve his computer skills, even better."

Some of that cold shoulder Maria had shown him that morning melted, and the smile she sent him warmed him from the inside. "Is it stupid that I'm happy for them?"

"You don't even know for sure that's what happened. It's pure speculation." Before he thought better of it, he added, "It's not like he could tell by talking to us that *we'd* spent the night together."

"Only because they didn't call while we were still in bed." Some of the warmth left her smile. "What time did you get up, anyway?"

He'd never lied to her before, but for some reason, he didn't think she'd be happy with the truth. "Three."

A mix of emotions crossed her face that he couldn't quite read. Before he could ask about it, she asked,

"Should I strip the bed? Your mother already doesn't like me. I don't want her going in there and—"

"Trust me. My mother won't be in here. She has people for that."

Maria shook her head, mildly amused. "I can't imagine having *people*. It's a whole different life, isn't it?"

He stepped over, and despite her holding onto her bag, he managed to strip it from her shoulder and put it on his. "It's different. I'm not sure it's better, though."

Tilting her chin up, he added, "And to be clear, my mother's opinion of you doesn't matter to me, and I don't want you to let it matter to you. I hope mine is the only opinion you care about when it comes to us."

A little bit of that spunk returned to her eyes as she challenged him for the truth. "And what opinion is that?"

He leaned in for a kiss, brushing her lips with a simple, tender kiss and let it linger. When he pulled away, she might have had excessive moisture in her eyes, but she blinked, and it disappeared.

"My opinion is that you and last night are the best things to happen to me in a very long time."

Of all the things Maria thought Finn might say the morning after—that them having sex had been a good thing—hadn't been even a footnote on any of her mental lists of probabilities.

She stomped hard on that little bit of hope that something more may develop between the two of them. She would be setting herself up for heartbreak if she allowed herself to envision more than what Finn was able or willing to give.

Orgasms were one thing.

Relationships were another.

She wasn't quite sure why he'd allowed her to sleep in as long as he had unless it was to give himself some time alone to process the redacted report.

After all this time, the document could be the key to knocking the investigation wide open.

It would be a lot to wrap his head around.

At least she had been able to offer a bit of a distraction.

Her mind immediately went to all the deliciously naughty things they'd shared the night before.

Finn must have sensed where her mind had gone because he dropped their bags and trapped her against the kitchen wall.

Tilting her chin up, he kissed her again, lingering for a breath or two before pulling away. She wanted to pull him back into bed and—

He chuckled when he saw the needy look on her face.

"What's so funny?" she said, unable to hold back her smile.

"You looked like you would have been less surprised if I said I'd regretted last night than me kissing you."

"Do you? Regret it?"

"Oh, baby…"

He brushed the pad of his thumb over her lower lip. "Not for one second."

Those words would have been more of a relief if she hadn't had one nagging question. "Can I ask you something?"

Finn only hesitated for a fraction of a second before his features softened. "Anything."

She may regret hearing the answer, but she wanted to ask it before losing her nerve. "About last night…"

One of his brows raised, his interest piqued, but he didn't interrupt her.

"Why didn't we…"

He looked at her.

She looked at him. Was he really going to make her finish that sentence?

"Fuck?" he finally filled in for her.

That now-familiar heat flashed in his eyes, and the only regret she may have seen was the regret that they hadn't. He slid his thigh between hers. "You didn't enjoy it?"

She placed her palm on his chest, the thump of his heart against her hand tattling on him and telling her he wasn't nearly as cool and collected as he appeared.

"You know damn good and well I did."

The grin that spread across his face was a lethal, panty-melting mix of smug cockiness and unadulterated confidence.

But beneath all that, she knew what he was doing. He was avoiding answering the question.

Maybe you're not good enough for him? His mother certainly doesn't think you are.

That spark of flirty playfulness she had died, sunk in her belly, and rolled over. She broke eye contact and tried to push him away.

He took a step back because he wasn't the kind of guy to force her to stay where she didn't want to be, plus she knew that he knew she could make it painful for him with a well-placed elbow or knee if she chose.

Instead of completely losing all physical contact, he wrapped a hand around her wrist, his grip loose enough to break if she wanted. "Maria, whatever you were thinking right then is wrong." She glanced up at him again. "You don't have to fuck to have fun."

She wrenched her wrist free. "You don't think I know that?"

Finn closed his eyes and ran his hands down his face, all hints of playfulness gone, and the serious, no-nonsense man she'd come to know and love stood before her.

He opened his eyes. "If my failed marriage has taught me anything, it's that I'm not the man people think I am. Shondra found that out the hard way. I'm a hard man to love, Maria, and I suspect, an even harder one to live with."

She wanted to tell him he was wrong, but he had more to say.

"I didn't want to take it too far and have you find that out too late and regret it the same way Shondra came to."

"I'm not Shondra," Maria said, holding a finger up to shut him up when he tried to speak. "And I know what I want and what I don't. I don't have a problem with not fucking. I have a problem with you projecting and assuming what is best for me like I don't have free will. Like I don't have agency.

"So fuck me or don't fuck me, but make damn sure it's what *you* and *I* want, and it's not your ex-wife calling the shots."

Maria shut up and took a breath, not knowing what kind of reaction to expect. A broad, spreading smile, wasn't it.

Taking her hand, Finn pulled her into his arms, and she went willingly. He kissed her temple. "You're not afraid to say your mind. That's a quality I've always admired and loved about you."

Loved.

He didn't mean he loved *her.* You can love a person's finer qualities without loving *them.* But tell that to Maria's stupid heart that chose that moment to do the first couple kicks of a happy dance.A cloud passed in front of the early morning sun, dimming the light in the kitchen.

"Since we won't be able to meet Quan until this afternoon. We have a little time to kill. I was thinking about going for a run to clear my head. Do you want to join me?"

Maria glanced through the window over the kitchen sink. Light splatters of rain hit the glass. "I don't have rain gear with me."

"My parents stored some of Ali's things in the closet in your room. She might have something you could wear if that wouldn't be too weird."

Maria thought about it for a moment. It was clothes. It was fabric. And if wearing them gave her a chance to get her blood pumping and maybe clear her mind for the day ahead, then she didn't see a good reason why not.

"That's fine with me. As long as you're good with it."

"Yeah. Sure," Finn said.

Even though Maria had her doubts, she took him at his word.

Maria went into the bedroom to get dressed for their run. She'd brought her running shoes, shorts, and a T-shirt.

Once dressed, she opened the closet and thumbed through the hanging clothes, looking for something suitable to wear.

In the back of the closet, she found what she was looking for, a black and purple running jacket. The sleeves were a little long, but they fit well enough for a short run.

She left the room, trying to zip the jacket as she stepped into the den. Finn glanced up from the couch where he was tying his shoes. "Need help with that?"

"Yeah," Maria said. "I can't seem to get it zipped."

He fiddled with the zipper, tugging and pulling until he finally got it to zip partway. Then they both heard it. A weird, crinkly sound.

"What was that?" Finn held onto the front of the running jacket. He unzipped it, and she took it off. They felt the front of the jacket next to the zipper.

"There's something in there."

"Hang on," Finn said, let me get my pocket knife."

Finn disappeared into his bedroom and came back with his pocket knife. They laid out the jacket at the kitchen table, and Finn carefully worked his knife into the seam between the fabric and the zipper, ripping the threads. Inside the jacket lining, they found a thin stack of microfiche strips.

"*A la verga!*" Maria said. "This has to be your sister's. Forget the run."

Maria held the strips up to the light. "Let's get these to the library and see what your sister has to say."

15

————

At the Franklin Public Library, Finn stepped ahead of Maria and held the door open for her. The drive into D.C. from his parents' house seemed like it had taken a day instead of an hour.

It had been one of those times Finn would have preferred to use his father's helicopter to get into the city, but he wasn't ready to say anything to his parents about what he'd found until he had more information.

A part of him felt guilty for not giving his father a heads up, but considering his father had kept the redacted files from him for years as well as other vital info when he knew Finn had been investigating Ali's death, made the passing guilt easier to swallow.

As they walked in, he tried to tell himself not to get his hopes up. Tried really hard. He couldn't say he'd been too successful at it.

They hustled through the library, taking the basement stairs, in too much of a hurry to get to the microfiche readers to waste precious seconds at the elevator.

The long strips of the cut-up microfiche made it difficult to read on the microfiche reader, but eventually, they found a way to make it work. What they found looked like Ali's journal entries that she'd converted to microfiche. Instead of reading directly from the machine, they made copies of every page, tucked the microfiche strips safely away, and left the library.

Their shoes slapped in the puddles on the pavement as they jogged back to the rental car. Once inside, Finn couldn't wait to read the journal entries. He divided the stack roughly in half and handed a short stack to Maria, and kept the other half for himself.

They didn't have enough time to find a hotel and get unpacked before they had to drive across the Potomac to meet with Quan, so they settled into their seats and read.

"Wow," Finn said. More of the same commentary followed as he read through his sister's detailed journal.

If the journal entries had been a movie he'd been watching, he would have had a hard time suspending his sense of disbelief to allow himself to enjoy the story. It boggled his mind that this had been his sister's real life and not fiction.

The timer on his phone went off, and he reluctantly set the papers aside, started the car, and shifted into reverse.

The rain continued to fall, not a hard drenching, but a soft lazy misting on his windshield that his wipers swept away with a slow *swish, swish*. The traffic into downtown D.C. was heavy, and Finn had to fight the urge to lay on his horn.

"What did you find?" Maria asked. "All those 'wows' you kept saying. You must have found something mind-blowing."

Finn didn't even know where to start, but he had to start somewhere. "Ali was on assignment in the Soviet Union, gathering intelligence as the country was splitting apart. Tensions were high between the US and the Soviet Union, as you can imagine, and Ali and other agents were doing their best to gather what information they could in that ever-changing landscape.

"Turns out, some agents were more zealous than others about how they gathered that information. There had been rumors about brutality, even going so far as torture to get what they needed. It doesn't sound like Ali had seen any of that firsthand, but the rumors were rampant. There had to have been some truth to them."

"Damn," Maria said. "Sounds like a potentially dangerous situation."

"There's this one agent out there, Marcus Wright. I think he could be the same agent the congressional hearing is about. He'd heard the rumors too. And he must've had some first-hand knowledge because he reported it up his chain of command back at Langley, but from what Ali said, nothing came from those reports, and the beatings and the torture continued. Then Wright threatened to give all of his evidence to reporters at the Washington Post. He was supposed to meet with Ali that morning at a café before contacting the Post.

"He was supposed to give Ali copies of his evidence in case something happened to him. She was running late to the meeting and took a shortcut through some sketchy alleys, trying to get there in time."

Maria linked her fingers with his over the center console. "I don't like where this is going."

Finn couldn't agree more. He glanced over at her before returning his attention to the road.

"She heard the muffled bark of a silenced shot and dropped behind a dumpster in the alley. When she peered out from behind it, she saw Wright laying, unmoving on the ground. A panel-type van pulled up. Three men got out and shoved Wright inside. But not before Ali recognized one of the men. It was another CIA agent also assigned to Moscow."

"Fuck." It sounded as if someone had knocked the breath right out of Maria. "The CIA really killed one of their own?"

Finn didn't want to believe it was true. But he believed his sister's words. Believed every single, solitary one of them. She had no reason to lie.

In fact, with Wright dead, she had every reason to turn her head and look the other way. But apparently, that's not what she'd done.

A fresh wave of grief filled his chest and clogged his throat. And his pride for his sister only grew that much stronger. He didn't believe he'd ever known anyone with a clearer sense of right and wrong.

"Certainly looks like the CIA had been involved."

"That explains more of what I read," Maria said.

Finn turned on his blinker and slowed, pulling into the parking garage across from D.C.'s FBI headquarters. He glanced at the clock. They still had about fifteen more minutes until they met with Quan.

Finn unbuckled and turned in his seat to face her, almost afraid to hear what she had discovered. "What did you find?"

"Ali laid low for a couple of weeks after the incident, it sounds like. Then she reported it to her handler, which was Fitzhugh. He said he would take care of it. He said he'd make sure there was an investigation. But months later, after she'd returned to the States, she found out that Fitzhugh hadn't done a damn thing. So being the Finn that she was, she went up her chain of command. At first, they paid her lip service. And then they pushed back. And then she started to fear that she'd end up like Wright."

"Which explains the hidden microfiche," Finn said. "But who would have been so concerned about this information getting out that they would risk killing her? On American soil, no less."

"I don't know." Maria shuffled back through the papers she'd read and skimmed her finger down a page until she came to a name. She looked up and said, "but maybe we should ask Abe Carter."

"Abe Carter?" *Uncle Abe?* "Fuck."

"Wait. You know him?"

It couldn't be the same guy, but then again...

"My dad had a friend when we were growing up that was around so much that we started calling him Uncle Abe. He..."

Finn thought back to his childhood, and a memory hit that he'd never associated with his sister's death before. "He pretty much stopped coming around after Ali's funeral. My father said that work kept him busy, and he couldn't come by."

But it couldn't be him. Not the same Abe Carter. Could it?

Finn didn't ask the question out loud because, with everything his father and sister had been involved in, more than likely, they were the same person. It would be too much of a coincidence otherwise.

Maria let the papers fall back into her lap. "According to your sister, he was Director of Counterintelligence at the CIA at the time."

Finn let that sink in. It was all he could do to breathe in. Would Carter know who killed his sister? Or know who ordered her assassination? Or... was he involved himself?

Finn felt like he was so close to the answers yet still a galaxy away. "Is Carter still alive?"

Maria pulled out her phone and did a quick Google search. "According to the CIA website, he retired in '05. He'd be old, but he may be still alive."

Finn pulled out his phone to do a quick search of his own, and it rang in his hand. He held the screen up for Maria to see.

"What do you think Ronan wants?" Maria asked.

Ronan couldn't help keeping tabs on Finn. He wanted to roll

his eyes. "Probably checking up on me and making sure I haven't gone off the rails."

"That was my job. Hopefully, I've succeeded."

"So far." Finn smiled.

Maria had done more than keep him from going off the rails. She was good for him in more ways than just his career. For the first time in a long time, he had a lightness to him.

Even with all the darkness surrounding his sister's death, his life was brighter with her by his side.

Finn answered Ronan's call and put it on speaker before it went to voicemail, knowing that if he didn't answer, Ronan would keep calling and calling until he did.

"I didn't think you were going to answer," Ronan asked by way of greeting.

Finn thought it best not to affirm Roman's suspicion. "What can I do for you?"

"I wanted to see how things were going."

"As my friend or as my boss?"

Ronan sighed heavily enough for it to be heard over the connection. "I'm worried about you."

Finn couldn't tell if that was the boss talking or his friend. Sounded more like his friend.

As the silence stretched out, Ronan said, "How's Soto?"

"What do you mean?"

"You know what I mean," Ronan said. "We talked about this. Have you two—"

"Have we what?" Maria asked. She threw Finn a saucy smile.

"*Jesusfuckingchrist, Finn.* Why didn't you fucking tell me I was on speaker?"

"You're on speaker," Finn and Maria said at the same time with a laugh.

Ronan groaned and let whatever he'd been about to say drop. Good thing because Maria didn't need to know that Ronan had encouraged him to start seeing her before she'd agreed to join him in D.C.

"Any new developments in the case?" Ronan asked.

Finn glanced at Maria. They had more leads and more lines of investigation open up in the past forty-eight hours than he'd had in all the years he'd been working the case.

He tried to keep his optimism in check. It was entirely possible the leads would be a dead-end, and he would go back to Wyoming not any further along in finding out who'd killed his sister. Though, he didn't feel that way. Maybe it was because Maria was there.

Or maybe it was because he had someone beside him who cared.

"There's been a lot." Finn checked the clock again. If they didn't head inside soon, they'd be late for their meeting. "Look, I need to let you go. We've got a meeting with Quan in a few minutes. I'll fill you in when—"

"Quan?" Another groan followed by a heavy sigh emanated from the other end of the line. "Anita Quan?"

Before Finn could answer, Ronan added, "Christ, please tell me you told her you weren't there in an official capacity."

Finn almost messed with Ronan and told him he had, but he didn't have time to rile up his friend. "She knows I'm here on my own time. Now, we really need to go. You got anything else for us?"

"I heard something about that investigation into Maria's shooting."

Maria reached over, took Finn's hand, and gripped hard enough to make the blood blanch from his fingers. "What about it?"

"They're saying a video has surfaced and that Maria had been compromised. That she intentionally started the shooting. That she wanted to take over the operation."

"What the fuck?" The words spilled out of her mouth, thickly coated with incredulity.

"If this is a joke," Finn said, "it isn't even remotely funny."

"No joke. I wouldn't do that to you."

"This is insane." Maria dropped his hand and grabbed the phone. "Who's saying this? Where did this mystery video come from? Why didn't this come out before and addressed during the initial investigation by OPR? Why—"

"That's what I'm trying to find out," Ronan said. "I'm hoping to get to the bottom of this. I just wanted to give you a heads up on what was going on. Don't worry too much about it. But I wanted you aware of the allegations."

Finn took the phone back and ended the call. Maria stared out the window at the drizzling rain, a cloud hanging over them literally and figuratively. Would they ever catch a break?

Before they got out of the car, a text came in from Quan. He gave Maria a nudge with his shoulder. "Quan wants us to meet her at the back entrance."

Maria came back to herself and opened her car door. "Let's go. Let's see what your girlfriend has to say."

THE CAR BEEPED behind Maria as Finn locked the rental. He jogged to catch up with her. "She's not my girlfriend. And where the hell did that come from?"

That had been a shitty joke and an even shittier thing to say. Especially when she knew that Finn had no romantic interest in Quan. They'd broken up all those years ago for a reason, and nothing had given Maria any indication that either one of them carried a torch for the other.

Besides, Maria had no claim on him. "Sorry. I—"

Finn gave her shoulder a reassuring squeeze as if he knew

that her insensitive remark had nothing to do with him and everything to do with the report from Ronan. "Ronan's going to get this thing sorted. He's got your back. Put that investigation out of your mind, and let's see what Quan has for us, yeah? I've got high hopes for this."

"Yeah," Maria said. "Me too."

They worked their way around to the backside of the building. They would still need to go through security to get in, but there was less traffic at that entrance and fewer people who would see them coming and going. Maria guessed that had been Quan's intention.

By the time they arrived at the back entrance, Quan stood in the open doorway and ushered them inside.

"Afraid to be seen with us?" Finn asked Quan as the door closed behind them, and they approached security. Quan didn't answer, and Finn hadn't expected one.

Once through, Quan badged them into a back elevator. She didn't speak until the doors closed and the elevator started upward. "I'm not afraid to be seen with you. But let's say that it would be better all-around that fewer people see us together."

Maria agreed. Finn didn't say anything, so apparently, he agreed as well. Quan was doing them a favor. She didn't have to give them any updates, which spoke to the relationship Finn had built with Quan that she was willing to help him out when they all knew it could backfire on her and possibly damage her career.

They made it to Quan's office with little more than a head nod to a couple of passing people that didn't seem to raise any eyebrows. Quan held her office door open for them and firmly closed the door behind her.

"Have a seat," Quan said.

Finn and Maria sat in the leather chairs across from Quan's desk, and she slipped into her office chair across from them. Her office was a decent size. And she had a nice view of scaffolding on the building across the street.

Quan logged into her computer and extended the display to the large screen hanging on the wall to Finn and Maria's left. What showed on the screen was a still shot from the video from the hidden camera Maria had found in Fitzhugh's bushes.

Maria recognized the view of Fitzhugh's pool. She sat up straighter and focused all of her attention on the screen.

Quan hit play, and the video started rolling. "Fitzhugh will come into frame shortly, along with a young lady friend. We're still trying to identify her to see if she had noticed anything off that evening. It seems that Mrs. Fitzhugh's concerns about another affair had been warranted."

They watched a sped-up version of the video. Fitzhugh and the woman came out of the house and laid out by the pool. The camera was too far away to capture any identifying features of the woman without any enhancement.

While the FBI would be interested in identifying the woman, Maria and Finn were looking for Ali and Fitzhugh's killer. They weren't interested in looking for Fitzhugh's fun-time fuck.

As time passed, Fitzhugh's girlfriend came and went, and night was falling by the time Fitzhugh emerged from the house in his bathing suit, a towel around his neck. He had a drink in one hand and a plate of food in the other.

He sat down on a lounge chair, his back to the camera facing the setting sun. A dark figure passed in front of the camera. The camera had no sound, but the mystery man's approach had been stealthy enough that he hadn't alerted Fitzhugh of his approach.

In mere moments, the man wrapped an arm around Fitzhugh's neck, catching him by surprise. The drink and the plate of food fell to the pool deck as Fitzhugh tried to fight back.

A man of Fitzhugh's age—with the potbelly of a man who'd

given up taking care of himself years before—made it relatively easy for the attacker to keep him held against the lounge chair.

Fitzhugh struggled, his arms flailing back to hit the man, but to no avail. One moment Fitzhugh was pinned to the chair, and in the next, the man yanked the lounge chair back. Fitzhugh's feet shot up in the air as his head hit the pool deck with what looked like a hard thump and a bit of a bounce.

It hadn't knocked him completely unconscious, but it took the fight out of him. The man came around and straddled Fitzhugh's body, his gloved hand squeezing Fitzhugh's lower jaw.

Fitzhugh started struggling again, but even though the man wasn't enormous, Fitzhugh was over-matched.

"What's he putting in Fitzhugh's mouth?" Maria asked.

Quan slid a preliminary report across her desk for them to see.

"How the hell did you get this so fast. Normally, it takes weeks?" Maria picked up the toxicology report. "Fentanyl?"

"It's amazing how fast you can get something back when the office of the United States President asks you to put a rush on it," Quan said. "According to the report, Fitzhugh had enough fentanyl in his system to kill him ten times over. A dose like that would suppress his respiration in a minute or two."

Quan paused the video, and Finn said, "The ghost does like using drugs as his weapon of choice."

"We don't know this is the person who killed your sister. We don't know if he's the ghost," Quan said, pushing back against Finn's assumption. After all, at this point, they had no verifiable proof.

Finn looked at her for a long quiet moment. "No. Not for sure. But that would be my guess. Do you have any other suspects?"

Quan shook her head. "No. I'm afraid you're probably right."

The rain continued to fall outside the window, shrouding

D.C. in gray clouds and gloom, but on the inside, the sun shined brighter. Maria could only imagine what Finn would be feeling after all these years to finally see the man he thought responsible for his sister's death.

Quan restarted the video, and they watched as the ghost stripped Fitzhugh of his bathing suit and put it on him backward.

It didn't take him long to roll the body onto the pool deck and into the pool. Fitzhugh floated there, lifeless, his extra fat keeping him afloat before he finally started to sink.

"Was Fitzhugh dead before he was dumped into the pool?" Maria asked.

Quan leaned back in her chair and linked her fingers over her stomach. "No. The medical examiner found chlorinated water in his lungs. But the drowning was a formality. With that much fentanyl in his system, he would have died very quickly, even if someone had been around to administer Narcan."

"Was a prescription for fentanyl found for Fitzhugh?" Finn asked

Maria knew why Finn asked since his sister had a forged prescription he believed had been planted at her house. It would've been one more piece of evidence that the man they watched on the video was the same man who'd killed Ali.

"No," Quan said. "But I think, in this case, the man is much less worried about making Fitzhugh's death look like an accident. He's good. He knows he's good. He knows he can get away with murder because, if this is the ghost, he's been doing it for years."

They watched in silence as the ghost—and yeah, they might as well be calling him that because that's what they all suspected —righted the lounge chair, picked up the spilled food, laid the towel over the back of the lounge chair, and placed the drink glass and plate on the nearby outdoor table. The plate and glass must've been fancy plasticware because neither one of them had shattered on impact.

The ghost walked toward the camera, leaving Fitzhugh's place the same way he'd come. Quan paused the video, giving Maria and Finn the best view of the ghost's face that anyone had probably ever knowingly captured.

The man's medium build, nondescript features, and every-man haircut with his short-cropped beard pretty much guaranteed that he could walk by nearly anyone and be overlooked. There was a reason why this man was considered a ghost. He could easily blend in and disappear.

Quan's printer grumbled to life. Within seconds, the print cartridge buzzed back and forth across the paper and spit out a still image of the ghost from the video.

She reached behind her, pulled the picture from the printer tray, and handed it to Finn. "I'll send a digital copy to your phones as well." And without giving him the expected warning to stay the hell off the case, Quan added, "I hope this helps. I hope you find him."

16

___

They left Quan's office the way they had come, through the back entrance. At least the drizzling rain had let up, and the sun attempted to peek out from behind a rain-heavy, gunmetal-gray cloud.

Finn took her hand. Maria liked that the gesture had seemed like a perfectly natural thing for him to do. His fast, long strides ate up the concrete sidewalk as they headed around the building to the parking garage. They both held their tongues until they got into the car, not wanting to be overheard.

As soon as their car doors slammed, Maria turned and said, "Can you believe that? We got a photo of the ghost."

"Thanks to you. If you hadn't found that hidden camera, we would have little else to go on."

"I was just lucky the sun reflected off the lens the right way. Though, I'm not opposed to a little luck. It's about damn time you had a little on your side."

"Agreed." Finn buckled up. "Are you hungry?"

Maria sagged against the car seat. "Starving."

They hadn't eaten since the night before. The discovery of the microfiche in Ali's jacket had started their morning off with a jolt. Finn had barely spent a few minutes telling his parents goodbye before they'd thrown their luggage into the rental and sped off for the library in D.C.

Finn started the car and pulled out of the parking garage. "I know a good place to eat."

They ended up at a café with an outdoor seating area underneath a covered canopy. Being past the lunch hour and with the sky still threatening to open up, Finn and Maria had the patio to themselves. A few brave pedestrians walked by, but they walked with the purpose of people who didn't want to get wet, not the steps of somebody taking a stroll through the city on a beautiful day.

After their meals arrived—Caesar salad for Finn and the chicken Parmesan for Maria—they took a few bites before starting their conversation.

"My vote," Maria said, "is to find a hotel after lunch, get settled, and plan our next course of action."

"A nap sounds fucking good to me," Finn said around a bite of lettuce.

"God, that's so tempting." Despite her hunger, Maria's chicken Parmesan sat heavy in her gut. With as much good information as they'd discovered so far, they still didn't have a clear path moving forward. How would they find this guy in a city the size of D.C? *If* he was even still around.

All they had was Massey's thought that he was still in town waiting on another job. With a man like the ghost, it would've made sense for him to skip town right away, so if he'd stayed the way Massey suspected he had, he would have to have a damn good reason to.

Finn took a few sips of his iced tea and washed down his lunch. Maria had barely had four bites of hers, while Finn had practically licked his plate clean. She pushed her plate over to him. With a raised brow, Finn asked if she was sure. Maria nodded, and Finn started in on her lunch.

A breeze kicked up, and some of the water dripping off the canopy splattered them and the table. Finn was so engrossed in her chicken Parmesan that he didn't seem to notice.

Finally, he came up for air. "I'm sure Quan and her team have all the nearby airports, train, and bus stations covered and are scanning the security footage in Fitzhugh's house, but that's a long game. By the time they're likely to find anything, even if he is hanging around now, she can't have that many people fanned out across the city looking for him. Even for Fitzhugh, she wouldn't have that kind of budget. Eventually, she'll have to pull her team back, and it'll allow the ghost to escape the area unseen."

"Have you heard anything from Massey?"

Finn put his fork down long enough to pull out his phone. His face scrunched up when he looked at his screen. "Damn. I missed his call. We must've been in with Quan when he called."

Finn quickly redialed Massey's number and put the call on speakerphone, glancing around to ensure they were still alone.

"What do you have?" Finn said as soon as the line connected.

"Damn." Massey had a smile in his voice. You could hear it over the hiss of the tires in the puddles as the traffic passed by. "I don't even get a kiss first? Just Wham! Bam—"

"*Massey.*"

"Okay, okay. I think I've got something you'll like."

"Spit it out," Maria chimed in. "You're killing us here."

Massey chuckled. "But it's going to be worth the wait. Get this. Your guy connected to the DeadMoney website from an internet café called Bytes near George Washington University forty minutes ago. I tried calling you, but you didn't answer."

"How do you know it's him?"

"The guy accessed the same CoinIt wallet from Bytes that the DeadMoney bet for Fitzhugh paid out to."

Finn switched to the map app on his phone. He pulled up directions to Bytes. "That's like a ten-minute walk from here. What are the chances the guy is still there?"

"Slim to none," Massey said, but by the tone of his voice, he clearly hated delivering the bad news. "But criminals get caught because they do stupid things. Maybe you'll get lucky, and he's watching porn and still at the café wanking off under the table."

"If only we could be that lucky." Maria stacked up their plates and waved a hand at the waitress who'd stuck her head out the door to check on them. "Can we get the check please?"

The waitress nodded and disappeared inside.

Finn folded his arms and rested them on the table as he talked into the phone. "Anything else you can tell us about this guy's internet habits?"

"Only that he seems to go to Bytes once a day. He's usually online for about ten to fifteen minutes tops before he logs off."

The waitress brought their bill, and Finn pulled out three twenties to cover their meal and the generous tip. They both stood and exited through the little gate in the outdoor patio's fence and headed down the block with Massey still on the line.

Maria had to nearly jog to keep pace with Finn's long strides.

Bytes may have been a ten-minute walk from where they'd had lunch, but Maria calculated they might get there in five.

Maria caught up and grabbed Finn's wrist, the one holding the phone. "Anything on that redacted file I sent you this morning?"

"You do know I'm on a job myself, right?" The words would have sounded chiding if she hadn't heard the humor in Massey's voice. "I'm hoping to start on it tonight. As long as things stay quiet on this end. I'm hoping I can get it to you sometime tomorrow at the latest. No promises, though. It's going to be hard to remove those redactions digitally."

As much as she and Finn wanted to know what was in the report his father had given him, they had a pretty good idea of what had happened to Ali after reading his sister's journal entries.

They were only a couple of blocks away from Bytes when they ended the call. Maria glanced at the map directions on Finn's phone and stopped him before they turned the last corner.

"What?" Finn asked, clearly annoyed at being slowed down.

"Wait here. I'll go in and see if our guy is still there."

"Not gonna happen."

She raised a brow at him. She understood Finn's perspective, but if they had any intention of catching this guy, boiling through Byte's front door like a bull charging an arena full of red capes was a great way to scare the guy off if he was there.

"Let me go in. The ghost catches one look at you, and he'll immediately know you're a Fed."

"I don't look like a Fed."

Maria stared at him, giving him a chance to hear what he'd said. "I'd stop somebody and ask what they think you do for a living to prove the point, but we don't have that kind of time."

He blew out of breath and leaned against the side of the building. When she held out her hand, he reached into his back pocket and pulled out the folded sheet of paper with the ghost's picture printed on it.

"Okay," Finn finally relented. "But if we're going to do this, I want you to call my phone and put yours in your front pocket with the camera facing outward so I can see what's going on. I want an open connection when you go in there. I don't want to be around the corner wondering what the hell is going on."

EVEN THOUGH HE sent Maria into the internet café with her phone shoved in the front pocket of her pants, he still didn't like that he hadn't gone with her.

She was completely right—and completely competent—but he still didn't like it.

He waited around the corner from Bytes until he heard the tell-tale tinkle of the café's bell against the glass. He crossed the street at the light and watched the video feed in the shade of the building.

Directly across the street from the café was a fashion store with a window of skimpily clad mannequins wearing revealing outfits. He pretended to be looking through the window while he divided his attention between his phone screen and the reflection of Byte's in the glass.

Quickly, he scanned the area around him, not expecting to come face-to-face with a ghost, but he had that little niggling at the back of his neck where the hairs stood at attention, making him wonder if the ghost was watching him.

The weather kept the pedestrian traffic to a minimum, affording Finn a better view of the café in the reflection than he would have had otherwise, but it also made him stand out.

He didn't want to look too suspicious if the ghost were still around.

Or—according to Maria—too much like a Fed.

The audio came through muffled with Maria's phone in her front pocket. It might have been easier to hear over the street traffic noise with earphones, but his were stuffed in his luggage back at the car.

In the video, Finn watched Maria walk through the few rows of computers in the café. Each station had short dividers between them, so the user couldn't see the people at the stations next to them unless they went out of their way to lean over and look at the other person's computer screen.

The café had been styled with a retro '70's vibe with garish orange and olive green paint. Or maybe that was more of a '60's hippie style. Finn couldn't be sure. He knew the cut of a quality suit when he saw one, but home fashion and decor weren't his thing.

What he could be sure of was that the ghost wasn't in Bytes.

Even though he knew Maria could handle the conversation with the person behind the counter, Finn had to be there. For himself.

And for Ali.

He clicked off the video chat, watched for oncoming traffic, and jaywalked across the street.

The kid behind the counter couldn't have been more than college-age. His fingers flew across the keyboard with a loud *clackity clack clack*, barely looking up from the keyboard when Finn walked in.

The kid missed the eyebrow Maria raised at Finn that said, *You didn't think I could handle* this, and Finn knew he'd probably catch hell from her later.

She stepped up to the counter, pulled the paper from her back pocket, and unfolded it on the counter, flattening out the creases before sliding it across to the attendant.

"Have you seen this guy?" Maria asked.

The kid took a glance at the paper, not even long enough to register if the photo was of a human, but the kid said, "Who's asking?"

"I am," Finn said.

The kid did a double-take. His fingers finally left the keyboard. For a second there, Finn thought he might have to pull out his FBI credentials, but then Maria leaned across the counter, her cleavage working its magic. When the small smile spread across the kid's face, Finn decided he probably wouldn't have to flash his badge for a case he had no official business working. Maria had a way with her.

Especially with men.

The kid looked at the photograph again. "What the fuck? Yeah. I've seen him. He's been coming every day or every other day for about the past week or so. Stays for a little bit. Never uses up his time.

"Do you ever look at his search history? Or have a way to track it here?" Finn asked.

The kid narrowed his eyes at him, truly confused. "Why would I do that?"

Maria straightened. "Curiosity?"

What else did the kid have to do?

"Trust me. You don't wanna be looking at people's search histories in here. Some things you can't unsee. Besides, the guy always clears his history."

Maria smiled at him with one of those *gotcha* kind of smiles. "Aaah, so you did look."

He'd been caught, and he had the flush rushing up his cheeks to prove it. Finn hoped the guy never decided on a life of crime because he couldn't lie worth shit.

"This isn't the most exciting job. Sometimes you have to do what you can to amuse yourself."

It was all Finn could do to hold back all of his questions so that he didn't scare the kid mute. Or worse, make him start asking some questions of his own. "Is there a specific computer that he uses?"

The kid pointed to the far corner. "He always uses that one. It's got a good view of the front door, and it's steps from the rear one. Not that he could go out that way without the alarm sounding, but if he needs to exit through the back, I figured at that point he wouldn't care if he sounded the alarm. I always thought he was up to no good, the way he kept scanning the front door to see who came in. There have been a couple of times that that particular computer had been in use, and he left and came back later when it was free."

"Do you have any kind of data on the people who use your computers?" Maria asked. "Like their names or credit card information? A reservation list?"

"No, ma'am. Unless they paid with a card, but I can tell you right now this guy always paid for his time with cash, and he was always a walk-in, never one to reserve the computer ahead of time."

Finn held back his disappointment. It's not like he hadn't expected as much. But he'd still hoped for something more to go on. Finn glanced around, looking for security cameras. Bytes had one pointed directly at the entrance.

Maria must have noticed it as well because she asked, "I don't suppose you could give us a look at the security footage, could you?"

The kid's eyes grew suspicious as if he wanted to report the whole conversation to his boss. "You know that's something I'd have to ask my manager about."

Maria leaned across the counter, bracing her weight on her forearms, a conspiratorial tone in her voice when she said, "Look, I'm not trying to get you in trouble. But this guy," she tapped her finger on the ghost's picture, "this guy is my ex. He wants custody of my kids. And me and my friend here are determined not to let that happen. He's bad news. But I'm sure someone as smart as you knows that."

"I already said it was him. Why do you need the security footage?"

"Because he's on probation for child pornography. He's not legally allowed to use computers. If I show that he's broken the rules of his probation, they can violate his probation and send him back to prison. Where he belongs."

Finn smiled to himself. He loved how Maria could come up with a lie on the spot and make it sound convincing. Undoubtedly, it was what had made her such an amazing and successful undercover agent.

He'd known that she was good, but truthfully, he had never seen her in action like that. It made him wish all over again that she hadn't left the task force, but she'd done what was best for herself, and he respected that.

"Come on, dude," Maria said, "can you help a desperate girl out?"

The kid behind the counter glanced down at the killer cleavage she'd aimed in his hapless direction, then back up at her engaging smile.

Hell, if she looked at Finn that way, there's no telling what he would do for her. Did the kid even stand a chance of refusing?

Finn took a step back and allowed the kid to make his decision. Finn could always pull his badge out if he had to, but it would work out best for everyone if he didn't have to.

Actually, it would work out for the best for Finn. If Quan found out that he'd used his badge when he wasn't officially on a case, Ronan would definitely hear about it.

And the last thing Finn needed was Ronan on his ass for one more thing.

Maria batted her lashes and smiled at the kid. Had anyone ever refused her when she looked at them like that?

Finn seriously doubted it.

After what seemed like a terminally long time, the kid behind the desk sat back and said, "Okay." He glanced around the store as if he expected his manager to pop up out of nowhere to discipline him, but they were the only ones in the café.

"Come with me," the kid said. "The video footage is on the office computer."

Finn and Maria followed him into a small office behind the counter. The kid left the door open in case anyone were to walk in. Until then, it was the three of them.

The kid flipped through the security footage as if he did it all the time. He backed up to the time before the ghost entered and then pressed play.

They fast-forwarded through about fifteen minutes of footage before the door opened. But it was only a young college-aged girl who quickly signed in and went to the computer closest to the window.

They fast-forwarded through more footage until they saw the ghost. Finn reached over and clicked pause with the mouse and filled his lungs with a deep breath.

Maria looked up at him with an empathetic smile. She knew how much this moment meant to him. How much it meant to Ali.

The kid had a questioning gaze, but before he could ask them anything Finn didn't want to answer, Finn pressed play, and they watched as the ghost walked into the establishment.

Finn leaned in closer, but even from a distance, it was plain to see that the guy in the video footage and the man caught on the hidden security camera at Fitzhugh's place were the same person.

"If you don't mind me saying," the kid said, "this guy doesn't look like much of a threat."

Maria stifled a snort. "Well, looks can be deceiving."

"I guess you're right," the kid said. "Looks like you chose better this time around."

Finn did a double-take that the kid caught.

"Or not—I mean—"

"What he's trying to say," Maria said, "is that we're not

together."

The kid looked between the two of them and shrugged. "Whatever."

Maria asked, "Do you think I can get a copy of this footage?"

The kid pulled a thumb drive out of the desk's top drawer and pushed it into the USB drive on the computer. "I've gone this far. Seems a shame not to go all the way."

The kid had a sly grin, and Maria played into the double entendre. She seemed happy enough to do whatever it took to get the job done.

She grabbed a pen and a fluorescent green Post-It note from the desk and scribbled her number on it. "If we're talking about going all the way, can you give me a call the next time he comes in?"

The kid hesitated before taking the paper. Then a smile spread across his face. "Yeah. I'll text you."

"When the guy comes in." Finn laid his hand on the kid's shoulder to clarify.

The kid swallowed hard. "Yeah. Sure. That's what I meant."

Finn slipped the kid a hundred-dollar bill before they left with the thumb drive deep in his pocket.

He scoured the area around them as they left Bytes. No one remotely fitting the ghost's description was anywhere in sight. He blew out a breath and shook out some of the tension in his shoulders.

Not that the ghost should have any idea what Finn looked like. But as Maria said, he looked like a Fed. He didn't want to take the chance of spooking the ghost and have him find some other corner of D.C. to hole up in.

They walked back to their car, the rain starting to spit down again—big, soft splats that they could almost run between and not get wet. Neither one of them said anything on the way, not wanting to be overheard on the street.

After they both climbed in and closed the doors, Finn laced his fingers with hers. He kissed the back of her hand. "You were brilliant back there. You know how to think on your feet."

"Yeah, well, when I was on the streets, a skill like that could be the difference between life and death."

He squeezed her hand and only let it go long enough to start the car and put it in reverse. He couldn't let himself think too hard about that whole *life or death* comment Maria had made because it reminded him of how ridiculously close she'd come to not surviving.

"Are you going to tell her?" Maria asked.

Finn didn't even pretend not to understand who Maria was talking about. "Yeah. I'll tell Quan. It's only right after she shared information with us that she didn't have to."

"Agreed. No need to make an enemy. When are we going to start sitting on the café?"

Staking out Bytes could mean hours or days of sitting around, twiddling their thumbs, and waiting for something that might not happen. But they couldn't *not* do it, and Finn appreciated that to Maria, staking out the cafe was a given, not a question.

Before they did anything else, though, they needed to find a place to stay. He drove to his favorite hotel and drove up to the valet.

Maria looked around, her eyes wide. "What are we doing here?"

"Getting a room?" Finn said. With the rise in his voice, he couldn't help sounding as if he were asking a question instead of making a statement.

"Yeah, but this is the Obsidian."

"I'm aware. I pulled in here, remember?"

"There are cheaper places to stay in D.C."

Finn grinned. "Yeah, but not many nicer than this one."

17

Finn handed the valet the keys to the rental and gave their luggage to the bellhop. Maria followed Finn through the revolving door, past the smartly dressed man at the concierge desk, and under the multi-tiered crystal chandelier on their way to reception to check-in.

The gentleman looked up at them with bored eyes under a deep-set brow. "Did you have a reservation, sir?"

"No."

The man's expression shifted from bored to bored and pained, making him look constipated. "I'm sorry, but there's a convention in town. The only rooms we have available are the two-room suites."

"That's fine." Finn pulled out his wallet and glanced at Maria. "Do we want one suite or two?"

"Sir, those rooms are—"

Before the receptionist said the price, Finn leaned on the counter and lowered his voice. "I'm well aware of the price."

Finn glanced at Maria and her raised brow. A suite? Let alone two suites? Had Finn lost his ever-loving mind? "I'm sure we can find a room someplace else."

"Here is fine," Finn insisted.

"Will that be one suite or two?" the receptionist asked again. Two more people got into line behind them, and Maria didn't want to stand there and discuss it with Finn while everyone else waited.

"O-one." No way would she have Finn cough up the money for her own two-room suite, even if he could afford it. She wouldn't be able to get a wink of sleep knowing he'd spent that much money on her. And it wasn't like they hadn't shared the same bed the night before.

Unless he didn't want to share it with her. "If that's okay with you?"

Finn's expression softened, and he leaned over and pressed a kiss to her lips. "Yeah, baby, that's more than all right with me."

Maria turned her attention back to the man who looked like he'd rather be shoving tiny splinters under his fingernails than standing there while they decided what they wanted to do.

"We'll take one suite then."

The receptionist checked them into a room with singular, practiced efficiency, and handed over two key cards. They headed for the elevator, and Finn caught the bellhop's eye. The man followed them into the elevator with their luggage.

In the span of a few minutes, they arrived at the second to the top floor, the bellhop depositing their luggage in the bedroom. The man left with a hefty tip from Finn and a wide smile on his face.

Maria didn't quite know what to do with herself. She spun around the suite's living room, then went over to the floor-to-ceiling windows and looked out over the city. Even with the cloud cover and the drizzle, from that high up, the city was beautiful.

Finn came up behind her and threaded his arms around her waist, tucking her head beneath his chin. "Would you like something to drink? They have a fully stocked drinks fridge. Or I can order food up from room service."

"That's okay." Maria covered his hands with her own. "I'm more tired than anything."

"You could take a nap."

"We could both take a nap." She turned in his arms and raised a brow at him. While she knew he didn't regret what had happened the night before, she wasn't convinced he would allow himself to repeat it.

"I don't think I could sleep. I'm too keyed up."

Maria buried her disappointment. Not that she'd expected more to happen than a little snuggling. She stepped back, and his hands dropped to his side. "Then let's get some coffee brewing and get some work done."

"You know you're allowed to take a break, right? My inability to sleep doesn't mean you can't either."

"You're not paying me to sleep, Special Agent. You're paying me to work."

His eyes narrowed, bristling at her for calling him Special Agent. "Fine."

They separated and unpacked their equipment on the table near the suite's efficiency kitchen. She doubted they'd be doing any cooking, but it was nice that they had the option to at least reheat leftovers if they needed to.

Maybe that would save a buck or two. Not that Finn seemed to care about that.

Finn got the coffee started, and while it gurgled and spit, he booted up his laptop and tapped a few keys. "I sent you a copy of the redacted file my father gave me so you can look at it on your computer. Probably won't do us much good until Massey can work his magic."

"That's fine. I still want to skim through it and see if I can pick up on anything. And I probably need to check in with Wyatt to update him on our progress.

Finn nodded, his attention divided between her and whatever he'd started working on. "I want to see if Uncle Abe is Abe Carter. Either way, he seems like someone we should talk to."

Maria only nodded because the call to Wyatt picked up on third ring. She quickly filled her boss in on tracking the ghost to Bytes and their plan to stake it out first thing in the morning.

She didn't have much else to add. She promised to keep him updated.

"Stay safe," Wyatt said before ending the call.

After Wyatt, she attempted to reach Massey to see if he'd had time to work on the redacted file, but it went straight to voicemail.

"Massey and Isaac must be on a stakeout," Maria said. "Either that, or they're too busy fucking to answer the phone."

Finn did a double-take, and Maria laughed.

"What did you say?"

"Nothing," Maria went back to her file. "It was a stupid comment."

"Do you think they're together?"

Maria cocked her head in thought. "Yeah. No. Maybe?"

"Or is that wishful thinking on your part?"

"Wishful thinking? I don't have a stake in their relationship. But apparently, Isaac has a thing for Massey. They both seem like great guys. Is it such a bad thing to hope that they got together?"

"Not at all." Finn turned his attention back to his screen. "It's a beautiful thing when two people find each other."

Maria stilled and stared at him. She'd never pegged Finn as the romantic type. Go figure.

It was early evening by the time Finn sat back and scrubbed his red, screen-irritated eyes.

He blew out a heavy sigh. "I looked at the CIA photos of Abe Carter. He's Uncle Abe. After my search for him, I'm not surprised Carter was CIA. All traces of him on the internet disappear after his retirement. No social media. No events. No awards. He sold his property a month after he retired, and after that, nothing is popping up on real estate ledgers. At this point, he could be giving the ghost lessons on how to disappear."

"It tracks that he would want to keep a low profile." Maria swallowed a swig of cold coffee and grimaced. "But somebody has to have a way of contacting him. Maybe Ronan—"

Finn groaned. "I'd rather keep Ronan out of this as much as possible. It took an act of Congress for him to give me these two weeks off as it was."

"You could always ask Quan. She's been in D.C. awhile. I'm sure she has plenty of contacts within the CIA. Maybe—"

Finn grimaced, looking as if he'd swallowed a bunch of cockleburs that pricked and poked all the way down. "Even worse."

"Maybe. But she was willing to help before. What makes you think she won't help again?"

"I'll keep it in mind. Last resort sort of thing."

"Fair enough." Maria's phone rang, and she snatched it up. She held the screen up for Finn to see. "It's Massey."

She answered the call. "Did it work?"

She put the phone on speaker and set it on the table between her and Finn.

"I'm here," Finn said. "Maria put you on speaker."

"Do you want the good news or the not-so-good news?" Massey asked.

In the background, Isaac said, "Don't tease them. Tell them already."

"You're no fun." Massey chuckled, his voice quieter as if he'd turned his head away from the phone to direct the comment at Isaac.

"Give me what you've got." Finn scrubbed his hands through his short hair. His eyes drooped, and he looked like he could've used that nap.

Or at least that run that they'd missed in their rush to get to the library that morning. Had it just been that morning, right?

"The not-so-good news is that I'm having difficulty removing the redaction. My algorithm is going to take more tweaking. Could be a few days. Things are kind of heating up here, and I don't have that much time to work on it."

"That's fair." Finn sounded more defeated than Maria had expected. It had been a long shot anyway. But she understood Finn's disappointment. They'd come so close to finding out some important information, but without removing the redactions, the report Finn's father had held onto for so long was basically worthless.

"The good news is that I think I found the reason the ghost is still in town. If I'm right, you have until Saturday to catch him."

Finn reached for her hand on top of the table. Blood pulsed in her hand as he gripped it. "Who is his target?"

It wasn't a difficult guess. The ghost was an assassin. The only reason he would stay in town and not get the hell out of Dodge was if he had a chance to make even more money.

"Get this," Isaac's voice came on the line. "There's a concert on the National Mall on Saturday. Rival punk rock bands. One stage will be at one end of the mall, the other stage at the other end. At least that's what the fan sites say."

"What does this have to do with the ghost?" Finn asked.

"The frontmen of both of the bands are having a war on social media. The story is that one of them had sex with the other one's girl, and it devolved from there," Massey said. "And now there's a DeadMoney bet on the both of them. It's fucked up, man. Fans must have gotten wind of the site, and they're all throwing down bets."

Maria couldn't believe what she was hearing. "That's so fucked up."

Massey laughed, but it held that note of incredulity to it. "Tell me about it. At least that's my best guess as far as Dead-Money is concerned."

"How has the concert not been shut down?" Finn asked. "Surely the government, or at least the Metropolitan Police Department, has eyes on this."

"No doubt," Massey said. "But you have to remember, nearly all of these bets come and go, and absolutely nothing happens. Most of these people betting have no idea that people are really dying. To them, it's all fun and games."

Maria still couldn't believe it. "Yeah, it's all fun and games until your favorite punk rocker dies."

Finn sat back in his chair. "And with the concert happening at the National Mall, security is going to be a nightmare. For a guy like the ghost, killing one of those guys and escaping into the crowd with all the confusion will be child's play."

"If that's why the ghost is hanging around," Massey said. "He's keeping tabs on the DeadMoney site for a reason. It could be something else entirely that we haven't picked up on yet."

In the background, Isaac reminded Massey that it was time for them to go.

Finn stood and picked up Maria's phone. "Hey, thanks for all the hard work you're doing. I know you have your investigation to contend with."

"Happy to help where I can."

They ended the call, and Maria stepped into Finn's embrace, wrapping her arms around his waist. She looked up at him. "I think it's time we took a break."

"Go ahead. I'll—"

"No. *We're* taking a break." At this rate, he'd work himself into an early grave if she didn't step in. She took a half step back.

"We're going to go down to the gym. We're gonna take that run that we missed this morning. We're going to relieve some of the stress and hopefully get a rush of endorphins along the way. After that, we're going to come back here, take a shower, and order room service. Then, and only then, are you allowed to go back to work. Understood?"

She had no compromise in her voice.

A slow, tired grin spread across Finn's exhausted face. "I like a woman who takes charge."

"Remember that. Now, get your ass changed and meet me down at the fitness center."

An hour and a half later, they had returned from their workout, freshly showered, and a little less stressed—if not better rested—when room service arrived.

Maria dug into her burger and truffle fries as if it were her last meal. Finn made a trip to the drinks fridge and held up two small whiskey bottles. "You want?"

Maria swallowed her food, surprised Finn had gone for the alcohol. "If there's a Coke in there that you can mix it with."

Finn squatted and searched through the mini-fridge and popped up with a can of Coca-Cola. "Bingo."

From the kitchen cabinets, he pulled two glasses from the open shelving, emptied one bottle of whiskey into his glass, and mixed the whiskey and Coke in the other for her. "Ice?"

"Please. If we have any."

Finn went back to the fridge. "If they don't have any, I'll order some up."

But of course, there was a small tray of ice cubes in the fridge. Finn returned to the living area. Maria was sitting on the sofa, her plate of food on the coffee table. They had enough work spread out on the table that they didn't want to take the time to clean it up to eat. Besides, they'd be getting back to work after dinner.

Maria finished her drink and food around the same time Finn did. He stacked their plates and placed them on the room service tray. He held up Maria's glass. "Another?"

The surprise must have shown on her face because he added, "Don't look so shocked. I think we both deserve a bit of a break, don't you?"

"You're the boss."

They laughed. They both kind of needed that.

While waiting for her second drink, she laid a throw pillow against the armrest. She leaned back and stretched her legs out in front of her. As short as she was, there was still a whole cushion available for Finn.

He returned with their drinks and handed hers over. "Where am I supposed to sit?"

"Wherever you want." The first Jack and Coke already buzzed through Maria's system. She was a lightweight when it came to drinking, and she feared the second drink would put her out of commission for the night.

At least when it came to focusing on the case.

But that didn't keep her from accepting it and resting the glass on her abdomen.

Instead of taking the open spot on the sofa, Finn lifted her legs and sat down, placing her bare feet on his lap. He slouched down and rested his head on the back of the sofa.

He turned his head toward her, his eyes at half-mast. "Is this okay?"

Maria wiggled her feet. After their shower, which she'd taken by herself— regrettably—she'd changed into her shorty pajamas, deciding that if she was going to work half the night, she'd be comfortable. "Only if I get I foot massage."

His free hand went to her foot. Her body shivered. She hadn't expected him to give her a foot massage, but then again, she hadn't expected the orgasm he'd given her the night before either.

Finn set his drink on the coffee table and used both of his hands on her feet. He pressed his thumbs into the instep of her foot, and she couldn't hold back the grateful groan.

"Feel good?"

The ice in her glass tinked against the side as she held the cold surface to her forehead. Her eyes drifted closed. "You have no fucking idea."

Finn chuckled. "Do my feet next, and I'll find out."

"Anything, just don't stop."

Between the epic foot massage and the two Jack and Cokes, Maria was little more than a puddle of warm flesh on the sofa by the time late evening arrived.

She would need to get toothpicks to prop her eyes open if she wanted to get any work done. Maybe Finn could have someone from the front desk bring some to the room.

Finn finished the massage and shook out his hands. He moved her legs off his lap and stood. He pointed to the empty glass resting on her abdomen. "Are you finished with that?"

"Mmmm-hmmm," was all Maria managed.

The glass disappeared from her loose grip, and her eyes closed. She heard Finn in the kitchen rinsing out the glasses. She really should get up and get back to work.

The next thing she knew, Finn scooped her up in his arms and started carrying her into the bigger of the two bedrooms. "What are you doing?"

"I'm putting you to bed. What does it look like I'm doing?"

"Only if you come to bed too."

When he hesitated, she added, "In this bed, or the other one. Your choice. But we owe it to ourselves to get a good night's sleep so we can hit it hard tomorrow."

His shoulders sank, and the exhaustion on his face became

even more evident. The circles under his eyes had darkened, or it could have been the shadows thrown by the bedside lamp.

Finally, Finn relented. "Okay. Give me a second to turn off the lights and shut the computers down."

Finn deposited her on the bed. She rolled to her side and snuggled into the pillow, her eyes already falling closed.

A short time later, the bedside lamp clicked off, and the mattress sagged as Finn crawled into bed behind her.

He snuggled up against her, lightly laying an arm around her waist. She linked her fingers with his and squeezed his hand.

They may not have had any success finding Carter yet, but hopefully, come morning, they would have success catching a ghost.

FINN WOKE with his arm around Maria's waist, his hand cupping her breast, and his hard-on lined up with the crack of her ass.

She snuggled back against him and moaned a lazy morning moan. She stretched and rolled over, still half asleep, her dark hair in tiny tangles around her face. Finn brushed some of the stray hairs out of her face.

"Morning," she mumbled.

"Morning to you, too."

When Maria stretched again, her pajama top rose, exposing the soft skin of her midriff. Finn stretched his hand across her stomach, tracing the lower edge of her ribs.

No lie, it wasn't much of a sacrifice to wake up next to Maria in the mornings. Definitely, something he could get used to if he were looking for that sort of thing.

Which really, as nice as that sounded, he only had time in his life for one woman—Ali.

Maria knew that.

She was a big girl *and* the one who'd started this. As soon as they returned to Wyoming, he'd let whatever this was die down. But right now, he had a soft woman in his bed, and he would be a fool not to recognize how damn lucky that made him.

He kissed the cap of her shoulder and leaned up on one arm, kissing his way across her collarbone to the hollow of her neck. She tilted her head back, exposing more skin.

God, there was nothing that he wanted to do more than start at her neck and work his way down from there.

Thinking about the epic way she'd blown him two nights before, he immediately hardened more. He couldn't remember the last time he'd come that hard.

Or that fast.

His fingers slipped lower, skimming beneath the waistband of her underwear and running through the short-cropped curls at the apex of her thighs.

Palming the back of his head, she held him to her while the other covered his.

She didn't stop him. She guided him.

Fuck. She knew how the hell to turn him on.

She was already slick, warm, and wet as his fingers slid through her folds. He groaned as he nibbled on her collarbone. Maria ground against his hand and guided his pressure.

Her middle finger lined up with his, and she thrust against their joined hands, pressing their middle fingers inside her. They both hissed in a breath.

As much as he wanted to spend the whole morning in bed with her, bringing them both pleasure, he knew they didn't have much time.

He'd forgotten to set the alarm the night before. They'd had every intention of being staked out in front of Bytes before it opened.

But maybe, just maybe, he had enough time to bring her to orgasm.

Her phone pinged with an incoming text. Maria muttered, "Leave it. It's probably Wyatt checking in."

Finn did what she commanded, leaving her phone on the bedside table, and started kissing his way down her sternum. His fingers worked inside her, her hand still on top of his. That she was so brazen, so brash, so bold in the quest for pleasure, Finn had a hard time imagining himself with anyone else.

Then her phone pinged and pinged again with a series of incoming texts that Finn couldn't ignore. Maria's hand slipped off his and she relaxed back into the mattress.

"Mother fucker," she grumbled.

Reluctantly, Finn snatched his phone off the bedside table and leaned against the headboard.

He unlocked her phone with the password she gave him. "Oh, shit. I had no idea it was this late."

He jumped out of bed and went to his suitcase for his clothes. "Get dressed. The kid from Bytes texted. The ghost is there."

Maria scrambled to her feet, throwing on the same clothes she'd worn the day before, quickly tying her hair into a messy bun on the back of her head.

After a quick trip to the bathroom, they both threw on their shoes and ran out the door. The elevator wait was interminably long, but they were too high up to run down the stairs and beat the elevator.

They were only seven or eight blocks from Bytes, so they ran for it instead of waiting for the valet to get their car.

They burst through the hotel's front door and sprinted down the street. He texted the kid to tell him they were on the way and to try to stall the ghost if he tried to leave, but only if he could do it safely.

Then he tried calling Quan. At this point, she would be the only one who could help. He didn't have the time to call 911 and explain what was going on and why they needed officers dispatched to Bytes.

At least Quan would know they needed to approach the café without making it look like a police raid, and that could possibly end up scaring the ghost away for good.

They were still a couple of blocks away when Quan answered the phone. With this not being his case, he'd rather not step on Quan's toes and arrest the ghost himself if he didn't have to.

Though panting, he managed to update Quan. She held her hand over the phone and yelled some orders before coming back on the line.

"Don't go in there." Quan's voice was uncompromising. "Do you hear me? Wait for my team."

"If we wait, we'll lose—"

"I repeat, Finn, wait for my team. That's an order."

Quan didn't bother with goodbye. Finn disconnected the call, put his head down, and ran faster, trying to catch up with Maria. Though she had an almost imperceptible hitch in her stride from her healing gunshot wound, it hadn't slowed her down.

"Take a right," Finn called out as they neared an upcoming alley. "Shortcut."

Maria almost overran it but pivoted better than an NBA player at the last second, pushing off the brick wall of the building and changing direction on a dime.

The alley smelled like cat piss, rotten food, and big-city dirt and grime, but they were through it in no time. Maria's innate sense of direction had her turning left at the end of the alley as Finn caught up with her.

They skidded to a stop around the corner from Bytes, their

backs pressed against the building, their hands on their knees, trying to catch their breath. Maria's hair was falling out of her bun, her face flushed and splotchy from the run and the adrenaline dump.

She couldn't have looked more beautiful to him than she did at that moment.

"Are we waiting?" Maria asked between gulping breaths.

"Quan ordered—"

"Are we really going to take the chance that he gets away?"

"No. We're not."

Maria grinned that adrenaline-fueled grin. "You're not as *By the Book* as you make everyone think."

Finn didn't have anything to say to that. He took Maria's hand and regulated his breathing the best he could as they turned the corner and tried to walk casually to Bytes.

Finn knew Quan would have his ass for disobeying her, and there was a good likelihood she'd call Ronan, who would chew him out as well. At this rate, he'd never advance above special agent, but he couldn't take the chance of the ghost slipping through his fingers.

They'd almost made it to Bytes when the door opened a few feet in front of them. Maria stiffened, and tension coiled in his muscles as he prepared to pounce on the ghost if he had to.

But it was only the kid from the day before. He glanced up at them with a bored, disinterested look on his face. "You guys just missed him."

18

———

"What do you mean we missed him?" Maria asked, "You were supposed to distract him."

"Look, man," the kid said, "I just work here. I texted you when he came in. It's not my fault you didn't get here in time. That's a you problem. Not a me problem."

She dropped Finn's hand, but not before she felt the tension and frustration coursing through his body. As disappointed as she was that the ghost had gotten away, she couldn't even begin to imagine Finn's soul-crushing disappointment.

To be that close and miss the man who'd probably killed his sister would be devastating.

Finn motioned for the kid to go inside, and they followed him in. There were two customers at the computers, but they both wore headphones and didn't seem aware that they had been in the same room with an international assassin.

"Which way did he go?" Finn asked.

"How should I know? He was here, then I went into the backroom to get batteries for a mouse that had died, and he was gone when I got back."

Finn rubbed his hand across his forehead as if trying to stave off a migraine.

Behind them, the bell on the door clanged tonelessly against the glass. She and Finn both spun around to see Quan and two other agents, a man and a woman, walk in with her.

Quan cut a look at Finn that said they would discuss his disobeying her order later. "He's gone?"

You could look around the small café and see that the ghost wasn't there, so the question had been more rhetorical than anything.

Quan spoke into the mic hidden at the cuff of her shirt. "Stand down. He's not here."

She turned her attention to the attendant who'd moved behind the counter. "Which computer did he use?"

The kid pointed to the computer in the far corner. The same one he'd told Finn and Maria the man liked to use.

"I'm on it." The female agent with Quan headed to the computer station in question and took a seat.

She donned a pair of gloves and used a brush and powder to check for the presence of fingerprints.

Quan, Finn, and Maria gathered in the corner, looking over the agent's shoulder.

"Anything?" Quan asked.

The agent sat back. "He wiped it clean. There are no fingerprints anywhere on this keyboard."

The agent checked the top of the desk and the edges as well. "He wiped the desk down too."

Quan said, "Well fuck. See if he cleared his history, or if there's anything else we can trace."

Quan motioned for Maria and Finn to go with her. They followed her to the back of the store, and the second agent went to assist the other one.

Maria figured Finn was about to get the ass chewing he

deserved. Quan leaned in. "I thought I told you two to wait for me. I'm pretty sure that was a direct order."

Finn probably knew he had to make his case from the heart. Anything less wouldn't work. "I couldn't do that. I couldn't take the chance that he was inside and that he would get away before you got here. And I think you knew that when you gave me that order."

Quan pursed her lips but didn't dispute his words. "What would Ronan say if I told him what you did?"

Finn laughed, but nothing about the sound reverberated with anything remotely humorous. "He'd have my ass."

"If you're going to tell Ronan, then tell him. I'm not begging you not to. I had to do it. You would have done the same in my position, and you know it."

"The moment you walked up to Fitzhugh's estate, I should have sent you packing. That was my mistake thinking that I could trust you with any of this."

Finn didn't say anything. Maria knew he wasn't about to apologize, so what else was there for him to say?

"I suggest, Special Agent," Quan said, "that you go home and let my office handle this before you fuck it up for everybody."

Quan got in his face when he hesitated, which was quite a feat for a woman who was a head shorter than him. "That's an order, Special Agent. You remember what an order is, right?"

Her dark brown eyes never wavered from his. Maria felt fairly certain that if he didn't pack up his shit and leave D.C. that day, that Quan would do everything in her power to make him regret it.

"Understood?" Quan asked.

"Yes, ma'am. Understood."

Quan eyed Maria but kept her thoughts to herself. Probably had something to do with distancing herself from Finn to keep her career from being ruined. Well, that joke was on Quan.

Maria had already left the DEA. So career-wise, at least, Quan couldn't touch her.

Maria put her hand on Finn's arm and added a little pressure. "Come on. They've got work to do. Let's get out of here."

They left Bytes and started walking back to their hotel.

Finn hit the meat of his fist on a light post as they passed. "We should have been in position. We should never have missed him. That's my fault."

Maria had to tamp down on the feeling that it had been her fault, not his. She could have told him to stop, but she hadn't. "You can't beat yourself up about it now. It's done."

"With the way Quan and her people had shown up at Bytes, if the ghost had been anywhere around watching, chances are he won't be coming back. He'll find somewhere else to get anonymous computer access."

They continued walking. A block or two later, Maria said, "You're not going back to Wyoming, are you?"

She pitched it as a question, but it very well could have been a statement.

There was no hesitation from Finn. "No. I can't leave, not when I'm this close. But if you want to go, I can have the jet come and pick you up. I won't hold it against you. This is my fight, not yours."

"*Bullshit*. You made it my fight as soon as you accepted me onto your case."

"If I remember right, I didn't accept you. You insisted."

Maria smiled, and Finn, despite everything that had happened that morning, smiled as well.

"Damn straight. And I'm not going back to Wyoming. At least not without you."

That smile of Finn's widened. He wrapped his arm around her neck and kissed the side of her head with a loud smack, his sense of pride in her wafting off him like cheap aftershave. "Yeah, that's what I thought you'd say."

THEY SPENT the rest of the day and into the evening searching for Abe Carter. There was no point in having eyes on Bytes. It wasn't in the ghost's normal pattern to go more than once.

But by the time room service arrived with dinner, they were no closer to finding Carter than they'd been when they'd started.

Maria glanced over at Finn, who pushed his broccoli around on his plate, not even taking a bite of his lasagna while it was hot. "You know what you need to do, right?"

Finn dropped his fork onto his plate with a clatter and sat back against the sofa. They were like a couple of college kids never eating at the kitchen table. But that suited them fine. Besides, they had papers scattered all over the table.

"You're saying if I want to find Carter, I've got to call my father."

Finn said it like he knew it had to be done, but there were a million other things in the world that he would rather do.

Maria couldn't blame him, but if they had any hope of finding Carter, who better to have contact information on him maybe than someone who'd been in the CIA at the same time?

Finn flipped his phone in his hand again and again. "Which means I might have to explain everything else to him. I had hoped to know more before talking to him again, but we're running out of time before Ronan expects me back in Wyoming. The truth is, we probably only have until this weekend at the latest to catch the ghost if Massey is correct. The guy can't hang around D.C. forever."

Finn's phone rang as he flipped it in his hand again. He'd flip it and catch it without really even looking at what he was doing. Maybe he should have been a juggler instead of an FBI agent.

"It's probably Quan..." Then Finn's face soured. "Or Ronan."

By Finn's tone, Maria figured he'd rather not talk to either of them. Finn let it ring.

Flip. Catch. Flip. Catch.

"You going to let that roll to voicemail?"

"Thought about it."

Unable to take the ringing, she snagged it out of the air when he flipped it up again.

"It's Massey." She handed the phone over. At least it was someone they wanted to hear from.

"What have you got?" Finn asked as he put the phone on speaker, warning Massey that he'd done so.

"Hey, Maria."

"Hey, Massey," Maria said. "Have you had any luck?" She couldn't keep the anticipation out of her voice. They needed something to go on, and it seemed like all she and Finn were doing was spinning their wheels and slinging mud everywhere.

"I don't know if I have something or not." In the background, Isaac said something they couldn't catch. "Isaac isn't sure that it's anything, but I wanted to bring it up just in case."

Finn glanced at Maria, and she saw new hope building in his eyes. "Sure. Go ahead."

"Does the name Abe Carter mean anything to you?"

Maria sucked in a breath, and Finn got this look in his eyes, a mixture of curiosity and renewed determination.

"Yeah," Finn said. "We've only been looking for the guy all afternoon. But we can't find anything on him that doesn't date back to before he retired. Why?"

"I think I was wrong about the punk rock bands. I mean not wrong," Massey corrected. "But I think it's unlikely that the ghost is sticking around for them. It's potentially a lot of money, but it never really sat right with me that that's who he would focus on. He's always been more of a state-sponsored guy. Going after the government types."

Maria took a light hold of Finn's wrist and moved the phone closer so that she could hear Massey. "How did Carter get on your radar?"

"There's a new bet on DeadMoney that showed up a few hours ago. It's for Carter. I'd love to help you find him, but—"

A horn blared over the phone loud enough to make Maria wince.

"Go time," Isaac hollered out in the background.

"Gotta go." Massey hung up without saying goodbye, leaving Finn and Maria wondering what the fuck was going on on his end, but they had their own investigation to worry about.

"With Fitzhugh and now Carter on the list, it looks pretty convincing that someone is tying up loose ends," Maria said. "Call your father. I know you don't want to do it, but I don't think we're going to get anywhere in the time frame we need without some inside help."

Finn leaned back, blew out a heavy, defeated breath, and groaned. "I never expected this to be easy. But, deep down, a part of me never expected it to be this hard either."

The weariness and sheer exhaustion seemed to come over him as he allowed his shields to drop. Maria was probably one of the few people on earth to see that side of Finn, and she felt honored and frightened at the same time. Finn was a rock, but every geologist knew that even the hardest rocks had fracture lines.

It just took an incredible amount of force before some cracked.

Maria stacked the plates out of the way and sat on the coffee table in front of him. "If you want, you can put the call on speaker, and I'll be right here with you."

That Finn finally nodded, instead of taking his phone and going into the other room to make the call in private the way she'd expected him to, said a lot.

Finn thumbed over to his father's contact information and pressed call. It connected and rang on the other end. In a near whisper to Maria, he said, "I swear to God, if I find out my father had any involvement with my sister's death, I don't—"

For the first time since Maria started the investigation with him, his eyes got red and glassy. He swallowed hard as if what little dinner he'd eaten was about to come back up.

"Hello," Finn's father answered, but Finn couldn't, or wouldn't, speak.

"Oscar?" His father's voice came again, softer this time. "I know you're there. I can hear you breathing."

Finn cleared his throat. "Do you have a contact number for Abe Carter?"

The silence on the other end of the phone dragged on and on. Maria would have thought the call had dropped, except she heard the blowers from the gardeners in the distance.

"I do." The simple answer should have made Finn feel relieved, except he only swallowed harder.

"Is Abe Carter Uncle Abe?"

Again, that pause before the answer, as if Finn's father was trying to think of any way he could get away with lying to his son, or at least skirting the truth.

Maria would have missed Walter's answer if it hadn't been so quiet in their hotel room. "Yes." Then he said, louder this time, "Who do you think gave me the copy of the redacted report?"

The muscles in Finn's throat worked, his hands shook, and the last time Maria had seen anyone that white, they'd been bleeding out from a gunshot wound.

After a minute or two of silence, Finn's father asked, "Are you still there?"

Walter had a hitch in his voice, full of some kind of emotion that Maria couldn't name. It wasn't anything she'd expected from the man she'd met a couple of days before.

Finn had to clear his voice a couple of times to be effective. "I'm still here. I've got one more question."

Before her eyes, Finn gathered himself. His father waited him out with a patience Maria hadn't anticipated.

"Did—" Finn swallowed again. "Did you have any involvement in Ali's death?"

Maria took the phone from Finn's hand and held it as she crawled into his lap. He wrapped his arms around her, burying his face in her shoulder for a moment before his gaze went to his phone screen as if it were a video call and he could watch his father's expression.

"No," Walter said, the surprised hurt clear in that one softly spoken word. "How could you ask that?"

"At this point, how could I not?"

Now, the anger in Finn's voice dominated his emotions. "You let me search all these years for information on Ali's death, and you had some of the answers the whole time. How could you have kept that from me?"

"It won't bring Ali back. None of it will bring Ali back... You know that, right?"

"I'm not trying to bring her back, Dad. I'm trying to bring her killer to justice. You of all people should understand that."

"Trust me, I understand all too well. I also know that that's not something I could ever hope to have for Ali."

Finn's arms tightened around Maria when he admitted, "We almost had him, Dad. Today. Do you get that? We almost had the ghost. We missed him by only a few minutes."

"Yeah, see, but that's what ghosts do. They slip through your fingers."

It was clear to Maria that at that point, Finn and his father would be talking in circles. It didn't escape her notice that a couple of times Finn had called his father *Dad*. Maybe that had been a bit of the traumatized boy coming out. After all, Finn had been little more than a boy when his sister had died. It stood to reason that those traumatic memories would take him directly back to that time.

"If I could get that number from you," Finn said as if he couldn't handle the idea of talking to his father anymore. "I would appreciate it."

"I'll text it to you."

"Thanks. I appre—"

The call ended abruptly from Walter's end. Finned tossed the phone onto the cushion beside them, pulled Maria in tighter, and he shook.

He shook, and he cried.

Maria cried along with him—for Ali. For the boy who had lost so much.

And for the man who refused to give up.

19

———

Finn held onto Maria longer than he should have.

But not nearly as long as he'd needed.

He scrubbed his eyes dry with the heel of his palms and took a series of deep, cleansing breaths. He couldn't remember the last time he'd cried that hard over Ali. Probably not since the night his parents had told him the news.

On the couch cushion beside them, his phone pinged with an incoming text. Hopefully, that would be his father with Abe Carter's contact information.

Maria got up, giving his hand one last squeeze before she headed into the kitchen. She returned with a cold glass of water and handed it to him. He drained it in three long swallows, like a man who'd run a marathon in the Gobi desert.

He retrieved his phone and glanced at the text with a ten-digit number and nothing more.

Maria sat across from him on the coffee table again. "Maybe we should call it a night. Get some sleep. You can call Carter in the morning."

But Finn couldn't wait. He'd come so far, the journey so long and hard. It was way past time for it to end. "It's not going to get any easier in the morning. I might as well get it over with.

He added the number to his contacts and dialed Carter. Not surprisingly, it went straight to voicemail. Finn debated not leaving a message, but he had a feeling Abe Carter wasn't the kind of man who answered incoming calls from numbers he didn't recognize.

At the beep, all Finn said was, "This is Oscar Finn. My father gave me your number. We need to talk."

Finn hung up and tossed the phone away again. *Fuck.* That's wasn't how he'd expected his day to go. He thought back to his conversation with his father and his father's denial of his involvement in Ali's death.

He'd seemed sincere.

He'd seemed truthful.

But his father had lived a lie for longer than Finn's adult life. A man like that got exceptionally good at lying.

Then again, even Finn couldn't comprehend the cold-hearted nature required to be involved in your own child murder. Despite everything he knew about his father, he didn't seem capable.

But Finn had been wrong before.

Maria shut off the overhead lights, leaving the end table lamp on. She went to stand in front of the floor-to-ceiling windows overlooking the city.

He came up behind her. From that elevation, all he saw were the city lights—the office buildings still being cleaned, the streetlights illuminating the road, the traffic lights turning from green to yellow to red, the ribbons of red and white taillights and headlights. Up near the top floor, everything seemed peaceful.

Even if everything was in complete chaos.

Threading his arms around her waist, he kissed that tender

spot at the base of her neck where it attached to her shoulder. Goosebumps flashed across her flesh, bringing a small smile to his lips.

"I like your lips on me," Maria murmured, meeting his gaze in the reflection in the window.

"And they like being on you."

Maria laughed, turning in his arms and threading them around his neck. She glanced down at his semi pressed softly into her belly and caught his eyes again. "My lips like being on you as well."

The heat in her eyes when she looked at him that way almost overcame his bone-deep exhaustion. He would like nothing more than to take Maria into the bedroom and show her exactly how his lips could make her feel. But for the life of him, he didn't have the energy.

Maria let her arms fall to her sides. She took his hand and tugged him.

"Where are we going?"

Maria walked backward, tugging lightly on his hand. "You put me to bed last night when I'd needed it. Now it's my turn to return the favor."

Finn's feet stalled out. "I still have work—"

Maria glared at him. "We've been working all day. We've come so far. We've learned so much. You won't be any good to this investigation, or Ali, if you don't get some rest."

When he merely thought about disagreeing with her, she made that noise in the back of her throat. The kind of noise that stops you in your tracks and tells you whatever you'd planned to say or do next wouldn't be tolerated.

So, Finn kept his mouth shut. And that earned him the slyest, sexiest smile. "Good man. I like a guy who knows when he can't win."

Finn laughed and followed her into the bedroom and even

farther as she steered him into the adjoining bathroom. She dropped his hand and waggled her finger at him. "Strip."

"Excuse me?" Finn asked even though he hadn't misheard her.

Maria turned on the shower. Water cascaded down from the rain head fixture in the ceiling and jetted out from the nozzles on the sides.

He had a similar shower back in Wyoming, and he knew exactly how amazing all those jets would feel on his tired, aching body.

By the time he'd stripped naked, steam had started billowing up. Maria came up behind him, put her hands on his shoulders, and walked him into the shower.

"*Christ.*" His eyes closed. The hot jets of water felt amazing. Finn braced his hands on the cool tile and dropped his head between his shoulders.

He jumped when he felt Maria's hands land on his back. Glancing over his shoulder, he found her naked behind him.

Maybe he wasn't so exhausted after all.

Maria poured the rich, citrus body wash onto a washcloth. When he moved to turn around, she said, "No. Stay there."

He had no clue what she had in mind, but he had an idea. And he wasn't opposed.

She scrubbed him down from literal head to toe, leaving not even an inch of his body unwashed. She had gentle, calming hands that eased the knots in his shoulders and the tension at his temple. The long, slow strokes up and down his arms, his spine, over his quads, and the curve of his calves made him have to brace one hand on adjacent walls to keep himself from falling over.

If this woman ever decided the security business wasn't for her, she could make good money as a masseuse.

He heard a soft splash and a plop behind him as the washcloth hit the shower floor.

"Turn around," she said.

Finn liked it when she ordered him around with that confident authority in her voice. He turned around, his arms out to his sides, with a *what now* gesture.

She planted a hand in the center of his chest and pushed him into the corner, the tiles cold against his warm back, but the built-up steam in the shower kept him from breaking out into goosebumps.

She poured more body wash into her hand, added a little bit of water, and lathered up her hands. She held her hands palms out for him to see. "May I?"

Finn swallowed, but all he could manage was a nod, curious about what Maria's naughty, delightful, dirty mind had planned.

Even though she'd already washed him thoroughly, she re-lathered his chest and started working her way down from there.

His veins buzzed with anticipation as she worked her way down and down some more. The blood rushed south faster than her hands, his erection standing straight out from his body.

She stepped closer, straddling one of his legs as she reapplied soap to her hands and lathered up again. This time, she worked her fingers through the cropped hair around his cock, and took his heavy balls into her hand. He let his head fall back as his eyes fluttered closed.

"Christ, your hands feel so good." Finn gave himself over to the sensations—to the slick slide of soap on his skin, to the beat of the blood behind his eardrums, to the fire flickering low in his belly.

She worked her hands around his cock, his base, his balls, avoiding the area where he wanted her hands and her lips the most. She ground against his thigh, leaving his skin wet and slick.

Her hand left his body for a mere moment, and for the span of that second, he thought she'd finished. But then her hand returned, lathered again as she took his shaft into her hand.

A rash of expletives fell from his lips as he bucked up into her fist, her warm chuckle bringing a smile to his lips.

He reached an arm around her, cupping one of the most perfect ass cheeks he'd ever seen, and squeezed it. He pulled her tighter into his thigh and her hand stalled on his dick.

Finn loved that he could make her body forget what she'd been doing. Liked that he'd taken her brain off-line, if only for a moment.

But then her brain must have rebooted because she started stroking him harder and faster.

She continued the slow grind against his thigh, dropping an unexpected moan here and there as she worked him from base to tip. He was already close to blowing. How could he not be with the way she rode his thigh, chasing her own pleasure as she simultaneously worked the head of his cock over again and again.

She tongued his sensitive nipple. A lightning bolt shot straight to his groin, tightening his balls, threatening to make them explode. He wrapped his arms around her head, holding her in tight.

He let one hand fall to her ass again, squeezing one of her amazing ass cheeks, encouraging her to go for what he knew she wanted. She stroked her hand faster, bringing him to the brink.

He felt the first pulses of his impending orgasm as Maria scraped her teeth across his nipple. The duality of the pleasure and the pain propelled him over the precipice.

He grunted and snugged her tighter into his thigh as he came in her hand.

Maria's body shuddered, and the sweetest little moan escaped her lips as she climaxed against his thigh.

She collapsed into him, and he collapsed against the wall. It was the only thing holding them up.

She released his spent cock as he went soft and stood on her tiptoes to kiss the underside of his jaw.

He held the back of her head, her hair still in that messy little bun from earlier that morning. He pulled the tie from her hair and let the strands fall around her shoulders. Leaning down, he took her mouth with his.

It was gentle, but no less passionate. He could die a happy man if all he was able to do was kiss Maria for the rest of his life.

Finally, he broke the kiss and rested his forehead against hers. "I'm—I'm speechless. And boneless," Finn said with a laugh.

"That was the general idea." Maria had a very self-satisfied expression on her face that was sexy as hell. "Hopefully, you'll be able to get some sleep now."

"So all this…" Finn gestured between the two of them, trying to indicate what had just happened. "All this was strictly therapeutic?"

"An orgasm is always therapeutic."

Finn laughed again. What was he going to do without her in his life?

Maria and Finn woke up to an early alarm they'd set, determined not to miss the ghost this time if he happened to show up at Bytes.

With street parking limited, Finn dropped Maria off on a corner. She walked down the street and entered the fashion shop across from Bytes. He drove around, waiting for a parking spot to open that would give them eyes on the café.

It took him a good thirty minutes, and it had become increasingly difficult for Maria not to look suspicious in the store. The clerk kept asking if she needed help, and she had to keep looking at the same four racks of clothes and tell the woman she was browsing.

Not that there was a whole lot to look at.

Between the four racks, there couldn't have been more than a few yards of fabric between all of the skimpy garments combined. Maria couldn't even imagine what kind of event she'd have to go to to make one of them a viable option. Especially the sequined or rhinestone-studded one.

Finally, Maria got an incoming text from Finn with his location, and she walked down the street in the opposite direction from where he'd dropped her off.

He waved to her from the patio of a nearby café. He had a steaming cup of coffee already in his hands and one beside him for her.

She went through the restaurant and exited onto the patio, taking her seat. The view down to Bytes was farther away than she would have liked. They would have to have an eagle eye on the place to recognize the ghost from that distance.

"Do you think you can recognize him from here?" Maria asked as she took a sip of the much-needed coffee. The beans were only slightly bitter, but the caffeine hit hard. With a few sips, the caffeine started leaching into her system.

"I brought my Nikon," Finn said as he lifted his camera with the short-range telephoto lens off his lap to show her. "It doesn't have as much zoom as I would like from this distance, but I think it will be enough if we need it."

With the weather improving, more people were out and about on the streets and the patio with them, so they had to be more careful about what they said. At least at that distance from Bytes, it would be unlikely for the ghost to spot them watching and make a run for it.

"What about Quan's people? Have you spotted any of them?"

Finn shook his head. "With the ghost a suspect in Fitzhugh's murder, she's bound to have them out here, though. But the whole time I sat here waiting for you, I didn't spot anyone obvious."

"Do you think they spotted us?"

Finn grinned and held up his phone for her to see. He'd already gotten a text from Quan that simply said, "Don't do anything stupid."

"So my guess," Finn said, "would be yes, they've spotted us."

"I'm surprised she didn't tell you to leave."

"She probably knows I wouldn't listen. I have no intention of getting in their way. But if somehow they miss him, I want to make damn sure that he doesn't get away again."

They sat there for a couple of hours until the morning crowd dissipated, and they were the only ones left on the patio. They started drawing suspicious looks from the waitstaff, and without the other customers around, they had a much greater likelihood of being spotted.

Luckily, a closer parking space opened up, and Finn went to move the car closer so that they could stake out Bytes from there. Maria paid their tab and met him at the car, sliding into the front passenger seat.

"Now we wait," Finn said.

And they waited, and they waited.

And they waited.

They waited until Bytes closed, having moved the car to different locations during the day as other spots became available.

They returned to the hotel feeling like they were playing the waiting game.

Waiting on Massey and hopefully the *un*redacted files.

Waiting to hear from Abe Carter.

Waiting for the ghost to show up in a location, he may never show up again.

Had they blown it?

Had the ghost been watching Bytes?

Had he been close enough that he'd seen her, Finn, Quan, and her people descend on Bytes like a drug raid.

Finn's days in D.C. were numbered, and she hated the idea that they would return home without Ali's killer under arrest.

There was only so much one man could take.

And even Finn had to have a point where he would break.

20

They woke extra early Thursday morning to get a good spot to watch Bytes. The long morning passed extremely slowly, but the street traffic had increased dramatically from the day before. As the sun came out and the clouds dissipated, the pedestrian traffic increased exponentially.

"Is it a holiday or something I don't know about?" Finn checked the date on his watch, but it wasn't any kind of national holiday that he was aware of.

"Look at the people walking around. Do they look like your typical tourists or college kids?"

Finn looked closer. Then it hit him. An inordinate number of multicolored mohawks, heavy black boots, leather jackets, ripped jeans, and body modifications walked the streets. "Has to be all the people coming into town for the punk rock concert on Saturday."

"That would be my guess."

"Not exactly working in our favor. It's going to be that much harder to find the ghost in this crowd."

"It's been hard enough looking for the ghost as it was. I don't think we've seen this many people going in and out of the café the whole time we've been watching it, much less in the few hours since it opened."

Even though Finn's confidence had started to waver, he said, "We're going to spot him. If he goes in that café. We'll spot him."

"Unless those delivery trucks keep coming. Maybe we need to get to a better location so we don't have to watch from across the street and have the trucks block our view."

"Agreed. Even though I'd bet my left nut that Quan has multiple eyes on the place."

"That's a pretty high level of confidence." Maria took a sip of her coffee, having to tilt her head back to get the last few drops. It had to have been ice cold by then. "I need a pee break. We're pretty close to a coffee shop. Do you want me to get you a cup as well?"

Finn handed her his empty cup to toss in the trash. That would be amazing."

She opened her door and took the two empties with her. The waiting, the being in limbo, stole a sliver of his soul minute by minute, second by second. While he mostly felt optimistic that they would catch the ghost, he couldn't deny that a part of him was waiting for one hell of a cluster fuck.

After all, they didn't call it Murphy's Law for nothing.

And for some reason, Murphy had taken a dislike to Finn from the very fucking beginning and liked to keep his foot on Finn's neck for grins.

At least that's the way it felt sometimes.

Finn started checking his watch, expecting Maria to return any second. He checked his rearview and side mirrors as well. The coffee shop was only a block behind him. He'd see her as soon as she exited the building.

Finn's phone rang, and he picked it up on the first ring. "Finn."

"Where are you?" It was Ronan. Maybe Finn should have checked the screen before he'd automatically answered.

"Where am I? You say that like a man who already knows where I am." And if Ronan didn't already know, he'd rather not be the one to tell him if he had another option.

"Answer the question, Finn."

"Did Quan call you?"

"*Jesus Christ*," Ronan muttered. Finn could practically see Ronan rubbing his temples with a thumb and forefinger. "Did you give her reason to?"

Okay, so Quan hadn't called Ronan to complain about him. That must be good news, right? "I'm watching the door to Bytes. It's the internet café the ghost has been using. Where did you think I was?"

"I mean where, *exactly*."

"Why didn't you track me on my work phone."

"You didn't bring your work phone."

Finn grinned to himself. So... Ronan *had* tried to use the work phone to locate him. One of the many good reasons Finn had left it at home. But that precaution did him little good if all Ronan had to do was call him up and Finn told him. "Why do you need to know?"

"*Finn*." Ronan's exasperation nearly made Finn laugh. Finn checked his side and rearview mirrors again. Still no sign of Maria. He was starting to get concerned, the little hairs standing up on the back of his neck.

"I'm near the corner of E street and 20th."

Finn spent the next five minutes or so filling Ronan on how they'd missed the ghost—at least the parts that weren't X-rated—when a car pulled in four parking places behind him.

"Hey man, you know I'm your friend, right? That I want what's best for you?"

What the hell was Ronan getting at? "What's wrong with you?"

Maria finally came out of the coffee shop with one of those cardboard drink trays with two coffees and a bag resting on top. She must have bought them something to eat as well.

Before he could contemplate what Ronan had alluded to, two men in classic federal-issued suits spilled out of the car that had parked four spaces back.

The men approached Maria, each taking one of her arms. The tray of drinks and food dropped to the ground.

"Got to go." Finn hung up on Ronan and jumped out of his car. He took one look across the street at Bytes then jogged down to where the two men were manhandling Maria, trying to get her into their car."

He came up to them, physically putting himself between Maria and the car, closing the open rear door with his hip. "What the fuck is going on here?"

"Official business," the guy with the mustache on Maria's right side."

The guy on her left, who couldn't have been three days out of high school, much less any law enforcement academy, added, "They warned us you might be difficult."

Who were these guys? And who the fuck told them anything about Finn and what he might or might not do? And obviously, they knew something about Maria. But it all had to be some fucking mix-up.

Or maybe these were Quan's men, and it was her method of getting him and Maria out of her investigative hair.

But that wasn't Quan's style. If she'd wanted him out of the way, she would have knocked on the car window herself and not had some lackeys do it for her.

Finn got into the kid's face. "Who said I was going to be difficult?"

Mustache Man seemed the more reserved of the two, or maybe he didn't get as hyped up as Babyface did. He must've been on the job a while longer. "Look, we're just doing our job here."

Mustache Man pulled out a pair of handcuffs and pulled Maria's arm behind her back.

She didn't fight. She knew the drill. "Are you arresting me?"

With a quick look up at Finn, maybe to make sure Finn wasn't going to bum rush him, Mustache Man said, "You're under arrest for the murder of Pablo Vazquez and Billy Gordon."

Maria took a step back, but both men quickly got a controlling hand on each of her upper arms. "What the actual fuck is going on here?"

Finn knew exactly who Vazquez and Gordon were. After all, he'd read every single one of the reports in the wake of the fiasco that nearly got Maria killed.

Billy Gordon had been the brains of the operation—if you could call him that—and his childhood friend, Pablo Vasquez, had been his right-hand man in everything illegal.

Maria had been undercover for months with his joint task force trying to bring their operation down.

Babyface said, "We have orders to bring you in. Agents are flying into Dulles airport to question you. They should be able to answer all your questions."

"Where are you taking her?" Finn asked. No way would he let her out of his sight for any longer than necessary.

"The FBI field office," Mustache Man said.

Maria's eyes rounded, her line of sight over Finn's right shoulder. "That's him, that's him. Finn, it's him."

It took Finn a second for his brain to reengage. Oh, *him*. He spun around in time to watch the ghost take his last two steps on the sidewalk before yanking open the door to Bytes.

With Finn distracted, the agents took the opportunity to open the rear door and deposit Maria inside.

"Don't tell them anything," Finn ordered through the open door as they buckled her into the backseat. She should know to keep her mouth shut. It went without saying. But Finn couldn't *not* say it.

"Finn," Maria said, "Go. I'm sure this is all a misunderstanding. Go. Go now. *Get him.*"

The fierceness in Maria's voice snapped Finn back to reality. Brought him back to what they were doing there.

He stepped back as Mustache Man started closing the door. Finn pointed at her and repeated loud enough to be heard through the closed door, "Don't talk. Don't tell them anything."

Finn turned and sprinted up the street. This was it.

The ghost was finally his.

Finn hadn't even made it to his car before the agents pulled out of their parking spot and zipped past him, Maria's face in the car window looking much less fierce and much more worried.

Finn knew what he had to do. There was no question.

He hopped into his car, the engine roaring to life. He pulled up the FBI field office on his map app and waited for the light to change so that the cars blocking him could go and he could pull out into traffic.

For a brief moment, Finn turned his attention back to Bytes. The door remained closed. The ghost was inside. Finn searched up and down the streets, expecting Quan's people to be approaching.

But no one came.

No one ran.

Did no one else have eyes on the ghost?

Finn couldn't have been more than a couple of minutes behind Maria, but the drive to the field office seemed interminable even though it was less than two miles away.

The traffic didn't help. The drive turned into a series of honking horns, him cutting people off, and a bunch of middle fingers aimed in his direction as he tried to make every light.

Unfortunately, they would take Maria through the private entrance, and he'd have to walk into reception and try to talk his way into that interview room.

He decided to use what little leverage he had. It would have been better if he'd been dressed in his suit and tie, looking the part, and not in his jeans and a button-up. But it wasn't like he had time to go back to the hotel and change.

The interior of the field office looked like a typical government building. It had marble floors and a security checkpoint almost immediately after walking through the front double doors. He tapped his feet, waiting in the line for his turn to go through security, losing patience with the old lady who didn't understand that she had to give up her purse long enough for the security personnel to check it.

When it was his turn, he tossed his wallet, credentials, keys, and spare pocket change into the little bowl before stepping through the metal detector. On the other side, he gathered his property and made a beeline for the reception desk. This was one place where he didn't have an issue flashing his badge.

He pulled out his credentials and showed them to the receptionist. "I'm Special Agent Oscar Finn..."

It was then that he realized he hadn't caught the names of either one of the agents that had arrested Maria. He could have kicked himself for that. But between the shock of the arrest and his divided attention on the ghost, he hadn't been in his best form.

"...Maria Soto was brought in a few minutes ago. I need to be brought back to the interview room."

Instead of buzzing him through, the receptionist scanned his credentials and gave them an expert once over. She stood from her desk. "One moment. Let me see what I can find out for you."

"Thank you." Finn tried to sound as if he fully expected to be allowed back, and all of this was a formality. He glanced around at the various people coming and going and making their way through security.

The receptionist came back and took her seat. "If you could have a seat over there." She pointed to the chairs surrounding a decorative rug with a coffee table and page-bent magazines laying on top of it.

At that point, Finn knew that he wouldn't get past reception so easily. "They're not gonna let me back there, are they?"

Something in her expression softened, telling him that he'd read the situation correctly.

"Please, sir, if you'll just have a seat."

Finn spun away from the counter, his hands on his hips as he scanned the lobby. The bank of elevators was nearby, but also several armed security guards were keeping their eye on the lobby. He didn't think he could make it into the elevators without the receptionist alerting security.

The last thing he needed was for both of them to be arrested.

He paced by the chairs. His stomach threatened to heave, his nerves too on edge to allow him to sit.

Pulling up Ronan's number, he hit the call button. It was almost like Ronan had been expecting Finn's call because Ronan answered it before it had a chance to ring on Finn's end.

He didn't wait for Ronan to say hello. "You motherfucker."

Ronan blew out an audible breath. "Trust me, if there had been any other way—"

"Any other way?" Finn practically yelled. He turned his back on the security personnel at the metal detectors when their eyes shot to him. He lowered his voice, but he was incapable of lowering his intensity. "How about telling me a warrant had been issued for her arrest? How about giving us a heads up instead of leading them straight to us?"

"It was an order from high above. I didn't have a choice."

"You had a choice," Finn said through gritted teeth. But he didn't want to hear any of Ronan's excuses. He'd expected much more from his friend. From his *best* friend. Or was that *former* best friend?

"I need you to get me in there. I don't care what you have to do, or who's ass you have to kiss, or what favors you have to call in. I want in that room."

"Finn, I don't have—"

"Do it, Ronan. Do it now."

"What happened with the ghost?" Ronan asked.

Finn knew Ronan was trying to change the subject and get Finn's attention off the shitty thing Ronan had done to him. "I don't know. I'm hoping Quan's people have him in custody by now. We had eyes on him, but I left the stakeout because of that stunt you allowed them to pull. What the hell do you think I did?"

"You had eyes on the ghost. On the man who probably killed your sister and you... left?"

"I didn't have a choice." Finn repeated Ronan's own words back at him.

"Bullshit. You really like this woman, don't you?"

Christ, Finn didn't have time for this nonsense. "Of course, I like her. She worked on my task force for—"

"Yeah. No. That's not what I meant, and you know it. Do you love her?"

"*Ronan.*"

"Okay, okay. Let me see what I can do." But before Ronan hung up, he added, "You know Maria is a big girl, right? You know she can handle herself in there with the best of them."

Some of the fight left Finn. He knew Ronan was right, but

that didn't make it any better. "Just... get me in there. You know those charges are bullshit."

Finally, Finn plopped down in one of the leather seats, his elbows on his knees, his head in his hands. He should probably give Wyatt a call. He'd want to know that one of his people had been arrested by some of Finn's people, but then he decided that he would have to wait. All of his focus was on getting Maria out of custody.

While she knew better than anyone not to talk to investigators without a lawyer present, he hoped she'd keep her mouth shut long enough for that to happen. Unfortunately, it wasn't like he had a D.C. lawyer on speed dial.

But... he knew someone who did.

He lifted his head and called his father, his weight still resting on his forearms on his knees. He hadn't talked to his father this much in years. He only hoped that his father would listen.

When the call connected, Finn said, "Dad, I need your help."

THE MEN who had taken Maria into custody—Special Agents Castillo and Little—had taken her to one of the FBI's interview rooms. There was a video camera high up near the ceiling and a recording device on the table. Maria rubbed at her sore wrists.

At least they'd had the decency to take off the handcuffs.

They'd already Mirandized her, a formality since she knew the Miranda Warning by heart. Even though they'd read her her rights, and she told them she wanted a lawyer, they kept asking her questions. But like any good officer of law enforcement, Maria knew anything she said would *definitely* be used against her.

"What are we waiting for again?" Maria asked.

"The agents from Wyoming." Castillo, the agent with the mustache, glanced at his watch. "Shouldn't be much longer. Their plane has already landed at Dulles."

"Why didn't they send somebody to take me back to Wyoming? Why are they doing the interview here?"

Little, the agent with the baby face, said, "You must be a big deal for them to come all this way to talk to you."

"These charges are bullshit," Maria said. "All they're doing is wasting government time and money."

Castillo said, "The FBI's budget concerns are above my pay grade."

Maria grumbled. "Anybody ever tell you you're an asshole?"

Little busted out with a laugh that he tried to cover with a cough, his cherubic cheeks flushing.

"So," Castillo said, "Did you waste those two drug dealers?"

Maria leaned back in her chair and stared at him with as bored of an expression as she could muster. When in reality, all she could think about was Finn and if he'd caught the ghost. They'd confiscated her phone upon arrest, so even if Finn wanted to get in touch with her, he had no way to do so.

"I want a lawyer," she repeated. She couldn't make it plainer than that.

Castillo folded his arms across his chest. "I'm sure they'll get to that as soon as the other agents get here."

As annoyed as she was, Maria didn't mind poking at the agents a little bit. After all, they'd gotten between her and helping Finn catch the ghost.

"So what? You lackeys are gonna babysit me until the other agents get here, in case I decide to confess and spill my guts?" She leaned forward and glared at them with disgust. "You know that's not gonna work, right?"

"Stranger things have happened."

Maria tipped her chair back until the front legs lifted off the floor, and she added a few more scratches to the wall behind her with the back of her chair.

"Suit yourself, boys. I'm sure your supervisors would rather have you here where they can keep their eye on you instead of out there catching the real criminals."

They didn't say much to that. Time passed by slower than it physically seemed possible. Slower than when she'd been waiting for the last bell of the last class in high school. Slower than a meal at a bougie restaurant when you hadn't eaten all day.

She would have gotten up and paced if there had been enough room to do so, and also if it wouldn't have shown the agents how concerned she was about maintaining her freedom.

Knowing the charges had to be total, utter, and complete fabrications and should never have been able to be brought against her in the first place did little to keep her calm. Her stomach flipped. She knew how slow the governmental and judiciary gears turned. It could be weeks or months before everything got sorted and she was released from custody.

But who had authorized the expense of sending two agents to D.C. to pick her up when Ronan knew she would be back in a little more than a week on her own? It wasn't like she was a flight risk. She hadn't even known she had a warrant for her arrest.

She groaned to herself. How long would all this take to clear up? She didn't relish being incarcerated for however long it would be if she weren't granted bail, which, with a double murder charge, seemed doubtful even for a decorated DEA agent.

The doorknob turned, and with a hollow click, it opened enough for a white man to push through. He looked at Castillo and Little and said, "We've got this."

He waited until the D.C. agents left before taking a seat across from Maria. His partner, a Black woman who looked like she could have held her own on the streets with Maria when she'd worked undercover, sat down beside him. By now, Maria's bladder was getting full, her stomach was getting empty, and all she could think about was Finn.

She rocked back in her chair again, trying to look bored and indifferent. They introduced themselves. The woman was Special Agent Turner, and Maria figured the other guy would be Hooch, with his saggy cheeks and the dewlap of a Neapolitan mastiff, but he introduced himself as Special Agent Long.

"I'm not talking without a lawyer. And since I haven't even been allowed to call one, you two are wasting your time."

Long had a paunch of a belly and a fringe of hair over his ears. He raised his hands as if in surrender. "Hey, we just want to talk."

Maria laughed. She didn't care that they probably weren't alone, and the whole thing was being recorded and videotaped. "You know, I'm former DEA. I know how this works. I'm not talking. Not until I have my lawyer." She started picking at her fingernails as if she had nothing but time on her hands.

Which, since she was in federal custody, that's all she had… time.

Special Agent Turner, who looked about Maria's age, tried her luck first. "We want to help you find a way out of this. We want—"

The door opened again, and a woman walked in wearing a navy-blue power suit with a Pianki briefcase hanging from her right shoulder. Long stood. "Who the hell are you?"

"She's her lawyer," Finn said as he stepped into the interview room behind the woman, a brow raised at Maria. One of those *Are you okay?* kind of looks.

She gave him a raised brow of her own, one that said, *Did you get him?*

His frown lines deepened as he shook his head.

Maria never thought the cavalry would ride up wearing a designer hajib, but here they were.

Turner gave up her seat for the lawyer, and she dragged it around to Maria's side of the table. She held out her hand to Maria. "I'm Amira Bashir, Walter Finn sent me. Please, call me Amira."

"Maria," she said as she shook her lawyer's hand and then glanced up at Finn. He'd leaned against the door and crossed his arms.

Maria couldn't believe her ears. Finn's father had sent a lawyer? But even without Maria asking, Finn nodded to verify she'd heard Amira correctly.

She turned her attention back to her lawyer. "Does this mean I can leave?"

Amira placed her briefcase on the table. "I've got my people working on it."

The two agents shared disapproving looks. They would have given Finn's mother a run for her money in a head-to-head contest. Certainly, they hadn't expected Maria to produce a lawyer so quickly.

"You arrested a decorated DEA agent injured in the line of duty," Amira said. Her soft voice had a hard, uncompromising edge that surprised the agents. "I hope, for your sake's, and for your superiors' sakes, that you have something very compelling."

Turner glanced at Long, pulled her phone out of her pocket, and set it on the table.

"There's a video." Turner almost sounded apologetic. "It's compromising. Are you sure you want him to see it?" Turner shifted her gaze to Finn, indicating who *him* was.

Maria had no idea what the hell could be on the video. All she knew was that she hadn't done anything to be ashamed of or anything she'd be embarrassed for Finn to see.

And she damn well would prefer to have him in the room rather than somewhere else, especially after he'd probably had put up quite the fight to get in there, to begin with.

"He stays." Maria glanced at Finn. Maybe she shouldn't be making decisions for him. "Unless he wants—"

"I'm staying," Finn asserted.

Of course, he was. Maria had expected nothing less of him.

Long put his hands out to his sides, with a shoulder shrug that said that it wasn't something he would have advised, but it wasn't any skin off his nose who stayed or who went.

Turner stood and turned on the screen hanging on the wall almost directly across from Maria and her lawyer. Finn had a decent angle, but the two agents had to turn and crane their necks to see it. Maria didn't feel bad for them.

"We got this from one of Billy Gordon's men," agent Turner said.

"Play the video already." Maria's bladder felt like it had swollen to the size of the Goodyear blimp, making her even grumpier than she otherwise would've been.

Turner mirrored the video from her phone onto the screen and hit play. The first thing Maria saw was her ass in the air as she went down on Billy on his bed. The video had audio, but to be honest, there hadn't been a whole lot of talking going on in the video.

Relief flooded through her at the sight of that video. If all the feds had was her having sex with Billy Gordon, then they had nothing on her. Was she supposed to have sex with the people she was trying to build a case against while she'd been undercover?

No.

But life didn't always go according to plan.

And sometimes, your life depended on you bending the rules.

Maria pasted and Gorilla glued her apathetic expression into place. "Well, at least they got my good side. And if you watch closely, Agent Turner, there's a technique I use here that drives all the men crazy. If you're into that kind of thing."

Long looked away, and Finn had to cover his mouth to stifle his laugh, and that ball of anxiety that had been sitting in Maria's belly stopped bouncing.

Turner let the video continue playing. They let it play until Billy pulled her up, and she rolled a condom down his dick before straddling his hips and climbing on board.

At least she'd been able to convince Billy to use a condom.

Amira eyed the two agents. "Is this all you have?" When they didn't answer, she added, "If I'd known I was coming here to watch two people have sex, I could have stayed at the office and logged into a porn site. You do know it's perfectly legal for two consenting adults to have sex, right?"

"Sure," Long said. "But things get a little more complicated when one of them was working undercover, and the other one ended up dead." He turned his attention to Maria. "Tell me, Miss Soto, why did you want to take over the prostitution aspect of Billy's illegal operation?"

Before Maria could even say *for fuck's sake*, her lawyer said, "I'd like a few minutes alone to speak to my client."

The agents looked at each other and then stood before cutting off the video feed. Finn moved out of their way and held the door open for the agents. "You want me to stay, or do you want me to go?" Finn asked Maria.

"You can go. I'll be fine."

With a brisk nod, Finn followed the agents out, softly closing the door behind him.

"Catch me up to speed," Amira said. "The Cliffs Notes version."

Maria filled Amira in on how she'd worked undercover as a

sex worker on the streets of Alpine and Murdock. Their objective had been to gather enough evidence to take down a particularly vicious group of men using sex workers as a cover for other illegal activity such as drugs and human trafficking.

"Over the months, I earned Billy's trust and eventually became Billy's girl. But there's only so much diversion and so many excuses I can make for not having sex with him before he would become suspicious, and it would threaten my cover.

"I avoided having to see a bunch of John's by convincing Billy to let me run his girls. But doing sex work and having sex with your 'boyfriend' are different things. It would have raised a lot of questions and suspicions if I always refused him."

"Which explains the sex tape," Amira said.

Maria rolled her eyes. "I had no clue Billy had been filming us, though I should have suspected. I wouldn't be shocked to find out he'd uploaded some of it to the porn sites. That's gonna be fun to explain to my mother."

"I was this close," Maria said after a beat, holding her fingers mere millimeters apart, "to having enough solid evidence to shut them down. I wanted every last one of those bastards to go to jail. I sure as fuck didn't want to take over."

"Tell me how Pablo and Billy died."

Maria raised her hands and let them drop in her lap in exasperation. "That's why I don't understand any of this. OPR has already investigated the shooting. I was cleared of any wrongdoing. Now I have these two come out of nowhere and pick me up off the streets—"

"I know that has to be upsetting. But let's focus on this other bit. Can you do that?"

"Yeah. Sorry." The last thing Maria wanted to do was drag this thing out. The sooner she could get out of custody, the better.

"It wasn't me who wanted to take over. It was Pablo," Maria

said. "He and Billy fought for control. They did that a lot. This time, Pablo picked the fight. A fight that ended with Billy shooting and killing Pablo. I don't think that's what Billy had intended, but that's what happened. And there's ballistic proof that the bullet that killed Pablo was fired from Billy's gun. But then Billy turned his gun on me. I don't know if he'd suspected me or if he was overly paranoid at that point, but after killing Pablo, we fought for his gun, and he ended up shooting me in the leg before I wrestled it away and shot him with it. He died at the scene."

"You killed Billy with his gun."

"Yes."

"Any other witnesses there to verify your version of events?"

Maria's heart sank for the first time since being cleared in the shooting. "No, I—"

The door to the interview room opened, and Long straddled the threshold, a sour, curdled expression on his face. "You're free to go."

"Wait. What?"

Maria's lawyer stood, collected her briefcase, and took a slightly dazed Maria by the arm. She leaned in and whispered in Maria's ear. "I was stalling long enough for Walter to get through to some of his contacts."

Maria shuffled past Turner into the hallway where Finn stood with his father and a disgruntled agent Turner.

The relief on Finn's face said that all he wanted to do was scoop her up in his arms and never let her go again, but instead, he turned to his father and shook his hand. "I appreciate the help."

Finn shook the lawyer's hand. But before he could usher Maria down the hall, his father handed Finn a pair of handcuffs.

"These were your sister's. I want you to have them."

Finn only nodded as he pocketed them. Maria suspected it was because his throat had closed too tightly to speak.

They stepped into the elevators and, after a short detour to the restroom, out the front entrance.

It wasn't like Maria had been incarcerated at a maximum-security prison for the last thirty years, but damn, the fresh air smelled sweet. She had no idea what kind of favor Finn's father had called in to get her released from FBI custody, but she didn't care if he'd had to suck every dick until he'd gotten to the President himself.

"What happened with the ghost?" Maria asked as Finn took out his phone and dialed.

"I'm calling Quan right now. I haven't heard a thing."

What did he mean he hadn't heard? He'd been right there, right?

Quan must have answered the phone because Finn said, "Did you get him?"

His grip tightened on Maria's elbow. "What the fuck do you mean 'no?'"

Maria's hand covered her mouth. No. The ghost had been right there. He couldn't have gotten away.

21

After talking with Quan, Finn ended the call without comprehending everything she'd said. Scratch that. He *understood*. He just didn't see how the ghost could have gotten away.

Maria's face blanched whiter than it had been when the agents had nabbed her off the streets.

"What did she say?" Maria asked with her face screwed up, like a wince, already prepared not to like what he had to say.

He took a couple of deep breaths to calm himself enough to speak. Finally, he said, "I think the ghost might have seen the feds take you away, or something else tipped him off. Whatever it was, he ran before Quan's people could get close enough to him. He disappeared into the crowd as they chased him south toward the National Mall. They've established a huge perimeter, but it's been a while since anyone has had eyes on him."

Maria's shoulders sank, and the tears welled in her eyes. She brushed them away before they could fall.

"Let's go," Maria said. "I'm sure they can use all the help they can get."

She took a step away, but he grabbed her wrist before she could leave. "Hang on a second."

"But we have to—"

"Let's take a second, alright?" He held her wrist tighter when she tried to pull away. "Quan has handled this for the last few hours without us. I don't think a couple of minutes more is going to make a difference one way or the other."

Maria stared at him but stayed put. Finn released her wrist and stroked a thumb across her cheek. "Are you okay?"

"Of course. I'm fine."

He cocked his head at her, not completely sure if she was telling him the truth or if it was her stubbornness refusing to admit anything different.

"When this is over," he said, "we need to talk. Right?"

Her eyes welled up, her voice wavering when she said simply, "You came."

He hauled her into his chest and wrapped her tightly in his arms. "Oh, baby. Of course, I came."

She shuddered once, but Finn knew that was all she would allow herself with the ghost still on the run. When this was over, they would have plenty of time to process everything that had happened.

Maria put her hand on his chest and lightly pushed him away. She swiped away her tears as he took her hand. They ran to his car. They couldn't be more than a couple of miles from the mall.

They fought their way through traffic, trying to get as close to the National Mall as they could. They finally found street parking—farther away than they would have liked, but they didn't have time to drive around hour after hour looking for the perfect place to park.

They got out of the rental and jogged toward the Washington Monument. As they approached, they saw the crowds walking up and down either side of the reflection pool, the Lincoln Memorial in the distance.

Along with the crowd, there was also the added chaos of the road crews and support personnel preparing for the concert in two days. They'd erected the orange-mesh temporary fencing around the stages' substructures.

There was a heavy police presence, and Finn knew that Quan had been responsible for that. They weren't idly making sure the tourists didn't do anything they weren't supposed to. They were actively searching for someone.

There were officers on foot, on bicycles. They even had mounted patrol riding their horses as they searched the crowd for the ghost.

"Where do we even start?" Maria asked, having to take a jogging step every few feet to keep up with Finn's ground-eating stride.

"Quan said she's confident that they have him cornered between the mall and the end of the peninsula of the East Potomac Golf Links. Looks like they've blocked off car traffic coming into the area and are checking the cars on the way out. She has people all along the perimeter, and they're slowly collapsing the net. They've got multiple dogs within the perimeter trying to track him."

Maria spun around in a slow circle and stopped again when facing him. "I don't see how the dogs can catch a scent with this many people around."

"Probably won't be easy. Quan has most of her people holding the perimeter around the Lincoln Memorial and the Washington Monument. I think we should head down to the FDR Memorial and the golf course. If they're collapsing the human net on him, that's the only direction he can go. If they have the ramps off 395 blocked, there's no escape that way unless he's a damn good swimmer. I think he's going to try to find a place to hide out long enough that he can get by the searchers and get to safety."

"Let's go then."

Finn didn't think it was possible to smile under the circumstances, but he found himself smiling at Maria's dogged determination. God, he loved that woman.

He didn't have time to contemplate that thought or the feelings for her that welled up and warmed his chest. Like he'd told Maria earlier, they'd have plenty of time later to process everything

They started jogging south in the direction of the golf course located on a peninsula between the Potomac River and the Washington Channel just past the Boy Scout Memorial. Finn remembered his father taking him and his sister to Hains Point at the tip of the peninsula. It had amazing views, looking out over the water at Washington National airport to the west and Joint Base Anacostia-Bolling to the east.

But between the golf course's open fairways, there were plenty of trees and other places for the ghost to hide.

The farther away from the mall they jogged, the more the tourist crowd thinned, and the ratio of law enforcement to civilians increased dramatically. But they still had a ton of land to cover.

There were so many potential hiding spots. It wasn't very encouraging. And that's if the ghost hadn't already squirted through the throng of law enforcement stationed around the National Mall.

Finn spotted a man walking along the path heading away from them wearing the same jeans and tan T-shirt that the ghost had been wearing when he'd walked into Bytes.

He tapped Maria on the shoulder and pointed in the guy's direction.

"Let's go." Maria poured on the steam even though they were

both out of breath, and Maria could no longer mask the limp in her injured leg.

They were no more than forty yards away when Finn told her, "Stop running if you have to."

All Maria managed was a breathless, "Fuck you."

Finn would've laughed if he'd had enough breath to do so. Maria fell a little behind, but she was stubborn enough to stay on his heels. The man in question must have heard them running up on him, but instead of running away, he spun in surprise. "What the—"

Finn skidded to a stop and barely avoided running the man down. "Sorry," Finn said, the words coming out between panting breaths. "I thought you were somebody else."

The man looked them up and down and turned his back on them, continuing down the path in the same direction he'd been heading. Finn and Maria both stopped, their hands on their knees as they caught their breath. Then Maria straightened, her hands clasped above her head as she walked small circles to work off the lactic acid build-up in her muscles.

When they'd both sufficiently recovered, she said, "Maybe we should head back to the mall. This thing's a dead end. He would've been much more likely to stay in the crowd and try to blend in up there."

"Unless he didn't know D.C. well enough to know there's no way out from here. If you want to go back, I'll—"

She rounded on him and pinned him with a glare. "We're not splitting up."

Finn grinned. He gave her a quick nod, then wrapped his arm around her neck and planted a kiss on the side of her head. "God, I love you."

What the fuck did he say?

Maria had the same *wtf* expression on her face that he must've had. But fuck it if he felt like taking it back.

"Let's put a pin in that," Maria said.

"Deal."

Maria pointed to a long line of trees dividing the fairways. "Let's look over there."

They took off again, this time at a more sustainable jog. They must have checked three hundred yards of treeline, ducking shanked drives from the tees, with no sign of the ghost. They even looked up into the trees in case the ghost could climb like a monkey. Still no luck. Finally, they caught up with another one of the searchers, an officer from the US Park Police that had a station near the head of the golf course.

"I've checked down to the end of the peninsula," the officer said. "He's not down there."

Looking at the satellite view of the area on his phone, Finn and Maria were nearly a quarter-mile from the end of the peninsula. After the golf course, there was a small park and playground to search.

Definitely, too much real area for one person to clear well on their own. Finn wouldn't be satisfied until he'd gone all the way to the end himself.

They spoke with the officer for a few minutes, then parted ways. Finn and Maria never stopped their scan of the area the whole time they talked.

Maria glanced at him as the officer strode away. "Don't lose hope."

Finn blew out a hot breath. As much as he tried to keep a positive outlook, those three little words hit him hard because if he looked inward, *really* looked inward, that's what he'd been doing—losing hope. "Easier said than done sometimes."

Maria clapped him on the shoulder. "Come on. Let's find this motherfucker."

In answer, Finn took off at a jog again, Maria doing her level best to keep up.

Along the way, they checked every place that could hide a human being. The golf course restrooms placed at strategic locations along the fairways, miscellaneous outbuildings, and pump houses.

Near the end of the peninsula, Finn spotted a drainage culvert heading into some trees and overgrown brush. They slowed and carefully checked the area.

"You go ahead," Maria said. "I'll keep an eye out and make sure he doesn't run around behind us and get by while we're distracted."

Finn continued the search, ducking under tree branches and pushing others aside as he crouched and crept forward. The ground had mostly dried after the rainfall earlier in the week, but the lower areas that drained through the culvert still had mud and standing water.

Finn did his best to stay on the higher ground to avoid contaminating the area with his footprints.

He sucked in a breath when he saw the single foot and a handprint. The footprint was more of a skid mark, the person's hand going down to keep them from falling on their ass. There were a couple of other partial shoe prints, but whoever the person had been, it looked like they'd decided the culvert was not a good place to go.

To be thorough, Finn crouched and shined his phone's flashlight into the culvert and saw that it was clear.

He worked his way through the trees and brush, twigs snapping beneath his feet and branches slapping at his face.

"Anything?" Maria asked as she swung around to glance at him before turning back and scanning the area.

"I think so. A sliding footprint and a handprint. Not sure if it was him, but I can't see a good reason for anybody else to go down there."

"He could have hidden there long enough for the other officers to pass him by. You wouldn't be able to see anyone down there unless you got close enough."

"My thoughts exactly."

They left the culvert and ventured out into the park. There were a bunch of trees, but they were clear of underbrush, and they could easily tell no one hid behind them. Besides the picnic tables, there wasn't much else to see. Finn and Maria checked the garbage cans to be on the safe side, but it didn't look like a man of the ghost's size could have fit into one of them even if he'd wanted to.

It was getting easier to see the water on both sides as the peninsula narrowed near the end. As they started running out of land, the hope Finn had of catching the ghost wavered.

Maria took Finn's hand and whispered under her breath, "Go with it."

Confused, Finn attempted to glance around without looking like he was doing just that, all the while pretending to be a regular couple walking down the path and enjoying the view. Maria shifted their joined hands and used them to point inconspicuously to her left.

She pulled him to a stop and turned into him, hugging him with a view over her shoulder in the direction that she'd pointed. She linked her hands behind his head and pulled him in as if to kiss him but instead whispered in his ear. "That man over there near the point, he's got mud on the cuff of his left pant leg, and what looks like a swiped muddy handprint on his right ass cheek."

Maria must've had telescopic lenses for eyeballs, but after a second or two, Finn saw the mud print on the back of the guy's pants but was too far away to see the mud on the guy's pant leg. He'd take her word for it.

Finn ducked his face into Maria's shoulder and whispered, "Looks like he's contemplating swimming for it."

As Finn said that, the man put his hands on the top rail of the fence separating the path from the water and rested his foot on the bottom rung. The man would have to be one hell of a swimmer to make it across without drowning. Especially dressed in street clothes.

No, not a man, *the ghost*.

It had to be.

The shirt didn't match what he'd worn that morning, but the ghost wasn't a stupid man. He would have found a way to change his shirt, even if that meant he had to steal one off a tourist.

"Let's fan out," Finn said as he let go of Maria's waist and shot a text to Quan. He didn't want to call her and risk his voice carrying.

As he and Maria fanned out and started their approach, Finn expected to be more wired than he was. Yes, the excitement and nerves were there, but also an unexpected sense of calm. An inevitability that settled over Finn.

They had him.

The ghost wouldn't get away.

He and Maria got within thirty yards of him before Finn witnessed the man's body stiffen. The ghost slowly looked over his shoulder at Maria and then in the opposite direction at Finn.

Against all expectations, the ghost didn't run. Maybe the man felt a sort of inevitability himself. After all, he'd had quite a long run. It was about time for his luck to change or for him to get sloppy.

The ghost turned his attention to the water, allowing Finn and Maria to close the distance to about twenty yards when the ghost said, "That's far enough."

Finn and Maria stopped, checking in with each other with a quick glance. They had no idea if the ghost had weapons. From where they stood, he had no visible print of a gun under his shirt, but they couldn't see the front of him or his hands. It was entirely possible he had a gun.

"You'll never make it across," Finn said. "And even if you do, you've got the base on one side and the airport on the other. You won't escape either of those places."

"Maybe not," the ghost said. "But there's only two of you. And even if you called for backup, they're a long way from here. I think I like my chances."

The ghost went from casually leaning against the railing to bum-rushing Maria. It happened so fast that even though Finn had been looking straight at him, the ghost caught him by surprise.

While they had only been about twenty yards from the ghost, he and Maria had spread out to cover more ground, more of a zone defense than a one-on-one tactic, which put Finn farther away from Maria than ideal.

Finn took off at a dead sprint, but even with his speed, there was no way he'd get to Maria before the ghost did.

The ghost rammed Maria like a fucking freight train. Finn knew he'd think that she would be the easy target—thought that he'd be able to go right through her and disappear up the peninsula before backup arrived.

If Finn had been in the ghost's situation, he probably would have thought the same thing. The ghost didn't realize Maria wasn't a pushover— intellectually, and most importantly, not physically. She may not have been more than about five foot four, but she was scrappy as hell, and those lean muscles could land a solid punch, or in this case, a solid roundhouse kick.

She dodged the ghost at the last possible second and spun around, doubling him over with the full force of a kick to the stomach. Before he recovered, she jumped on his back, locking her ankles around his waist and her arms around his neck, locking him in a chokehold.

The man stumbled to one knee, his hands grabbing at her arm. When that didn't work, he tried hitting her in the face and head.

She only held on tighter.

* * *

MARIA HELD on to the ghost with all of her strength, trying her best to keep her head behind the ghost's to protect herself from the blows, but he still managed a few glancing hits that left her ears ringing and made her head spin.

But she refused to let go.

All she had to do was hang on long enough for Finn to get there. The ghost went down on one knee, and with him unbalanced, she twisted and intentionally fell back, taking him with her. She landed with him on top of her, but she held on like a human-sized spider monkey.

Finn grabbed one of the ghost's arms and slapped a cuff onto his wrist. Maria didn't think she had ever heard a more beautiful sound than the *clack clack* of the cuffs as they locked around the ghost's wrist.

Those being Ali's cuffs that Finn's father had given him only made the sound sweeter.

"Let up," Finn said to her. "We need to roll him onto his stomach."

Maria hated to let go, but she knew they wouldn't be able to get him cuffed until she climbed off him and they had him on his stomach. The ghost fought the entire time, but between the two of them, they managed to get him rolled over. Maria sunk a knee into the middle of his back while Finn cuffed his hands behind him.

They rolled him onto his side to make it easier for him to breathe. The last thing they wanted was for him to die on them and miss all of those glorious years he could have spent in a maximum-security prison.

"My advice," Finn said to the ghost, "is to stay the fuck on the ground."

The ghost fought to regain his breath, the color returning to his face after the chokehold Maria had on him.

Finn must have called Quan because the next thing Maria knew, he was on his phone and said, "We've got him. We're at the tip of the peninsula, past the park."

After a pause, Finn added, "No, we're fine. Just get someone down here."

Finn ended the call, and he winked at Maria over the ghost's body.

The sense of pride that one wink supplied warmed Maria's chest with a blossom of heat that could have boiled the Potomac dry. They'd accomplished the near impossible.

They'd caught the ghost.

"Who the fuck are you?" The ghost hadn't directed the question at either one of them in particular, so Maria let Finn answer for them.

"I'm Ali Finn's brother."

"Who?"

Whether the ghost honestly couldn't remember Ali's name, or whether he refused to give Finn the satisfaction, Maria couldn't be sure, but Finn didn't even flinch.

Finn squatted to get closer to the ghost's eye level. "Don't worry. By the time the jury convicts you of her murder, I'm sure my sister's name will forever be etched in your brain."

The ghost grunted but didn't bother replying. His chest still heaved as he tried to recover from his oxygen debt.

Throughout her life, Maria had always been a big fan of horses. She loved their beauty as they ran and the way the ground shook when they galloped.

But nothing was more beautiful than three of Washington D.C.'s mounted patrol officers galloping down the peninsula straight at them, the horses' manes and tails flying in the wind.

The last few hundred yards only seemed like it took them a few seconds to travel the distance. They dismounted before their horses came to a complete stop. One of the officers held all the reins while two others latched onto each of the ghost's arms and hauled him to his feet.

The horses' lungs billowed, their big nostrils flaring as they caught their breath. In the distance, sirens wailed. That would be Quan and her people on their way.

Finn's knees must have gone weak with the relief because he put an arm across Maria's shoulder, and she supported his weight. She glanced up at him at the same time he looked down.

"Are you okay?" they asked at the same time.

They both laughed, but there was an undercurrent of near mania to it. Maria tried to steady him but decided to help him sit instead.

His ass hit the grass and must have knocked some words back into him. "Honestly, I don't know how I am. Physically, I'm fine. Emotionally... it's a lot to take in. To think that it's over after all these years seems impossible."

She settled beside him, the grass cool beneath her. He brushed his thumb over the swelling on her bottom lip. She winced, and his thumb came away with a smear of blood. "Thanks for taking one for the team."

Maria started to smile, but that only made her lip split more. Then he did the one thing that she'd never expected him to do. With the sirens nearly on top of them, the emergency vehicles pulled in and stopped. Finn leaned down and gently kissed her in front of everybody.

He pulled away and rested his forehead against hers. They

breathed in the same air, the same relief, the same disbelief, and the same euphoria.

He leaned back to get a better look at her, skimming the tips of his fingers down the sides of her face, brushing back some of the sweaty tendrils that had escaped her messy ponytail.

The intensity in his eyes made it impossible for Maria to look away.

"I meant what I said," Finn said.

But that was the kind of man Finn was. He wasn't the kind to tell lies or mistruths. He usually said what he meant and meant what he said. But for the life of her, Maria had no idea what he was referring to.

There was a bit of a commotion behind her as Quan and her people assumed custody of the ghost.

Maria ignored all that, trying to figure out what Finn was trying to say to her. "What do you m—"

"I love you."

"Oh…" Maria's exclamation was so slight the light breeze coming off the Potomac River could have easily swept it away.

"'Oh?' That's all you have to say after more than three years of pushing my buttons? After making the task force meetings nearly unbearable as you tried to get my attention? That's all you have to say?" There was no animus in his words, only humor.

"I already figured out you loved me when you sacrificed catching the ghost this morning to follow me to the field office. But up until then, I didn't think you'd noticed the subtle hints, so I'd had to turn up the heat a few notches."

"'Turn up the heat.'" Finn shook his head. "You nearly did me in. I love you now. I loved you then. I couldn't—We couldn't—"

"Yeah, I get it. Mr. *By the Book* couldn't break any of the rules. I think that was one of the things that made me fall in love with you first," Maria said. "Your integrity. Even if it vexed me to no end."

"'Vexed?'" Finn laughed. "I'm not sure I've ever used that word in a sentence." It must've finally dawned on him what Maria had said. "Wait. You love me?"

"Yes, Oscar. I love you, too. All that I'd done wasn't just a ploy to get in your pants, though to be honest, so far, I haven't been disappointed."

Finn threw his head back and laughed, engulfing Maria in a hug. "Keep that thought."

Quan hollered at them. She leaned against one of the unmarked squad cars, the lights in the grill still flashing blue and red. "We need a minute to talk."

As much as Maria hated to disturb the little bubble that she and Finn had created, there were things they needed to take care of before they could ignore the rest of the world.

Finn stood and helped her to her feet, but Maria was sorely mistaken if she thought he would let her go after that conversation. Finn slipped his hand into hers as they walked over to meet Quan. She clocked their joined hands briefly but didn't comment.

Then Quan's eyes went to Maria's bloody lip, and the one or two bruises Maria knew must be starting to turn purple.

"Do I need to call a paramedic?" Quan asked.

"It's all superficial," Maria said. The last thing she wanted to do was waste time having the paramedics tend to her lip. There was little they could do for it, and even less they could do about the bruising. All she needed was a little time to heal, and she'd be fine.

Quan retrieved a small notepad from her pocket and pulled the pen from within the spiral. "I need to get a statement from you two."

Before Finn could respond, Maria took the initiative. "Look, it's been a long, hard, stressful day. Can we come by your office in the morning and give you our statement?"

Quan must have reconsidered the exhaustion on Finn's face or the bruising on Maria's. She put her pen and notepad away. "Zero nine-hundred. My office. Don't be late."

22

Finn and Maria accepted a ride back to his rental from one of the squad cars. When he retrieved his keys from his pocket, Maria stuck out her hand. "Let me drive."

"I'm perfectly capable of driving."

"I'm aware. But this once, let me take care of you."

Finn offered up a soft smile. "You know what? I think I'd like that."

Maria drove them back to the hotel, dropped the car at the valet, led Finn up to the room, and ordered wine and dinner. Then she made Finn strip and pushed him into the shower.

He turned around and looked at her, the cascade of water soaking his hair, the wall jets massaging the sore bits on his body. No lie, he was kind of disappointed when she didn't follow him into the shower.

"You're not joining me?"

"I'll take my shower after you," Maria said. You and I both know that if I step in there with you, I won't get out until we run the hotel out of hot water, and we don't have that kind of time before the food arrives."

Finn hated to admit she had a point.

Coming out of the shower, he found a T-shirt, pajama bottoms, and a clean pair of briefs on the bathroom counter. He quickly dried off, got dressed, and walked out into the living room to find Maria talking on the phone.

From the sounds of it, it was either Wyatt or Massey. Finn came up behind her, rested his hands on her shoulders, and massaged the huge knots between her shoulder blades.

As she angled her head, he took advantage of the expanse of her exposed neck, kissing the soft spot between her neck and shoulder. She reached behind her with her free hand, cupping the back of his skull. He almost yanked the phone out of her hand and told whoever was on the other end that they would have to call back, but then a knock came at their door. With great reluctance, Finn left Maria to answer the door.

He ushered the man from room service inside and directed him to leave the food on the coffee table. Work still lay scattered across the kitchen table along with their laptops.

He tipped the man and went searching for Maria, hearing the water running in the shower as soon as he turned into the bedroom. Instead of climbing into the shower behind her, he pulled his softest dress shirt out of his suitcase and retrieved a pair of her blue panties. Like she had done for him, he laid them on the counter in the bathroom and stole her pair of shorty pajamas.

He returned to the living room, laid out their food and condiments, and opened the wine to let it breathe.

After searching through the kitchen cabinets, he found two stemless wine glasses and set them on the coffee table.

Finn collapsed on the sofa, resting his head on the back cushions. Stretching his legs out in front of him, he crossed them at the ankles and listened to the squeak of Maria's feet on the floor of the shower, and the water hit the shower pan.

He considered going in and checking on her since she'd been gone a while. The next thing he knew, she shook him awake with a light hand on his shoulder.

"I can put your food in the refrigerator if you'd rather go to bed," she said.

Finn sat up and rubbed the sleep from his eyes. He hadn't expected to be so exhausted after catching the ghost. All those years that he'd been searching for the man, Finn had always imagined the elation he'd feel at finally catching him. He thought that he'd be so hopped up on adrenaline that he wouldn't be able to sleep for a week. He hadn't expected to be hit so hard with the sheer exhaustion.

All those years of searching and hunting were over. What was he going to do with the rest of his life?

"No," Finn said. "I'll eat. I wanted to wait for you."

Finn finally got a good look at her. He grinned and took her hand, appreciating the way his dress shirt skimmed her thighs and how the three unbuttoned buttons of the shirt arrowed down between her breasts.

"*Ooof*," Finn said, her exquisiteness hitting him hard. He took her other hand and guided her onto his lap. She straddled him and wrapped her hands around his neck. "Or we can both put our meals in the refrigerator and heat them later."

"Mmmm," Maria moaned as she pressed her lips to Finn's. "So tempting, but I'm starving."

She crawled off and sat beside him on the couch, taking the silver domes off their plates. She picked up one of the fries and fed it to him. "Eat up, Special Agent. You're going to need your strength."

Maria hadn't ordered anything fancy for dinner, just a couple of hearty blue cheese hamburgers and an order of fries to split between them. The burgers paired well with the wine, and Finn took a healthy swallow.

"Do you wanna talk about it?" Maria took a big bite of her burger.

"Talk about what? About your arrest? The ghost? About what we said after? There's so much that happened today. I don't know where to start."

Maria couldn't suppress a wince when Finn mentioned her arrest. It was hard to believe everything that had happened in a few short hours.

"Any of it." Maria stuffed a bite of her burger into her cheek like a hamster. "Or all of it."

"Yes. I'd like to talk about everything. But can we save it for tomorrow? All I want to do is hold you, and love you. What I have in my heart is too complex for words."

Maria swallowed hard and washed her food down with a gulp of wine. "I think I'd like that, too."

As hungry as Finn was, sitting there beside Maria with her wearing nothing more than a pair of panties with his dress shirt rolled up her forearms made him hungry for something else entirely.

He pushed his half-eaten food away and turned to Maria, brushing her hair away from her neck and easing the collar of his shirt away. He planted a row of kisses along her collarbone.

Maria let out a breath. "What are you doing, Special Agent?"

"A little... side investigation."

Maria almost choked on the wine she was sipping. She put her glass down and took his hand. "In that case, I think a better, more thorough investigation might be warranted.

Maria pulled Finn to his feet. The seductive smile on her face made Finn's heart beat faster. While the food had been a great idea, he'd rather eat it cold than wait any longer to get his hands, his lips, and the rest of his body on her.

He allowed her to haul him into the bedroom. Maria slapped

off the overhead light. With the blackout curtains in the bedroom, the only light that filtered in came from the living room.

But he wasn't looking for total darkness. He wanted to see, taste, and touch every single part of her.

Finn stopped her at the edge of the bed, threaded his fingers through her damp hair, and leaned in for a kiss.

He brushed his lips across hers, a little breathless as he snugged her up against him and deepened the kiss. She opened her mouth, inviting him in. She smelled like the hotel's expensive citrus shampoo and tasted like a two-hundred-dollar bottle of wine.

For the rest of his life, Finn didn't think he'd ever be able to drink that wine without having the taste of it going straight to his dick.

She ran her hands down his spine, raising an army of goosebumps on his back. Then her hands skimmed down to his pajama bottoms and slid beneath the waistband, grabbing his ass and snuggling him even closer. She straddled his thigh and ground against him.

If she kept that up, this wouldn't last for more than a minute or two. He wanted nothing more than to be buried deep inside her, to make her his, and for her to make him hers. He'd waited so very long for this, never expecting it could happen. His luck never ran that well.

At least it hadn't.

But it seemed like his luck had changed. After all, they'd caught the ghost.

And Maria said she loved him.

How incredibly lucky was that?

Maria broke the kiss and leaned away to see his face. "Hey. Where did you go?"

He loved how easily she read him, how she noticed the slightest changes in demeanor and mood. "Nowhere important," he said, trying to play the moment off. "But I'm back."

She eyed him for a second, then stepped out of his arms. The wicked glint in her eyes brought a smile to his lips. More blood drained south, filling his dick. He hadn't thought he could get any harder than he'd already been, but having Maria stand in front of him, looking at him like she wanted to spend all night savoring him, taking control, and driving him mad did that to him.

She reached a finger into the front of his pajama bottoms, grazing the tip of his hard dick. He sucked in a breath, and that devious heat in her eyes only got him more excited. She tugged at the elastic waistband. "I think you need to lose these."

Being an intelligent man, Finn lost the pajama bottoms and kicked them to the side faster than Maria could have said, *come fuck me.*

One of her dark brows shot up. "Commando, huh? I like."

She took a half step back, resting her chin on her hand as she pointedly looked him up and down. Her eyes touched every bit of his skin. It shot another salvo of goosebumps across his flesh like a gentle, barely-there caress.

"What do you think?" Finn said, dropping his voice. "Do you approve?"

The question was too little too late, considering what they'd already shared. However, he couldn't deny that he anxiously awaited her response.

"You'll do. As long as you know how to use that thing."

If he only went by her words, he might have felt the need to impress her, but the spark of humor in her eyes and the way they kept involuntarily dropping to his junk and her naked hunger told him she was more impressed than she'd allowed herself to let him believe.

He stepped closer, his cock standing out straight. He scanned a finger along the unbuttoned edge of his dress shirt, hooking his finger at the button and giving it a curious tug. "I think we need to take care of this. You're wearing entirely too many clothes."

"May I?" Finn asked, his finger tracing the outline of her breast. The thin shirt did nothing to hide her peaked nipples.

"It's not going to unbutton itself, Special Agent."

He gripped each edge of the fabric and yanked. It was a four-hundred dollar Italian dress shirt that he ruined, but hearing her little squeak of surprise and witnessing the heat that came to her eyes and the sexy grin that came to her face made it worth every damn penny.

"*Ooof*," Finn said as the shirt front fell away. His eyes dropped to the thatch of hair at the junction of her thighs.

She hadn't put on any underwear either.

And he'd exposed a pair of the most beautiful, full breasts he'd ever seen. The number of times that he'd had to give her his FBI windbreaker or his suit coat to wear when she'd come to the task force briefings dressed in her street garb for her under-cover work to prevent him from popping a boner in front of all of his people were too numerous to count.

Now, he never wanted to cover them up again. He circled her waist with her hands and ran his thumb under the soft curve of each breast before lifting one into his hand. Unable to wait a minute longer, he closed his mouth over one of those luscious nipples.

FINN'S warm mouth and talented tongue sent sharp shards of need shooting to her core. Her hands threaded through his soft, damp hair as he went from one breast to the other. He made a sound in the back of his throat as he wrapped his arms around her and pulled her closer.

A pain went up her side, and she winced. Finn immediately pulled back. "What's wrong?"

"I think I'm a little beat up from this afternoon, but don't stop. I promise you, I'll live."

Finn must not have believed her because he settled on his knees and turned her body into the light streaming in from the den area. His hands ghosted over a bruise on her side that she hadn't even known she'd had. More would probably be popping up over the next day or so.

Small price to pay to know that the ghost was off the streets.

He skimmed his hand over the bruise so lightly it tickled instead of hurt. "We don't have to—"

Maria took him by the ears and forced him to look up at her. "Yeah, Oscar. We do. We do *have* to."

A slow grin spread across his face. "Does that mean you're in charge now?"

"Now. Before. Forever. If you want me for that long."

Maria closed her eyes and groaned. It was too early, *way* too early, to be talking about forever. They might love each other, but love didn't always equal forever.

She knew that.

She wasn't naïve.

Finn stood and threaded his hand through her hair, his thumb brushing across her jawline. She managed to hide the wince that time as he skimmed over a developing bruise.

"Look at me." Finn's soft command had her opening her eyes as the heat rushed up her face. At least in the dim lighting, he probably couldn't see her flash of embarrassment. Would she ever learn to keep her big mouth shut?

"What was that about? Why are you embarrassed?"

She didn't want to lie to him. So she blurted it out. "Because it's stupid of me to talk about forever. We haven't even had the chance to define our relationship. To talk about moving forward. About—"

Finn shut her up with a light kiss. Then he pulled away when he remembered her fat lip.

"Sorry," he said.

"It's a long way from my heart. A split lip isn't going to kill me."

"So it is," Finn said. "Now, about forever…"

Maria's heart stopped beating, at least she thought it had because she no longer heard the blood rushing behind her ears, and she had that light-headedness people complain about right before they faint.

She needed to swallow but was afraid she wouldn't hear what else he had to say over the sound.

"Forever…" he started again. "Forever may not be long enough."

Her heart slammed against her sternum as it restarted. "Yeah," she said, her voice sounding breathless. Had her lungs stopped functioning? "I like the sound of forever."

The smile that erupted on Finn's face could have lit the entire city of D.C. during a winter blackout. He scooped her up, and she yelped, wrapping her legs around his waist.

His hard cock lay trapped between them. He carried her to the bed, laying her crossways on the mattress. The edge of the bed dipped as Finn's knee landed on the mattress. He crawled on all fours over the top of her, leaning down for a kiss that went on and on.

Maria skimmed her hands down his back and grabbed his hips, encouraging him to cover her body with his.

One thing about Finn was that he was pretty good at

following orders, even the silent ones. He settled between her legs and leaned in for another kiss as he braced his weight on his forearms. He ran his fingers through her hair and started kissing his way down her exposed neck.

She loved the feel of him, the weight of him, the way he pushed her into the mattress, the way his chest hair rubbed against her skin, the way his whiskers tickled her neck, the way his cock rested between her legs at the apex of her thighs, the head leaking precum and mixing with her slickness.

She still couldn't believe that Finn had risked losing the ghost to come after her when the FBI had arrested her.

Her lungs constricted, and it had nothing to do with Finn's weight pressing on her. Maria couldn't remember when anybody in her life had made her that kind of a priority. When had anybody given up something so desperately important to them to look out for her?

Never.

That Finn would do that for her, that he would make her feel worthy for the first time... it made her feel valued. It made her feel like she *mattered.*

Dios. She was going to fucking cry.

She tried to blink back the tears, but they fell anyway. She swiped at them even though these were happy tears. That didn't make it any easier for her to show her vulnerability.

She was the one who'd always looked out for herself.

She was the tough one.

She was the brave one.

She was the one who took care of everyone else.

She sucked in a breath, and a strangled sob escaped.

Finn immediately stopped, his hands cupping the back of her head. His thumbs lightly traced her hairline. "Oh, baby, what's wrong?"

Maria had seen many phases of Finn over the years. The

determined man, the uncompromising boss, the loyal brother, the dutiful son.

But the total, utter, and complete tenderness in his eyes as he glanced down at her almost had the tears flowing again.

"What is it?" he asked again.

"You came back," Maria said. "You put me first. You—"

Maria took a deep breath to keep from completely falling apart. Finn wrapped his leg around one of hers and rolled them to their sides, drying her tears with his thumbs. He pressed tender kisses to her eyelids, her nose, her tear-stain cheeks.

"I've never been anyone's priority," she managed. "And you made it clear from the beginning that Ali was yours. I never expected—"

She swallowed hard, and the constriction in her throat eased. "I never expected you to give up catching the ghost to chase after me."

Finn grimaced. "I'm sorry if I ever made you feel like you weren't important. That you weren't enough. That was wrong. I had a bad habit of getting tied up in Ali's investigation and shutting out the rest of the world. But then you dropped everything to help Ali and me, even when I tried to push you away. You put in long nights and hard work. And the truth is, while Ali was my sister, you're my heart. You're my priority. I will always put you first."

She had no reason not to believe him because he had already proven himself with his actions, not just with his words, showing her that he was the man she'd always thought him to be.

"I love you." Maria took his jaw and pressed a light kiss to his lips.

Finn smiled. "I love you, too."

Maria took his words in. It was the first time in her life that she could remember somebody saying those words to her and was able to feel it deep down in her marrow, deep down in her soul.

She believed him.

Having Finn love her back had never been something she had ever expected to happen. She'd pretty much resigned herself that what she'd felt for him would forever and always be one-sided.

She tried getting closer to him, but she couldn't get close enough. She wanted him on top of her, inside her. She wanted him everywhere.

Maria took his half-hard cock in her hand and stroked him from base to tip and back again. His eyes fluttered closed, and he pressed his forehead to hers. "You fucking slay me."

Maria skimmed her thumb over the precum gathering at Finn's slit. By the time she slicked up his sensitive head, he was fully hard again and thrusting into her hand.

He hitched her leg over his hip and squeezed her ass cheek. "That's so damn sexy." He gave it an extra squeeze for emphasis.

"I could stroke you or suck you all night," Maria said, "but I really want you inside me."

Finn patted her on the ass. "Hold that thought."

Finn rolled over her, sprawling across her body as he stretched to reach his wallet on the nightstand. She gave him a playful slap on his ass as he pulled a condom out of his wallet and handed it to her. He rolled back to the spot beside her.

"Leave it to *By the Book* Finn to always be prepared."

Finn laughed. It was this adorable self-deprecating sound that made Maria's heart beat double time. "Well, you might want to check the expiration date before you say that."

Maria held it up to the light and found the information. "Thank fucking God," she breathed out with a laugh. "It's still good."

He snatched the condom from her hand and tore the top off

with his teeth. He spit the strip of wrapper out of his mouth and removed the condom. Before he could roll it on, Maria took his wrist. "I want to do it."

He laid back on the mattress, his beautiful cock sticking straight out from his abdomen. "Be my guest."

23

———

At that moment, Fin couldn't remember wanting anyone as much as he wanted Maria. His hand ghosted over hers as she rolled the condom on. Before he could roll her over, Maria pushed him firmly onto his back and straddled his hips.

"Oh," Finn grinned. "It's gonna be like that, is it?"

"Oh, yeah, Special Agent. I think you've done enough for today. I think you should lay back and enjoy the ride."

Instinctively, his hands went to her hips, following the curve of her waist up to her rib cage until his hands held her heavy breasts.

Lightly, he pinched her nipples, and she ground against him, a soft moan escaping her lips. She raised on her knees and reached behind her, lining him up with her slick entrance.

"Are you ready for this?" she asked. She said it like there could be an answer besides *yes*, but there wasn't one.

"Yeah, I'm ready."

Turns out, he hadn't been ready.

He'd had sex plenty of times before, but nothing could have

prepared him for Maria's slow slide down his dick as she took him all the way down to his balls.

Internally, she gripped him tight, and he settled his hands on her hips again, thrusting up as he pulled her onto him, seating himself even deeper.

"You feel so fucking amazing," Finn said.

"*Dios mío*. I'm pretty sure there's a heaven now because you shot me straight up into it."

How could she wreck him and make him laugh at the same time? "It's a dick," Finn said. "Literally, every other person in the world has one."

"No." Maria dropped down, her hands on either side of his head. "I don't want *any* dick. I want *your* dick. Every long, thick, girthy inch of it. And as amazing and beautiful as your dick is, what's more amazing, is the man attached to it."

"Has anybody ever accused you of talking a lot during sex?"

She leaned in and kissed him, taking his bottom lip between her teeth and giving him a bit of a nip that went straight to his groin. "A few."

Her answer didn't come as a surprise. "Hey, Maria?"

"Yeah?"

"Shut up and fuck me already."

Maria chuckled. It was this low, throaty, devious chuckle that wordlessly told Finn he didn't know what he was asking for. Good thing he was more than willing to find out.

"Gladly."

She braced her hands on his chest, her eyes drifting closed as she rocked her hips back and forth.

He caught her rhythm and thrust every time she rocked back, sinking balls deep again and again and again until his eyes wanted to cross, and his lungs threatened to burst. His breath came rough and fast, and his heart knocked around in his chest.

Her pace quickened, and she ground her hips into his pelvis

as she rocked, seeking that friction, searching for that release.

"I've got you, baby." Finn reached between them and found that tight bundle of nerves of hers.

He gathered moisture on his fingertip and returned to her clit, using pressure and circles to drive her ever closer to the edge.

As much as he wanted this moment to last forever, his balls tightened, and the tingling at the base of his spine told him he wouldn't be able to hold out much longer.

But forever was a long time, and they'd have eternity to do this over and over again.

This wasn't a one-off.

This was a beginning.

She collapsed on top of him, her arms going around him, her mouth open and nipping at his shoulder. The pain of the nips and the pleasure around his cock sent sparks and spirals of heat straight to his groin.

She shuddered, squeezing him tight. She muttered something in Spanish he didn't catch. Then she moaned, her words catching in her throat. Her muscles clamped around his dick. Her frantic thrusts turned into a deep grind.

She used a guiding hand on his to help get herself off. "*Oh, my fucking God*. Right there."

She bit down on his shoulder again, and he wouldn't have been surprised if she'd tasted blood, but he was all in. He was there for it as she shattered on top of him. He held her together as she came apart, working that tight bud at the apex of her thighs until the contractions lessened and she relaxed against him.

He rolled them, taking her to her back and driving into her. He wouldn't last more than a few thrusts, and the knowing smile and the devil in her eyes told him that she knew as much.

She grabbed his ass and locked her ankles behind him.

And he lost it.

He called out her name, part surprise, part adoration, all love, as he shot inside the condom. His back arched with the final thrust. He collapsed on top of her, their bodies slick and sweaty—the air in the room smelling of musk, and sex and good decisions.

He shifted them to their side so he wouldn't crush her, his dick still inside her as he started to soften. As he went to pull out, she put a staying hand on his hip. "Not yet."

He kissed her face and her neck, loving how the aftershocks coursed through her body made her squeeze and clamp down around him. He didn't want to stop, but he needed to take care of the condom.

She grumbled at him when he pulled out, the pout on her lips adorable as hell. He gave her a quick kiss before disappearing into the bathroom. He returned with a warm washcloth and cleaned her up. "I'll be right back."

He ditched the used washcloth in the bathroom and settled in behind her naked. Maria rolled over and snuggled up against his chest. One leg laid across his hips as she rested her head on his shoulder. He kissed the top of her head and hugged her to him. "That was amazing."

Maria's fingers toyed with his chest hair, her body soft and sated beside him.

His mind drifted over the events of the day. So, *so* much had happened. If somebody had told him when he'd started his day on surveillance that he'd have to have his father pull strings to get Maria out of the fed's custody, he'd catch the man he'd been hunting for years, *and* he'd wind up making love to the woman who meant the world to him, he never would've believed it for one minute.

He thought back to the FBI interview. Business wasn't finished there. The only thing his father and the lawyer had managed to do was put off something that they'd have to face when they got back to Wyoming, no doubt.

But at least now, they would face the bogus allegations together.

The video that Special Agent Turner had shown them popped into his head. He loved and appreciated the way Maria had handled it. She hadn't cowed. She hadn't hung her head in shame.

Because there was nothing shameful.

He cupped the back of her skull and pressed his lips to the top of her head again. "I'm so proud of you."

Maria's fingers stilled on his chest. She pushed up on her arm and looked down at him. "What was that about?"

Finn could have kicked himself for bringing it up. It was a discussion for another day. Not that she had anything she needed to explain to him. He pivoted from the conversation. "You're amazing, that's all."

She shook her head. "No, Oscar. It's something else. Spill it."

The way she said his first name was both intimate and commanding at the same time. If she wanted to know what he thought, he'd tell her. "I was thinking about the video."

He didn't have to explain which video. There was only one. "You handled it like a boss."

"I'm not ashamed of what I had to do. If having sex with Billy meant I could keep my cover and not ruin a months-long investigation all while gathering evidence on some pretty serious shit, then I was going to do it. If that's a problem for you—"

"Whoa, whoa, whoa," Finn said. "I never said the video was a problem for me. If I remember right, I said I was proud of you. You're a strong, confident, intelligent, amazing woman. And that video is no exception. All I would like to know—and you don't have to tell me if you'd rather not—is if you're okay. Did he hurt you? Did he—"

"No," Maria said. "Billy wasn't a decent man. But surprisingly, he'd been good to me." Then she kind of laughed. "You know, good to me up to the point where he tried to kill me."

MARIA WOKE in a tangle of arms and legs, the sheets down around their waists. But waking up to Finn's gentle kisses and enticing touch was one hell of a way to wake up.

Five stars.

Would recommend.

Just wait until he read her Yelp review.

When she went to slip her hand beneath the covers and take hold of his morning wood, Finn caught her wrist.

"As much as I would love for you to touch me, we don't have that kind of time. We have to be at Quan's office in forty-five minutes, and if we want to have a shower and grab some coffee before we go, we need to get up now."

Maria snuggled closer, stealing his warmth and loving the way the muscles of his abdomen danced when she trailed her fingers over them. She shifted, resting her chin on her hand on his chest. "Maybe showers are overrated."

Finn smiled as if he considered the idea and liked it. "It'll smell like we spent the night making love—like sweet sweat and musky sex."

"Hmmm. If only we could bottle it."

Finn barked out a laugh.

Maria laughed with him and sat up. "When this is over, I want a week alone with you. No phones. No Internet. Just you, and me, and whatever trouble we can get ourselves into."

Finn rolled out of bed and stood, helping her to her feet. "You've got yourself a deal."

He kissed her, avoiding her lip, which swelled a little during the night. Maybe she could get some iced coffee. Maybe that would help bring the swelling down.

They claimed the car from the valet and drove to Quan's office. Along the way, Maria texted Massey, gave him a quick update, and told him that she'd call him later to give him the full update.

Finn's phone pinged with an incoming text.

Retrieving his phone from his pocket, he handed it to her. "Can you check that?"

She punched in the password he rattled off and checked his messages.

"It's from an unknown number," Maria said. "All it says is, 'We can meet.'"

Maria flashed him the screen so that he could see for himself. His brows went up. "That has to be Carter. But that's not the number my father gave me."

"Probably a burner phone," Maria said.

"That would be my guess. For a man retired from the CIA, he's certainly acting like he's still an agent."

There was one other option they hadn't thought too much about. "Or he's in hiding. Maybe this whole thing with the congressional testimony and Fitzhugh's death has made Carter realize he could be one of those loose ends that someone needs to tie up."

Finn turned onto a busy street, dodging a bicycle courier. "I wonder if he has any clue about the DeadMoney bet."

"It's possible. Though with the ghost out of the picture, Carter has very little to be concerned about on that front, I would imagine." Maria shifted in her seat so she could see Finn better. "We still don't know who's behind the bets and the assassinations. Who's so scared after all this time that they need all these people dead?"

"It would have to be somebody above Carter at the time."

"Not very many people at the CIA above the Director of Counterintelligence. That leaves the associate director, the deputy director, the director himself."

"We should tell Quan that we found Carter," Finn said. "Maybe she can help convince him to come in and talk."

Finn parked in the garage across from the FBI headquarters, but this time they went through the main entrance and regular security. From there, they were escorted up to Quan's office. They knocked on the jamb of her open door, and she glanced up from whatever she'd been typing.

She checked the time on her watch. "You're a little early."

"We can wait outside if you—"

Quan stood. "No. Now's good."

They spent the next hour going through Finn and Maria's statement, with Quan only stopping them to ask clarifying questions.

Near the end, Finn started fidgeting in his seat. Finn didn't fidget. At least he never had in the years that Maria had been on his task force.

He must have had a lot of questions for Quan about the ghost and was impatiently biding his time until he could ask them.

When they finished their statements, Quan cut off her recording device and sat back in her chair. "Now, ask me your questions."

Finn visibly relaxed and rested his hand on top of Maria's on the arm of her chair. Quan's eyes flicked down to their twined hands. Maria didn't know what she'd expected, but the softening of Quan's expression hadn't been it. It said something about a man when their ex seemed happy for him to have found someone.

Maria turned her hand over to thread her fingers through his and let him take the lead.

24

———

In Finn's opinion, he'd shown amazing restraint during their statements and not hammered Quan with questions as soon as they'd darkened her door. "What do you have on the ghost?"

Quan tossed her pen onto her blotter. "Quite a bit. Much more than I ever expected."

Finn held onto his skepticism. "He's talking?"

"The district attorney gave him good reasons to. First, his name is John Morris. At least that was his given name. He's had numerous aliases along the way, as you can imagine. But as much as we wanted him, we wanted the person or people hiring him more."

"Of course." He squeezed Maria's hand, and she tried to squeeze back, but he hadn't let up enough to allow her to do that. He loosened his grip and shot her a *Sorry about that* half-smile. She returned it before turning her attention back to Quan.

"He's given us Brett Iverson. And he has digital proof to back that up. At least as far as Fitzhugh's contracted killing goes."

Brett Iverson. The former Director of the CIA back when Ali

had been killed. The assassinations had been ordered straight from the top. The *very* top. It should have made Finn feel better that he had been right in his suspicions, but somehow, it didn't help. "I expected as much," Finn said.

While Finn had wanted to know who ordered Fitzhugh killed, that wasn't the reason he'd flown all the way from Wyoming. "And?"

He wanted to kick himself for how needy he sounded. But of all the people who knew how hard he'd worked to find the truth for Ali, two of the three people sat in that room.

Quan leaned forward, picking up the pen and giving it a couple of twirls on her fingers, studiously avoiding Finn's gaze as if she were trying to find an easy way to break something to him.

"It's okay, Anita," Finn said, calling her by her first name for the first time in a very long time. He appreciated her trying to spare his feelings. But he didn't need his feelings spared. He needed to hear the truth. "I already know Morris doesn't remember my sister. It was a long time ago. I get that. A guy like him—"

Finn couldn't finish that sentence, not without his voice cracking. He took a few deep breaths to steady himself.

"Finn." Quan waited until he looked up at her before she continued. She exchanged her soft, compassionate expression for one more closed-off. "This morning, I showed him a picture of your sister. He recognized her. He admitted she'd been one of his contract kills."

Air rushed out of Finn's lungs, leaving him without even one molecule of oxygen to circulate in his system. His head felt light, and his vision started to blur. All he could hear was the rush of blood shooting past his ears. His throat constricted as his stomach lodged somewhere behind his Adam's apple.

He bent at the waist, braced his weight on his forearms, and buried his face in his hands. He shook, then shuddered. Maria laid her arm across his shoulders, pulling him into her side as much as the two chairs allowed.

She kissed his shoulder, but he appreciated that she gave him this moment, that she didn't press, that she didn't say anything. She sat there with him after the news. It shredded him and somehow healed a part of him simultaneously.

Finally, he sat up straight and dried the tears for a life cut short way too soon and a mission to find the truth that had lasted way too long.

He didn't care who saw his tears. This had been a long time coming. But the look on Quan's face made his stomach drop. "Fuck. What's the bad news?"

"It's been so long. Morris has no proof that the Director had ordered your sister's killing. We didn't have the electronic paper trail back then the way we do now. Without further cooperation, it's going to be hard to pen her killing on orders from the Director."

Finn sat up straighter. "I think I have somebody who might be able to corroborate."

He pulled out his phone and scribbled the unknown number he'd received that morning with the text that could only have come from Abe Carter. "My father gave me a contact number for Abe Carter. He was—"

"Director of CIA Counterintelligence back in the day," Quan said. "I know who he was."

Of course, she did.

"I texted him the other day when I found his name in my sister's journal that we found. I asked him to meet with me. This morning he finally answered and agreed. I think he's in hiding. I think after Fitzhugh was killed, he knew that, in all likelihood, he would be next. Or at least somewhere on the cleanup list. He doesn't know that we caught the ghost—I mean John Morris. He doesn't know it's safe to come in."

Quan glanced up as Finn heard a soft knock on her open office door.

She stood abruptly, looking a tad confused. "Walter," she said as she greeted what could only be Finn's father.

Finn suppressed a groan and managed not to spit out an expletive. He stood along with Maria and turned to face his father. He half expected to see his mother pop up behind him, but he should have known better. Vivian only showed up for the company Christmas parties.

"You caught him," Finn's father said.

Finn wanted to say *No thanks to you*, but he held his tongue. Instead, he said, I think Abe Carter knows he could have been next. He's hiding and extra cautious. He could possibly corroborate John Moore's assertion that the CIA Director had been the one who ordered Ali's assassination. I need you to get him here. I need you to convince him to talk with Quan."

Finn's tone brokered no argument. He wouldn't for one second allow his father to refuse. Finding out that his father had known much more than he let on about Ali's death left Finn livid, severing any sense of loyalty he had for his father. "Get him here. *Now*."

Finn's father took a step back, and after a long, awkward, drawn-out silence, Walter pulled his phone out of his back pocket and dialed a number.

When the call connected, his father said, "I need you to come by FBI headquarters. I need you to talk to Anita Quan. You're safe, Abe. I promise you. They caught the guy. Come in. It's time you talked."

Finn's father hung up the phone and dropped it back into the front pocket of his slacks.

The whole time Finn faced his father, Maria stood beside him, a comforting hand at the small of his back, letting him know that she also stood *with* him.

It was a little thing.

It was a huge thing.

Finn didn't want to be there anymore. Not in Quan's office. Not in D.C. He wanted to be back home. He wanted to be with his friends, and he wanted to put this decades-long manhunt behind him.

He turned to Quan. "You got this?"

Quan didn't need him anymore. She could handle whatever the case threw at her. But most of all, Finn trusted that she would make a strong enough case that Moore and the former director never saw the light of day.

Her voice came out soft but no less determined when she said, "Go. I've got this."

He stepped around the desk, pulled her into an embrace, and whispered in her ear because his voice would crack if he spoke any louder. "Thank you."

She patted him on the back. "It's my honor."

Finn took Maria's hand. His father clapped him on the shoulder and stuck out his hand for Finn to shake, seemingly oblivious to his role in dragging out the search for Ali's killer. "Nice job, son."

Finn glanced down at his father's hand and then back up again. They'd never had the strongest of relationships, but somehow, it felt like this also signified the end of theirs.

He couldn't imagine ever being a father and not doing every little thing within his power to find the responsible for his child's murder.

And for that, for his father's disregard, for his father's inaction, he'd never be able to forgive him. He met his father's eyes for what he suspected would be the final time. "I think we're done here."

He practically dragged Maria out of the building, down the

stairs—because the elevator took too long—past the puzzled glances from security and out the front entrance.

The sun shined bright, and the breeze blew cool against his overheated skin. He tilted his head to the heavens and hollered. He hollered out all his frustration and pain and disappointment and rage and loss.

He hollered out to cleanse his soul.

He hollered out so that maybe Ali could hear.

The breeze swept away his darker emotions, and besides a few curious glances of a few passersby, he felt lighter.

Is that what it felt like to walk through the world unburdened?

If the breeze picked up even a tiny bit, it would sweep him off his feet.

"Are you ready to go home?" Maria asked.

He pulled her into a big hug, folding her tight against his chest. He kissed the side of her head, then held her out so he could see her face. "Yeah, I'm ready to go home."

They returned to his car. He started the engine, but he sensed Maria needed to say something.

He raised a brow at her, and she said, "If you want to stay, I'll understand. If you want to follow this through, that's okay. I know how difficult it would be to walk away.

"No. I'm ready. I trust Quan to do her job. If there's justice to be found, I trust her of all people to get it for us."

He pulled out his phone and punched in the number for his plane service. When he finished the arrangements, he turned to Maria, "The plane is finishing up in New York. They said they could be here and be refueled and ready to take us home in two hours. Enough time to get back to the hotel, grab our gear and some lunch, and head out to the airport."

Maria got that mischievous glint in her eye, and Finn knew

how her devious mind worked. Her lip twitched before she leaned in and pressed a kiss to his lips.

The swelling in her bottom lip had gone down a little from that morning, and she didn't wince at the pressure. "Maybe this time, we can do more than sleep in the bed at the back of the plane."

THEY LANDED in Alpine late afternoon with an incoming text from Ronan asking Finn to call him. Finn deplaned in his suit slacks and dress shirt, but he had the sleeves uncharacteristically rolled up to his forearms. He stuffed his tie in the pocket of his suit coat.

For years he'd worn his suit everywhere, and the members of his task force had jokingly suspected—or suggested—that he probably even wore it to mow his lawn, to sleep, and to have sex.

Well, one of those three had been correct—at least since the flight back from D.C.

He hitched his arm around Maria's shoulders and kissed her. Releasing her, he held her hand and waited while their luggage was loaded into Maria's car.

"Thank you," Finn said to the man, tipping him for his help. Before he sank into the passenger car seat, he called Ronan. He picked up on the first ring.

"You landed?" Ronan asked.

"Just."

"If you're up for it, I'm at Steele-Wolfe. You two can brief Wyatt and me at the same time."

Finn covered the phone with his hand and said to Maria, "Ronan wants us to debrief them tonight. If you're not up to it, we can—"

"No. I'd rather get it over with."

"We'll be there," Finn told Ronan. "Give us about an hour."

They drove back to the Steele-Wolfe headquarters in companionable silence, with Maria at the wheel. She'd left her hair down after they'd joined the mile-high club.

She still had a bit of a flush on her face and the beginnings of a baby bruise at the base of her neck from his teeth. But she didn't seem mad about it.

As they pulled into the Yates ranch, the That-a-way stood blocking them in the middle of the drive. The cow refused to move, so Maria had to maneuver around her.

Maria laughed. "*Ay Dios mio*. I love that fucking cow. She looks at you like she has absolutely no fucks left to give."

"Yeah, well, she may find one or two if she scratches your paint job."

Maria rolled her eyes. She had a way of doing that that made Finn smile.

"You're not the badass you pretend to be, Oscar. Beneath your *By the Book* exterior, you're soft and a bit of a rebel like the rest of us."

Finn couldn't argue. But hopefully, she was the only one that would see that side of him.

After parking, they climbed the steps to the offices to find Ronan talking to a woman Finn had never met before. They were in the kitchen, Ronan leaning casually against the counter and talking in low tones with her.

Something Ronan said must've been funny because the woman laughed, and Ronan smiled. It took a moment for Ronan to take his eyes off her and shift his focus to Finn and Maria. He finally straightened and came over to shake their hands.

"Why are you even here?" Finn asked.

"Had a case to discuss with Wyatt."

And then, as if remembering his manners, Ronan stepped back and introduced the woman he had been talking to. "Becca, this Oscar Finn, one of my special agents, and Marissa Soto. She used to be on his task force."

Becca shook both of their hands. "Maria Soto. Yeah. Wyatt said something about hiring you. As of this morning, I'm your new colleague."

"Wait," Maria said. "You're Becca? As in Geneva's sister?"

"Guilty."

"I thought Cassie said you were working for one of the local sheriff's departments."

Becca shrugged, and a flush Finn couldn't explain rushed up to her cheeks. "Yeah, well, it didn't work out."

She smiled, but it looked like one of those smiles you slap on when the last thing you felt like doing was smiling. "And now, I'm here."

Wyatt came out of his office. "You guys ready?"

Becca excused herself and disappeared down the stairs.

They spent the next forty minutes catching Wyatt and Ronan up to speed. By that time, Finn had tired of repeating himself, and it looked like Maria was done as well.

His stomach grumbled, and all he wanted to do was drag Maria back to his place and try to put the past twenty-five years behind him.

Wyatt sat back in his chair. He had a corner office with windows that overlooked the parking lot on one side and the obstacle course on the other. It looked like Gil had his young son, Jack, on one of the obstacles, holding onto his hand as his son tried to walk the balance log.

"About Maria's arrest..." Finn started

"Don't worry about it. Someone in OPR was trying to make a name for himself. Looks like that is about to backfire on him."

"Nice work. Both of you," Wyatt said.

Finn took Maria's hand. "Thanks." He shifted his gaze to

Ronan. "I still have almost a week left of that personal time I took. If it's the same to you, we'd like to take it."

"We?" Wyatt asked.

Maria swallowed, but she didn't shrink from her boss's gaze. "Yeah, we—"

"Would like some time to decompress," Finn finished for her.

Wyatt looked between the two of them, not missing their joined hands, not that they'd tried to hide it.

"I already have everybody assigned to our active cases," Wyatt said. "I didn't expect you two back for another week, so yeah, take it if you need it."

"Thank you," Maria said. "I appreciate it."

They both stood to leave. Wyatt and Ronan got to their feet as well. Wyatt said, "You two should stay for dinner. We're grilling burgers and hotdogs for anybody who wants them. Nothing fancy. But you're welcome to stay. Massey and Isaac should be back any minute."

A horn blasted, and they all turned and looked out Wyatt's window to see Massey and Isaac pull up in Massey's white panel van. That-a-way finally moved over enough so that she wasn't blocking the drive."

"Speak of the devil," Wyatt said.

They all filed out of Wyatt's office, and he said, "Why don't you three give me a hand. We'll load beer and soft drinks into a couple of coolers and bring them downstairs."

They loaded the coolers with a couple of kinds of beer and several different soft drink brands. They carried the coolers into the utility room, where Wyatt had installed an industrial ice maker. They filled the coolers and loaded them into the elevator.

On the ground floor, the doors slid open. Massey and Isaac stood not ten feet away. They broke their kiss and stepped apart.

A flush rushed up Massey's face. Wyatt and Ronan each took a cooler and stepped out of the elevator.

"Something you guys need to tell me?" Wyatt asked.

Massey and Isaac glanced at each other. Massey was the first to speak. "It's—"

"Complicated," Isaac finished for him.

"Well," Wyatt said, "do you think you can un-complicate it long enough to grab those chairs and drag them outside?"

"Sure," Isaac said. "We'll be right there."

Maria and Finn hung around while the food cooked, relaxing with beer and good conversation. When the food finished cooking, Wyatt's wife, Geneva, and her best friend Cassie ensured everyone got enough to eat.

Massey and Isaac sat close together in folding chairs, Massey's crutches laying on the ground at his feet. He glanced up from his phone and asked Finn and Maria, "What did y'all do to DeadMoney?"

Finn shook his head. "Do to it?"

Massey held up his phone.

Though Finn sat too far away to see much detail, even from where he sat, he recognized the FBI seal in the middle of Massey's screen. "What is that?"

Massey grinned. "I think the feds finally took the Dead-Money site down. When you go to it, there's an FBI seizure notice. It's about damn time."

Massey could say that again. Not that Massey would ever get the recognition he deserved for trying to get the feds to shut the site down a lot earlier.

Looked like Massey wasn't so crazy after all.

"That must've been Quan. Or her people. She tends to get things done."

It was one of the reasons why Finn could leave the rest of the case in her hands and trust her to deal with everything moving forward.

Finn glanced around and found Ronan over by the start of the obstacle course in another conversation with Becca. His friend had a smile on his face that Finn hadn't seen for a long time. Which only made Finn worry.

Geneva and Cassie walked over, and Geneva said, "Hey Maria, do you want to walk over to the pond with us? We can give you a tour of the houseboat."

Maria must not have seen Wyatt and Geneva's houseboat yet. She jumped up. "I would love to."

Then Geneva hollered out to her sister. "Hey, Becca, the girls are heading to the house. Do you want to come?"

"Be right there," her sister hollered back.

Geneva's sister had undoubtedly seen the house before, so Finn figured the tour was an excuse for the women to get some time alone without the men.

After Maria left, Finn excused himself from Massey and Isaac, not that they were paying Finn much attention. He walked toward the obstacle course as Ronan started walking back. They met halfway in the near dark between the obstacle course and the building. At the far end of the course, Gil had made it to the vertical wall with Jack, Gil's daughter strapped to his chest.

Ronan held his beer out to Finn. "Here. Take it. I didn't drink out of it."

Finn didn't take the beer. "Why do you think I need a beer?"

Ronan made a motion with his finger, indicating Finn's face. "I was hoping it would wipe that sour look off it."

"I don't have a sour expression," Finn said even as he felt his brows pinching together.

"Spill," Ronan said. "What's your problem?"

"You never told me why you wanted to have drinks last week."

Ronan waved him off. Forget about that. It's... settled. And that's not the reason you came over here."

That was the problem with old friends. You couldn't keep a thought in your head without them knowing that something was up. Fine. If Ronan wanted to go there, Finn would go there.

"Besides the fact Becca is Geneva's sister, that she's Wyatt's sister-in-law?" Finn asked.

Ronan widened his stance and crossed his arms over his chest. "Yeah. Besides that. It was harmless flirting, nothing else."

"From what I saw, that was more than just a little harmless flirting. You like her. You're interested."

"And if I am?"

"I—" Finn shook his head. "I remember what happened last time."

Ronan had a smile on his face that wasn't really a smile. Not to the people who knew him. More of a warning. "And you don't think I remember that? Because trust me, I do."

Finn glanced around, but they were still alone. "Does Becca even know you're bi?"

Ronan cut him a look, then finally blew out a heated breath. "It's not something I lead with the first time I meet someone. No. Just because I've been with guys doesn't mean I'm not into women. Being interested in both is kind of implied in the whole *bi* thing."

"I know that. You need to make sure she knows that. Or the same thing that happened last time will happen this time."

"You're way out of line. And not every woman out there is biphobic."

"I'm your friend. It's my job to point out the hard truths. I don't want you getting hurt again."

"I'm a big boy," Ronan said.

From the top deck of the houseboat, the women's laughter cut through the clear night over something one of them said.

Ronan's eyes landed on Becca for much longer than someone who only had a passing interest.

Ronan turned his attention back to Finn. "Why don't you let me worry about that?"

Footsteps approached behind Finn, and he turned to find Maria walking their way, little more than a shadow.

"I thought you were getting the grand tour," Finn said as she stepped beneath his outstretched arm.

She hugged his side. "I can see the boat anytime. I think what I need more is that week alone with you... for a start."

They said goodbye to Ronan, who didn't seem too upset to see them go. They skirted everyone else, Finn wanting nothing more than to get Maria home alone. He figured the guys would forgive them for not saying their goodbyes.

At her car, he held her door open but blocked her from climbing inside. "You want to be alone with me for a start," he said, repeating her words. "Then what?"

She stood on her toes and kissed him. It was the type of kiss that held a world of promise. "Then we start on that forever."

A LETTER TO MY READERS

Dear Reader,

Don't miss out on the series that started it all. The Lazy S Ranch series is where this world started and it is near and dear to my heart. It is chock full of book boyfriends you won't want to miss. It's a six book series with all the feels and adventures and you will get to meet some of Steele-Wolfe's favorite characters from the beginning.

Your next adventure starts here: Cowgirl, Unexpectedly (Book 1)

ADDED NOTE: After getting rights back for **Must Love Horses,** and **Hot on the Trail,** I changed their titles to better align with the rest of the series. Must Love Horse became *Cowboy, Untamed.* Hot on the Trail became *Cowboy, Undone.*

ROMANTIC SUSPENSE

Lazy S Ranch Series
Cowgirl, Unexpectedly (Book 1)
Cowboy, Untamed (Book 2)

(Previously published as Must Love Horses)
Cowboy, Undone (Book 3)
(Previously published as Hot on the Trail)
Cowboy, Undercover (Book 4)
Cowboy, Unbridled (Book 5)
Cowgirl, Unbroken (Book 6)
Lazy S Ranch Box Set (Books 1-3)
Lazy S Ranch Box Set (Books 4-6)

Wright's Island Series
Don't Look Back (Book 1)
In Her Defense (Book 2)

Steele-Wolfe Securities
Wyoming Confidential (Book 1)
Dealing With the Devil (Book 2)
Sweet Justice (Book 3)

CONTEMPORARY ROMANCE

Rockin' Rodeo Series
Luck of the Draw (Book 1)
Photo Chute (Book 2)
Reined In (Book 3)
Rockin' Rodeo Series Collection (Books 1-3)

MM ROMANCE

Black Stallion Studios Series
One Shot (Book 1)
Key Grip (Book 2)
Best Boy (Book 3)
Black Stallion Studios Box Set (Books 1-3)

<u>*Valley Boys*</u>
Art of Love (Book 1)
Flight of Fancy (Book 2)
Den of Thieves (Book 3)
The Valley Boys (Books 1-3)

ABOUT THE AUTHOR

Vicki Tharp makes her home on small acreage in south Texas with her husband and an embarrassing number of pets. When she isn't writing, you can usually find her on the back of her horse—avoiding anything that remotely resembles housework —smelling like fly spray and horse sweat.

Join my newsletter at: http://bit.ly/V-W-T
Join my street team and receive free Advance Reader Copies of my upcoming books at: http://bit.ly/S-W-S-T
You can find my website at: www.VickiTharp.com
I love to hear from readers. You can email me at
vwtharp@VickiTharp.com

Or you can stalk me at:

facebook.com/VickiTharpAuthor

instagram.com/author_Vicki_Tharp

bookbub.com/authors/vicki-tharp

amazon.com/author/vicki_tharp

twitter.com/vwtharp